THE TIGER'S GHOST

by Max Tucker

Copyright © 2023 Malcolm Tucker

The moral right of the author has been asserted.

ISBN 979 8862084 047

Malcolm Tucker was educated at Millfield School and Indiana University; he spent four years as a member of the British International swimming team, gaining a silver and bronze medal in the 1966 Empire and Commonwealth Games.

Enjoying a lifelong interest in Rolls-Royce and Bentley cars, in 1989 he launched *Pinnacle* magazine, The magazine for International Rolls-Royce and Bentley Owners on behalf of the Sir Henry Royce Memorial Foundation. He has also edited various souvenir books for the Rolls-Royce Enthusiasts' Club, the most prestigious being for Her Majesty The Queen's Golden Jubilee Celebration at Windsor Castle. He has been guest editor of the Club's magazine *Spirit & Speed* on six occasions.

He has written seven children's books (8 to 12 years old) on engineering subjects for Merlion Publishing, Chippenham. Apart from writing for motoring magazines he was a regular contributor to *The Nob Hill Gazette*, San Francisco, USA. He has authored four car-related 'coffee table' books for Dalton Watson Fine Books.

He is currently the Historic Archive Consultant for Rolls-Royce Motor Cars Ltd, at Goodwood.

Malcolm lives with his wife Clare in Hampshire.

The Tiger's Ghost is his first novel.

The Princely State of Cooch Sebah, India, 1909

Ajit Bakhat Singh is more frightened than he has ever been. Yes, it is his thirteenth birthday, and yes, he is surrounded by advisers and holy men who have instructed him for as long as he can remember. But he has become suspicious of their advice, seeing the hints of machinations, scheming and sycophancy that seem the norm for all but two of those who have guided him from birth. Those are his uncle the Acting Prince Regent Kuldeep Singh, and his governess, Miss Amelia Symington.

A single drum beat quietens the other musicians. Ajit takes a deep breath, he knows what he has to do, it has been rehearsed enough. He moves to stand in front of his uncle, who raises himself from the gold and jewel encrusted ivory throne of the Princely State of Cooch Sebah. It is the last time he will do so, for now he must relinquish his duties as Acting Prince Regent. Today Ajit, his late brother's son, has come of age, and will be crowned the next Maharajah.

Ajit takes his seat and looks out at the thousand invited guests standing or seated amongst the lush green lawns and fountains in the palace courtyard. All are shielded from the scorching sun by tented pavilions, dyed in the national colours of vermilion and lapis lazuli blue. Seated in the front rows are the great and the good of surrounding princely states, behind whom stand the lesser dignitaries from Cooch Sebah, not great enough to be witnesses on the throne dais. The most revered guests of honour are the luminaries of the British Raj, most important of whom are the viceroy's representative for the region, Sir Arthur Symington, his wife Lady Daphne, and their youngest daughter Miss Amelia Symington, governess to Ajit Singh. She has been willing him to remember all that has been rehearsed. Although she is nervous for him, she returns his gaze, and smiles, nodding her approval of his actions so far. She hopes he will take courage from her unspoken language; he does.

The culmination of the Coronation is now carried out in silence, but for the commands of a single drummer. Kuldeep Singh turns and approaches his nephew, kneels with head bowed and offers him the heavily bejewelled Sword of State. His equally jewel-encrusted State Collar of diamonds and emeralds is taken from him and placed around the Prince's neck. For his final act as Regent of the State, he takes the jewel turban-ornament, a single red diamond set in gold, from his own head and places it upon that of his nephew. Ajit Bakhat Singh is now the Maharajah of the Princely State of Cooch Sebah.

The musicians start playing in full celebration, competing with the well-wishing chants from the massed guests. The state's most influential men, the court officials, headmen of the fiefdoms, land owners and religious leaders approach the throne in turn and kneel to demonstrate their allegiance before the young Maharajah. He is more confident now. His glances towards Amelia Symington are less frequent, his need for reassurance waning. The drummer beats a tattoo, a signal for those on the throne dais to move to the sides. Only the Maharajah and his uncle Kuldeep Singh remain. The boy-king raises his hand, and the drumbeat stops as abruptly as it had started. A court official moves to the front of the dais, unfurls a scroll and reads a declaration in Punjabi.

Amelia Symington whispers to her father. 'Is this the declaration to Kuldeep Singh?'

'Yes.'

'Tell me what he's saying.'

'Only what I have told you, my dear. To stop any internecine squabbles between factions within the ruling family Kuldeep Singh, now his duties as Prince Regent are over, must leave the state of Cooch Sebah never to return. But he is allowed to take in one go as much gold and as many jewels as he can, without the help of man nor beast. That's the gist of it, Amelia, a Herculean task if he were greedy and decided to pull an overloaded handcart.'

'Where will he go?'

'Who knows, my dear, a friendly other State, to live out his days in quiet but luxurious retirement. It's even rumoured he may make his way to England.'

Amelia does not reply. She sits in silence, her eyes closed, her breath hardly under control, a hand resting on the brooch that Kuldeep Singh had given her. She secretly grew to love this man who had instructed the little Prince in the ways of the Court, as she, as governess, had tutored him.

A roar of astonishment from the entire crowd startles Amelia back from her musing. Kuldeep Singh has not had a chest of precious gems and gold placed before him. He has walked to the back of the throne dais and has pulled down the red and blue damask wall hangings, interwoven with gold and silver threads. A Rolls-Royce Silver Ghost limousine is revealed, the first automobile to be seen in Kooch Sebah.

Kuldeep Singh sits in the driver's seat. He starts the car and drives off the dais, down the palace steps, turning right to steer past the front row of honoured guests, then out of the palace courtyard to begin his new life.

No ordinary limousine, in place of the normally constructed aluminium panelling fixed to an ash wood frame, this car has gold panelling, painted in tiger-like stripes. In front of the windscreen sits a life-sized, solid gold, tiger's head, the eyes yellow diamonds, and an egg-sized ruby held in its teeth. As the car moves, the sunlight scintillates throughout the interior, which is studded with the finest gems taken from the Royal treasury.

Kuldeep Singh stops the Rolls in front of Lord Symington and looks straight at him. All eyes are on his Lordship; he says nothing while his mind races to form a judgement of the situation. The young Maharajah now stands at the top of the dais steps; his eyes dart from Lord Symington to his governess, Amelia, back and forth.

The only sound is a brief trumpeting from one of the Coronation Parade elephants. Lord Symington stands and addresses the Maharajah Ajit Singh. 'Your Serene Highness. The law states that a retiring Prince Regent of the State must leave the country within three days and may take as much gold, silver, and precious gems from the Royal Treasury as he is able, without the aid of man nor beast. Whilst the spirit of the law has been broken, the legality has not, for no other man nor beast is involved. Kuldeep Singh has every right to drive away in the first motor car to be seen in Kooch Sebah.'

Maharajah Ajit Bakhat Singh may only be thirteen years old, but that is old enough to swear to himself that he will avenge this immense theft from the Crown Treasury, however long it takes.

As Kuldeep Singh drives away, his only worry is what will happen when the young Maharajah is told the state secret, a secret held only by two high-ranking officials at any one time, that would be revealed to a new ruler immediately after his coronation.

The County of Berkshire, England, 2023

CHAPTER ONE

I poured two glasses of Mortlach whisky: large ones. 'Will you take twelve and a half million dollars?' Angelo Mitchelletti looked back at me, his downturned mouth showing his displeasure. 'Jesus, Ross, I'm asking fifteen.'

'Fifteen is what you think it's worth, not what the market thinks, believe me. Twelve and a half is a bloody good price.'

Mitch chewed his lip for a good ten seconds then downed his whisky in one shot. 'Okay, do the deal, Ross; on one condition.'

He'd been a client long enough for me to know he wouldn't renege on the sale. His one condition would be a tease for another car to find for him. It wouldn't be a problem; discovering, buying, and selling classic cars discreetly is my business, after all. We were standing by Mitch's up-for-sale 1960 Ferrari 250 Testa Rossa, in the old coach house now with glazed doors, showroom lighting, leather chairs, and a well-stocked bar.

'Let's go up to the office, and you can tell me your one condition, before I agree to reveal the buyer,' I teased.

'That's crap, Ross, you've got over half a million bucks in commission coming if the sale goes through. You'll reveal the buyer whatever.'

My humour had been lost on Mitch. Out in the cobbled courtyard he collected an attaché case from his rented Toyota and did a three-hundred-and-sixty-degree turn around. 'I like your place, Ross. I should visit more often.'

'It's a long way from San Francisco,' I answered.

We headed for the office, originally the grooms' quarters above the stables now altered to garaging for the cars. Mitch wheezing his way up the short but steep stairs, the attaché case clasped to his chest. At about five feet tall and almost as much around the waist he looked like an unfit Danny DeVito.

'So, this condition, what is it?' I asked again.

Mitch straightened himself up to his full height. 'I want you to find me The Tiger's Ghost.'

For a few moments I was speechless. 'Don't tell me you're talking about Maharajah Kuldeep Singh's gold and jewel-laden Rolls-Royce?'

'Yeah. That one.'

I crossed the room to a bookcase and pulled out a copy of Cars of the Indian Raj. 'Let me read you something about that car. I think it will save you some time and money.'

'Forget the book. I know what it says.'

'Okay, Mitch, so you also know that after leaving India Kuldeep Singh lived in England until 1912 when he decided to emigrate to the USA on the Titanic, along with a handful of his trusted servants. None of them survived, and it's a well-known fact that the car's still in the wreck of the ship.'

Mitch eyed me as he hoisted his attaché case onto the back of the sofa. He fiddled with the tumblers, popped the locks, and pulled out a padded bubble-envelope, the type used for mailing delicate contents. Lifting the flap he withdrew some glass photographic plates and handed me one. 'Hold the edges and be careful, it's fragile.'

I held it up to the light. The plate was obviously old, a black-and-white negative. Here and there were tiny chips on the edges. After a couple of seconds squinting, I could see that it was the side of an old liner shot from sea level. There was a smaller vessel towards the bow of the ship. Although the image was sharp, being a negative made it impossible to tell much more.

Mitch could see I was having trouble. 'Forget it, this'll make it easy.'

He handed me two positive prints, about eight by elevens. 'Tell me what you see, Ross.'

'The first one is a print from the glass plate negative I just saw. The ship looks like the Titanic, although it could be one of her sister-ships, the Olympic or Britannic.' I added this to show Mitch that I took nothing for granted. 'The picture is taken from low down and there's an out-of-focus line or bar running along the bottom of the image at a slight angle. It's probably a handrail of the vessel that the photographer was on. The smaller boat looks like a tug with its stern to the camera. There's something covered by a tarpaulin being winched onto or off its deck. The sky is overcast, and the sea is rippled but not rough. I'd say the ship is anchored in a bay, not at a dock or open water. There's land in the near distance behind the ship.'

I shuffled the second photo to the top. 'Next one is a blow-up of the big ship's bow. It shows the anchor chain, and it's difficult to see at the angle, but it says Titanic all right.' I glanced at Mitch to concede the point.

'And?' he prompted.

'It also shows the tugboat, stern on, still close to the Titanic's side. The Cionn Saile. About ten feet above her deck there's a tarpaulin covering cargo being lowered from the Titanic by a derrick.'

Mitch corrected my pronunciation. 'It's Ke-on So-lay, not See-on Sale. And why do you say, "being lowered," why not being taken on board the Titanic? You know, late cargo,' he asked as a teacher might of a not-so-bright student.

'Because there are four men on the tug's deck who have their hands raised to the load. They're getting ready to steady it as it comes down. Okay, it is the Titanic, but the load could be anything, taken any time.'

Mitch gave me a self-satisfied grin and handed me a third print. 'I also have the glass plate negative, but that one stays in my safe at home. Go on, tell me what you see.'

I looked at it for all of five seconds before answering. 'It's, ah, much the same as the last one. Probably taken a few seconds later, just time to change the plate in the old camera. The load is now down at the crew's shoulder level. They're manhandling it in line with the deck.' I gave Mitch a long glance and he nodded his encouragement. I cleared my throat. 'The wind must have gusted because the tarpaulin is blown up like a . . .'

'Like Marilyn Monroe's skirt over the air grating, you know,' said Mitch.

'I know, but this photo shows the front quarter of a Rolls-Royce Silver Ghost. The body is light in colour with dark stripes painted like a tiger's and you can see the left half of a tiger's head sculpture in front of the windscreen.' I looked up at Mitch who was slowly nodding his approval of my interpretation.

He confirmed my thoughts. 'Whatever happened to the Tiger's Ghost, one thing's for certain. It ain't two and a half miles down in the number two hold of the Titanic, and we're the only ones who know it.'

CHAPTER TWO

First business of the day had been to broker the sale of a 1964 Mini Cooper, one that had successfully competed in that year's Monte Carlo Rally.

That done, I walked over to the house, to which my home and business premises had been the stable block and coach house. I pressed the buzzer to Tegan Jones's apartment, one of ten into which the house had been divided. Tegan spends one or two days a week organising my desk and diary and seven days a week near Gwyn, her severely asthmatic husband. Until two years ago she had been a researcher at the Victoria and Albert Museum. If anyone could give me guidance on the chances of a long-lost gold and bejewelled car surviving it was Tegan.

She greeted me, with her hair wrapped in a towel turban. Rubenesque in stature, she had the dark beauty so typical of attractive Welsh women. 'Sorry about the look, Benedict, but I just had to wash it. Have you had any lunch?'

'Yes, thanks Tegan. Wouldn't say no to a cup of tea, though.'

We sat at the kitchen table. 'As you know, Mitch was here yesterday, and he agreed the deal on his Ferrari, but he's got another commission for me, a very generous fee, and I want your opinion on whether or not to accept it.'

'My opinion. You know cars aren't my thing, except some of them are quite pretty, but you might as well be buying and selling expensive wheelbarrows for all the difference to my office work.'

I had to laugh; Tegan was right. As office manager she really didn't need to know anything about classic cars. 'Well, this one is a bit different, and it's your experience as a museum researcher that makes me think you can help.'

'Go on then, what's it all about,' she encouraged.

I had bought Cars of the Indian Raj with me and read Tegan the story of little Maharajah Ajit Singh's Coronation and Kuldeep Singh's trickery.

Tegan gave a low whistle. 'That's some story, Benedict. So, the Rolls is worth millions?'

'Yes, but how many millions nobody knows as far as I am aware.'

'I still don't see where I fit in,' said Tegan.

'Well, nowhere yet, that's the next part of the Tiger's Ghost story. Singh had arranged with the British government to live in England, with a small retinue and of course his gold Rolls-Royce. This was when the car got its nickname The Tiger's Ghost, it being a Silver Ghost model. Singh became a famous socialite, invited to the grandest of aristocratic occasions, and was renowned for throwing the most extravagant house-parties. But for some reason in 1912 he decided to emigrate to America and chose the Titanic.'

'Don't tell me Mitch wants you to bring the Rolls up from the wreck?'

That's the thing. The whole world thinks the car went down on the ship, but Mitch has shown me absolute photographic proof that the Tiger's Ghost was off-loaded before it sailed for New York.'

'Off-loaded where?'

'I have no idea, but it could only have been Southampton, Cherbourg, or Queenstown. If I decide to undertake the search on behalf of Mitch, finding that would be a good place to start. Tegan, speaking as a trained researcher, do you think the chances of the car still being around are good enough to make a quest worthwhile?'

'What else do you know about the car?'

'Only that the Maharajah's extravagant lifestyle was paid for by selling off selected gems from the car as and when he needed funds. Willard's the jewellers would set them and sell them on his behalf, the spaces in the car being filled with paste replicas.'

'I think you should follow your own instincts, but I'll come over to the office when my hair's dry and play devil's advocate to you.'

When Tegan arrived, dark curls dancing around her smile, we debated the pros and cons of the search, me slouching in one of my scruffy armchairs, and Tegan at her desk.

'So, what do you think, Benedict?'

'I think that yesterday I'd have fallen over laughing at the idea of looking for the Tiger's Ghost, and now the truth is I'm as excited as I've ever been about a car search.'

'You really don't think the gold has been melted down and the jewels are all over the world by now?'

'That could be the case, but I reckon the car would have survived at least until Kuldeep Singh died, whenever that was.'

'And wherever,' added Tegan.

I nodded. 'Let's suppose that takes us up to the late 1930s, when Kuldeep would be getting on for seventy. If he had died, I think he would have willed the Tiger's Ghost to a secure future, and most probably it would have been secreted during the Second World War.'

Tegan picked up my train of thought. 'Or it became the spoils of war for someone.'

'It's all a helluva long shot,' I agreed.

I could see Tegan weighing up probabilities. 'Now if the car had been stolen during the war years, I reckon it would have been by someone with enough knowledge of fine things and enough wealth to keep it until values got back to normal.'

'Or that someone needed to give a Nazi or two a massive bribe to save their neck,' I countered.

Tegan nodded thoughtfully. 'Most likely though, Kuldeep hid the car safely, especially when the war started, intending to keep it for the rest of his life. He could have made it into the 1950s.'

'You've got a point. He could easily have lived well past seventy. So, you agree it's worth going for it?'

Tegan swivelled her desk chair around and tapped expertly at her computer; after a few seconds she spoke. 'You have the time, okay. The only thing you can't work around is California for the Pebble Beach Concours d'Elegance in August. You can't miss that; I know it's your best opportunity in the year for networking.'

'Too right.'

Tegan spun the chair back to face me. 'Plus, you said you've been offered a great fee and expenses by Mitch.'

I smiled briefly, remembering that he had suggested a very generous broker's fee. One that I would be happy to accept without negotiating. 'You don't think it was too easy, I mean, Mitch usually drives a bloody hard bargain?'

'No, from what you've told me, he really wants that car, and you would go down in motoring history as the man who found the Tiger's Ghost.'

'You're right, I'll do it.'

Our conversation was ended by a yell up the stairs from my mechanic, Smiler Harris. 'You there, Guv? I'm working on the 'thirty-five Bentley and need to lift the pistons out the cylinder block. Someone's got to push them up from underneath.'

A dyed-in-the-wool Londoner from the East End borough of Tower Hamlets, he had been a fitter in The Army Air Corps, and then a General Aviation engineer. Smiler had acquired his nickname over sixty-five years of looking, whatever his mood, as miserable as a bloodhound with nothing to chase. To my terrier Columbus he is a star, and when I'm away, the dog spends much of the time in his basket by the workshop entrance, ever ready to give warning of visitors.

As I pushed out the six pistons and their connecting rods I gave Smiler a synopsis of the Mitch story, which incurred the expected response 'Gordon Bennett! The Tiger's Ghost. J'er really think it's still about?'

'Put it this way, he's paying enough for me to keep you on for a few more days.'

Smiler was used to our ongoing banter of his imminent dismissal or the handing in of his notice. We both knew that he was the best old-car mechanic in England, and I had given him his dream job.

'Out you come, Guv, I've got to fiddle with number four piston.' Smiler kicked my leg gently as he spoke in the chalky growl that comes with that London accent.

'I'll be up in the office, yell if you need me again.'

Tegan was still at her desk. 'Have you started the Tiger's Ghost search?' I asked.

'Not yet, while I'm here I thought I would get your filing done, clear the desk. Also, these three letters that need your signature. Now be a good boy and sign them so I can get them in the post. We can look at this gold-car thing tomorrow when both our minds are fresh.'

Excited to get going as I was, it made sense. Using a computer search when you don't know the parameters is as much about instinct as science. A fresh mind is a big help, and as Scarlett O'Hara famously ventured, 'After all, tomorrow is another day.'

CHAPTER THREE

Tegan was at the computer bright and early. 'So, what do you think?' I asked her.

'I'm logged into Lloyd's Registry, to see if I can find the tugboat in the photo, the Cionn Saile. They have records of all British shipping since 1776.

I waited well back from Tegan, as she doesn't like anyone peering over her shoulder when she's working.

She called out without turning around. 'Found her. Cionn Saile. Built in 1898 by Denny's of Dumbarton for an Irish tugboat and dredging company, Black Pool Shipping Services. They owned her until she was scrapped in 1935. In 1912 her captain was one Dermot Cassady, and her port of registration was Queenstown, that's Cobh Island as it's now called. It fits.'

'Okay, just as a double check, let's run a Geomatch on Mitch's photo I scanned.' I scooted my chair across to see the computer screen. There's a useful little app that can match geographical features with their locations. Tegan punched up the scanned copy of Mitch's photo that showed the Titanic with the hills in the background. She drew a select-lasso around the hill formation and let the app do its work.

Seconds later we had a result. 'Look, there's an eighty-seven per cent match that the hills lie to the northwest of Cobh Island,' she said.

'We have our defined search point, then. So, what happened next? I don't think Captain Cassady would have taken such a valuable, heavy and large deck cargo far over open water, bearing in mind the tug's size. He probably headed back for land close by.'

Tegan cut in. 'But not within sight of the Titanic. The off-loading was all clandestine. The car was disappearing, as was its owner. Maybe the start of a reclusive life for the Maharajah.'

'That's a point! Did Kuldeep Singh skip the Titanic as well?' I answered my own question. 'Of course, he did. The story goes that in England, he even slept with the guarded car in sight of his window. He wouldn't let seawater separate them.'

I knew that one of the major transatlantic Irish ports, Queenstown, was the departure point for two and a half million of the six million Irish people who emigrated to America between 1848 and 1950. On 11 April 1912 Queenstown was the final port of call for the Titanic as she set out across the Atlantic. 'What was the nearest harbour to Queenstown that the tug could have gone to?' I asked.

A speedy tapping of keys from Tegan. 'To the north, Dungarven and Waterford, to the south Kinsale – that's the tug's namesake in English.'

'Okay, with those, notwithstanding the possibility that the car was shipped out on another vessel in Queenstown Bay, we have four probable onward destination sites. Geography won't tell us anything more, you're going to have to trawl through the computer for something.'

Tegan mumbled a reply, as she concentrated on her next moves. 'I'll search through the relevant databases of the National Maritime Museum at Greenwich. Apart from the Lloyd's stuff they've got shipping and crew records going back to the early 1700s. I'll play around for a couple of hours and see if I can get a lead on anything.'

Smiler bellowed up the staircase. 'You free, Guv? Them pistons are ready to go back in.'

'I'll be in the workshop,' I told Tegan.

An hour later, when Smiler no longer needed my help, I went back upstairs. Tegan was still sitting at the computer, now with head in hands.

'It's no bloody good,' she said. 'There are no specific records that I can find of a working tugboat's daily trips. We'd need the boat's logbook for that, and it's long gone. Even the company that owned her was taken over in 1925, and they ceased trading in 1937.'

'Take a break, I've got to deliver a little Amilcar to its new owner, near Glastonbury.' She looked relieved, although her frustration at failing to solve the problem was evident.

By 4:00pm, the Amilcar delivered, I was back at the Clock House. Tegan had typically ignored my instruction to have a rest, but she looked very much like the cat that got the cream.

'Don't tell me, you've found the Tiger's Ghost intact with all the gold and all the jewels.'

'Not quite that good,' she said. 'I've drawn a complete blank on the shipping records, but then I had an idea, a totally different line of attack.'

Putting down my briefcase and leaning against the back of the sofa, I encouraged her, 'Go on.'

'Well, what was the one constant during the time we know the car belonged to Kuldeep Singh?'

'Armed guards, with the car in sight of the Maharajah's window?'

'Yes, but not that, I'll give you a clue: money.'

'The jewels,' I replied instantly. 'When he was short of cash, he arranged for Willard's to take some gems from the car, and replace them with exact paste copies, then they would mount and sell the genuine items for him.'

'Exactly,' she said, stabbing her finger to make the point.

'So, I made a search of Willard's. They started business in 1775, gaining favour with the aristocracy in the 1820s following some spectacular commissions from George IV for his mistresses. In their day Willard's were just as well-known as Asprey or Garrard are today. They ceased trading in early 1945, following a direct hit by a German V-I flying bomb. The senior directors were in the building at the time and were all killed, the building being razed to the ground.'

'So that's a dead end surely, no pun intended.'

'No,' replied Tegan, with a radiant smile. 'It isn't. The basement containing the safes with most of their stock of precious stones and metals survived. Also saved were the company records, which today are happily tucked up in the library of the Goldsmiths' Company, in the City of London.'

She handed me a Post-it note with the address on it. 'You're off to Foster Lane first thing tomorrow to meet the Goldsmiths' Chief Archivist.'

CHAPTER FOUR

The Worshipful Company of Goldsmiths is housed in an impressive building at the junction of Foster Lane and Gresham Street, close to St. Paul's Cathedral. Built in 1835 and looking rather like a miniature version of Buckingham Palace, this is the third building to stand on the site, the first Goldsmiths' Hall having been erected in 1339.

The Goldsmiths are one of the City of London's twelve great Livery or trade companies. This I could believe, looking at the ornate and sumptuous interior. No expense spared here, I could have been in Blenheim Palace or the Vatican.

An attendant at his reception desk looked at me coolly. 'May I help you, sir?'

'I have an appointment with the Chief Archivist,' I replied, giving my best smile, as he checked his computer screen.

'Ah, yes, Colonel Levington will be with you in a minute sir, please take a seat,' he gestured to a small group of Chesterfield armchairs and sofas.

Five minutes later, the Colonel arrived, looking every bit the retired British Army officer of fiction; John Mills or Ralph Fiennes at their best.

'Mr. Ross,' this was a statement, not a question, and was accompanied by a brisk single shake of my hand. 'This way, please.'

Levington was a good twenty-five years older than me, but I could barely keep up with his lightning ascent of the marble staircase. We entered the library where a table had been prepared with stacks of Willard's leather-bound, gold-tooled account and record books. The Colonel handed me a pair of white cotton gloves. 'Please wear these to stop the acid from your skin accelerating the deterioration of the pages.'

I thought I would look like Mickey Mouse or Al Jolson: not a resemblance that the Colonel would appreciate.

'I'll be at my desk, Mr. Ross. Just come over when you have finished.'

Levington made an almost military about-face and left me to it. I had no doubts at all that whatever the Colonel was doing, one eye would be on me until I left.

Each book bore the company name, and a heading – Bought Ledger, Sales Ledger, Articles of Association, and more – all with the dates of the periods covered. On the way to London, I had thought about where the most helpful information might be and so I rifled through the books titled Gemstone Valuations. Each page was beautifully written up in black-ink copperplate, looking as if they had been penned by a character from a Dickens novel. There were six columns per page, headed Date, Gemmologist, Customer, Address, Stones, Valuation. Under Customer were names or, in some cases, just a word that I took to be a pseudonym. The Stones column had a coded jumble of letters and numbers, and the valuation list was in Pounds Sterling.

I started with the book dated 1910–1914 and, sure enough, there were entries in May 1910 and October 1911 for the Maharajah Kuldeep Singh, and his London address was given. In 1911 His Serene Highness had disposed of a huge ruby and three smaller diamonds for what seemed to me an astronomical sum, even now. There were no further entries in his name.

I moved on to the book dated 1935–1939. Obviously, the

Customer column was the place to start, and so I trawled through page after page for the whole five years; no Kuldeep Singh here, although twenty or so members of Indian Royal families of one sort or another were listed, but their details were complete and didn't fit the profile of my man.

I went through the book again, this time noting the names that were obviously pseudonyms in place of true identities. There were ten of them, but they all had a dash in place of the address. I added up the times the false names appeared and found the most prolific one repeated once or twice every year. Unhelpfully, it was a simple English name: George, but George was also listed in the 1910–1914 book, after the last mention of Kuldeep Singh. A random check of all ledgers in between also regularly listed George, but I could make no logical connection to Kuldeep Singh.

By now it was one o'clock and I asked the Colonel if I could continue my research after lunch. He consulted his watch to check that in his mind I was entitled to a break and grudgingly nodded his agreement. 'Two o'clock, shall we say.' The time was clearly non-negotiable.

The City of London, with its workforce of nearly four hundred thousand people, has many snack and sandwich shops that do a roaring trade from breakfast time to about 3:00pm. They then close as the out-of-working-hours population of the City dwindles to fewer than ten thousand souls. I took my egg mayonnaise sandwich, pecan roll and flat white to a just-vacated stool at the front window of such a place. It's near The Monument that supposedly marks the bakery where the Great Fire of London started. Food consumed, I decided to drink the coffee on the hoof, and amble through a few of the City's ancient streets on my way back to Goldsmiths' Hall.

This capital of commerce has seen more history than just about anywhere else in Britain, and the street names bear witness. I walked further along Cheapside, cheap being the old English word for a market. Past Bread Street, Ironmonger Lane, Milk Street, and Poultry, all named after the products once sold in the area. I turned left past the Bank of England into Prince's Street.

My mind was on the list of pseudonyms, and as I turned left again, into Gresham Street, I stopped dead in my tracks and looked back at the thoroughfare that I had just left, Prince's Street. Something was nagging at me about that name; I took the list of pseudonyms from my pocket and re-read them for the tenth time. Then it clicked. Before he became King, George IV ruled the country in place of his mentally ill father. During this period, his title was The Prince Regent, and in Kuldeep Singh's time as an interim ruler he was known amongst the British Raj as The Indian Prince Regent. Could the pseudonym George refer to Kuldeep Singh?

Back under the Colonel's watchful eye, I found the Willard's records for staff travel vouchers and reimbursements. I cross-referenced this against the gemstone valuation books, noting the dates that George was mentioned and the initials of the gemmologist who attended him – MAS. In each case, on matching dates, a Mr. M. A. Sidelski had an entry for reimbursements, and his destination was always the same; Clarecourt, County Cork, Ireland.

I closed the book and hissed a muffled 'Yess!'

Colonel Levington looked up from his desk. 'I take it you have found that which you were looking for.'

'Yes, thank you Colonel, I'll be off now.' I walked across to him, handed back my white gloves and added 'Thanks for keeping an eye on me. I may need to return.'

He looked dismayed at my last few words, but I kept smiling as I left the Worshipful Company of Goldsmiths.

Back at the Clock House, Tegan was still at her desk, impatiently waiting to know what I had found, and as always Columbus greeted me excitedly. Once the hound had decided his dog-chew was more interesting than his master, I slumped down in my favourite armchair and reached over for the glass of bubbly that Tegan had just poured for me. There is one weakness that I admit to: that's Perrier-Jouët champagne, and it had been a long day.

'Successful?' Asked Tegan.

'Too early to say yet, but I think we've got an exceptionally good lead, I'm going to follow it up.' I gave her a compressed version of my day. 'See if the Irish address still exists. After all, who knows what might have happened to a large country house over the last seventy-odd years.'

'The address is still there, at least its name; don't know the state of the building though.' After a short pause she went on. 'It's okay, there's a telephone number and the name of the person listed as living there, a Miss Caitlin Whelan.

No time like the present, so I dialled the number. I was just about to hang up when the phone was answered by an elderly but gentle Irish accent. 'Hello, this is Caitlin Whelan.'

'Miss Whelan, you don't know me, my name is Benedict Ross, I'm a classic car broker, and I'm trying to trace the ownership history of a particular car. I wonder if you can help me with some information about someone who I think once lived in your house?'

'And who might that be, Mr. Ross?' she asked, a little warily.

'An Indian gentleman named Kuldeep Singh, Miss Whelan.'

'You know about Mr. Singh, how exciting. I'll help you if I can, but I don't know very much about him,' she replied, her wariness gone.

'Miss Whelan, rather than talk on the phone, I'm coming over from England to your part of Ireland in a few days and wonder if I may call on you.' Tegan pulled a hopeful face and gave me the thumbs-up as I was speaking.

'Well, I'm not so sure, Mr. Ross. As you say, I don't know you and I'm a little nervous of having strangers in the house. My solicitor, Mr. Fogarty, will be visiting me on Friday afternoon. Could you manage to come here then?'

Tegan had been tapping away at her computer again and held up a scribbled note to me. Ferry arr Rosslare 06:45am Fri. She pointed at Columbus and mimed that she would look after him at home. A not unusual treat for the dog.

'That's fine, I can be with you in the early afternoon on Friday, Miss Whelan.'

'Shall we say two o'clock, Mr. Ross? It's quite a long drive up to the house, and I'm afraid it's a bit overgrown these days.'

'I'll look forward to seeing you Friday, Miss Whelan,' I said enthusiastically, hoping that the lawyer wouldn't be contrary. I really had no idea what to expect, a dead end or the Tiger's Ghost in all its splendour sitting in a heated garage: at best something in between.

CHAPTER FIVE

The ferry was due to leave Pembroke in South Wales at 2:45am and the satnav told me it would take three and three-quarter hours from home to ship. At 11:15pm there was still plenty of traffic about, but by the time I had left the dual carriageways of the A48 other road-users were mainly trucks and vans, a good few with Irish registration plates. I reached the ferry terminal just in time to stretch my legs before loading began and was in my cabin asleep as the Isle of Inishmore left port.

An hour to go before docking at Rosslare I was up and enjoying a full Irish breakfast, gulping down the last of my tea, just as drivers were called to their vehicles. The day promisedbright sun in a blue sky and Tegan called me to check that all was well. She's a real mother-hen, and although I always tell her to stop fussing, we both know I would miss it if she did. 'Just passing Waterford and should be in the Bantry area in another three hours,' I told her.

Ireland's postcode system is only a few years old, but the Land Rover Defender's satnav accepted the Clarecourt destination without hesitation, and by 1:00pm, after a quick lunch stop, I was in the village of Ballylicky on the east coast of Bantry Bay. The countryside was outstanding, and if Kuldeep Singh had wanted a beautiful area to live out his life in relative seclusion and anonymity this was as good a place as any. Having time to kill I walked about the village, with a brief stop at the Bay View Bar. Tempting as a pint of Guinness looked, I make it a rule never to drink before meeting clients or vendors, especially if they are little old ladies; a coffee with cream had to do.

It was another few minutes' drive to my destination, confirmed by the word Clarecourt chased into one of the weather-beaten stone gate pillars at the entrance. On top of the pillar was a large stone sphere, its mate missing from the other side. The gates themselves were ornate wrought iron, well on the way to rusty oblivion. They looked as if they hadn't been closed for many years.

The drive was about a quarter of a mile long, and Miss Whelan had been right: the borders were so overgrown that the Defender's mirrors on both sides were constantly brushed by the overhanging branches of unkempt rhododendrons. At five minutes to 2:00pm, the house finally came into view, and what a view. Clarecourt was a fine example of Irish Georgian architecture. The sweeping gravel drive widened out to an oval, bordering the Palladian-style property. Bantry Bay was the backdrop, and in the distance, across the water, the magnificent Bantry House could be glimpsed through the trees.

Walking up the steps to the double front doors I could see the house was showing severe signs of neglect. I didn't think Miss Whelan had a lot of spare cash. The doorbell was a china knob set in a brass saucer-shaped ring. The china was chipped, and the brass was gun-metal grey with flecks of green verdigris, but when pulled, a distant ringing came from the depths of the house. After two or three minutes I decided Miss Whelan had not heard me, but as I reached for the bellpull again the right-hand door opened slowly.

Miss Whelan looked to be in her mid-eighties. She was tall with shoulder-length white hair held in place with a tortoiseshell hairclip. She wore a baggy green cardigan over a high-necked cream silk blouse, and a pair of grey, pleated trousers, straight out of the 1950s, an elegant lady whatever she wore. She welcomed me with a smile and a definite twinkle in her grey-blue eyes. Quite a beauty when she was young and mischievous too, I thought.

'Mr. Ross, won't you come in?'

Miss Whelan ushered me into the entrance hall. It was a large oblong space with a wide staircase abutting the centre of the far wall. The landing served galleried corridors running both left and right, overlooking the hall on three sides. The lime-wash on the original Baroque decoration with its curves and swirls was now peeling in part, but nearly all the gilded highlights had survived.

On the wall each side of the staircase, for no apparent reason, were three marble sills at the level of a dado rail. I could only guess that large paintings had been supported by them in more affluent days.

Most striking of all was the hall's floor. Black and white marble tiles formed an obviously Asian criss-cross design of interlinked triangles surrounded by two concentric circles. I knew this was a geometric representation of lotus leaves, sacred flowers to Sikhs and Hindus. The space between the circles was decorated with groups of repeated symbols, maybe a religious text or prayer.

'Mr. Ross, we'll go through to the library, but mind the bucket by the door as you go,' Miss Whelan warned.

The container and three others were placed strategically on the hall floor. In each case there were the tell-tale signs of water coming through the ceiling, brown stains, flaking plaster and in one case bare laths.

'It's the roof you see, there's a deal of money needing to be spent. I'm saving up just now.'

I felt my hostess had been saving up for quite a long time.

The size of the library, about forty feet square, suited this grand old house. It was a welcoming room. To one side was a large marble fireplace with a carved wooden overmantel. High backed armchairs, some with faded linen coverings, some in worn and creased leather, were dotted about the room. At the far end, the sash windows had wooden shutters, typical of the Georgian style. Beneath the windows two of the chairs were separated by an inlayed rosewood side table, strewn with old copies of Country Life magazine and local newspapers. Miss Whelan's favourite reading spot, I thought. Mahogany bookshelves mainly covered all four walls. Most of the books were either bound in brown or red calf-leather, their titles embossed on the spines in gold leaf. I doubt any of them had been published in the last hundred years.

Miss Whelan was not slow to notice my interest. 'Many have been with the house since the first owner, you know. I'm afraid they're not for sale; the house would never forgive me.'

'I suspect they would buy you a new roof, Miss Whelan,' I replied.

'Something will turn up Mr. Ross, it always has. Now let me introduce you to my solicitor, Mr. Fogarty. Patrick, this is Mr. Ross.'

I had imagined Lawyer Fogarty to be in his sixties, dishevelled and overweight. The man before me was tall, smart and had yet to see forty. He had a vice-like handshake and a pleasant, open smile.

'A pleasure to meet you, Mr. Ross, you have a grand reputation in your world of rare motor cars.'

I was in no doubt the words were carefully chosen to let me know he had done his homework on behalf of his client.

Before I could come up with a suitably self-deprecating

reply, Fogarty continued. 'I'm sure there is no need for me to be present Mr. Ross, but as I'm here, I'll just sit quietly and listen to what you have to ask Caitlin, Miss Whelan.'

Now is it really Mr. Singh you want to know about?' she asked immediately.

I cleared my throat. 'Yes, I think he bought the house in 1912. Did you know Mr. Singh was an Indian Maharajah, His Serene Highness Kuldeep Singh of Cooch Sebah?'

Miss Whelan smiled, and her eyes twinkled. I could almost see the memories float behind those grey-blue eyes 'No, no, we only knew him as Mr. Singh.'

'He was trying to live a quiet life. Do you know much about him Miss Whelan?'

'Not a great deal, I was only ten years old when Father bought the house, and it was all done through Mr. Singh's solicitor, himself being dead, you see. I only met him the once. Mr. Singh invited the adjoining landowners and their families for tea here in the library one afternoon. It was just before Christmas 1944.'

'Please tell me anything you can about him and what happened to him,' I encouraged.

'Well, as I said, I was only ten at the time. We farmed on the adjoining land. My family came from Waterford and Father and Mother moved to Bantry in 1930. The war hardly affected us in Ireland, what with us being a neutral country, although most of us favoured helping any British soldiers that came our way. Shipwrecked or shot down, you see, although they were supposed to be interned for the duration.'

'No offence, Miss Whelan, but I thought the Irish were pro-German, what with the troubles and everything.'

'No, not at all,' she explained. 'A few diehards maybe, but there was a sort of unwritten truce during the war about the fight for Home Rule in the North. The powers that be thought there was a much better chance to do a deal with the British than with the Nazis if they won the war.'

Miss Whelan had a sharp brain, despite her frail-looking body, but I wanted to get back on to Kuldeep Singh and his car. 'So, how did your father come to buy Clarecourt?' I asked.

'Oh! Yes, the house. Well, Mr. Singh was a bit of a recluse. He was rarely seen, only his personal servants; all Indian you know, lovely people, very friendly. We respected his privacy, as he was good to the local people. Always gave generously to local charities. Did you know he paid for the grand village hall in Ballylicky; it's still there.'

'But you said he had died,' I prompted. 'Was he ill?'

'I don't think so,' Miss Whelan gave a sad shake of her head. 'He was found by the sea, near to the grounds of the house; washed up amongst some rock pools, the poor man. He had a nasty gash on his head and a fractured skull. Slipped on the seaweed and rocks, knocked himself out and drowned in a few inches of water. Papa said the body was found early in the morning. Most thought it was an accident, although a few said that the Indian servants had murdered him, as all four of them had disappeared: run off and were never heard of again.'

'Do you remember when this happened, Miss Whelan?'

'Oh! yes, it was early in 1945, just before the war ended. At the end of April, I think it was.'

'Didn't the Maharajah leave everything to his family, or friends maybe?' I asked.

'There was a sum of money I believe. Quite large, it was said, but that was between him and his solicitor. As to the house, all its contents and the land, well, they were to be sold by auction and the proceeds given to the parish for the benefit of the local people. Did I say, he seemed to like us all. There were quite a few locals worked at the house over the years, gardeners, maids and others, but one of the Indian servants looked after all the cooking, my mother once told me.'

'And that's how your father came to buy the house, in an executor's sale?'

'Oh yes, an auction. All the other bidders were builders who wanted to knock the place down for the stone. Father was determined to outbid them, as he wanted it as a home for us all. And of course, the land joined ours, so it was more valuable to Father than anyone else for both reasons.'

Now was the time to ask about the Tiger's Ghost. 'Miss Whelan, do you remember if the Maharajah, Mr. Singh had a big old car, painted with tiger stripes?'

She thought for a few seconds, before replying. 'No, no, I don't remember anything like that. His servants had the use of a large black car, an Austin I think it was, but I'm not very good at car names.'

Disappointed, I smiled. 'No reason why you should be Miss Whelan, but I don't suppose it's still around?' I thought that a pre-war Austin in sound barn-find condition could be better than nothing.

'I haven't seen it for years. It's in the barn, a lovely old building, but a bit ramshackle now, too dangerous to use,' Miss Whelan warned me.

'Do you think we could go and look at the car?' I asked hopefully.

'It's a little too far for me to walk nowadays, I get out of breath easily, but go yourself and Mary will have served tea by the time you get back. Take the track to the right of the house and then the right fork. You'll see within a few minutes.

Meanwhile, Patrick and I will finish our business.'

In less than five minutes I was standing in front of a beautiful but derelict stone-built barn. The roof with its missing slates had a ridge that dipped alarmingly. A portion of one end-wall had fallen away at a corner, and the vast wooden doors were weather-worn to a silvery grey. It took all my strength to force one of them open, but the old hinges, with vivid green moss along their top edges, were as sound as the day they were fitted. If ever there was a place that promised the discovery of a long-forgotten car, this was it. My searcher's sixth sense screamed at me that there was more than a derelict 1930s Austin just yards away.

Inside the barn was like a rural film-setting. The dusty remnants of long-gone straw bales were strewn across the floor. A set of rusting gang mowers lay against the opposite wall to the entrance, and pigeons cooed languidly on their roof-beam perches. To the right at the far end of the barn was a wooden partition, with a man-sized door to one side. In front of it were the sad remains of a 1938 Austin Iver limousine, a sturdy old car in its day: now too far gone to be worth recovering. The leaking barn roof and pigeons had seen to that.

I looked across the Austin at the wooden barn-partition, not an unusual feature for such a building, as it had probably been added to house a stationary engine for driving a water pump, or electricity generator. There was a good chance the engine was still there, a clue being a rusty exhaust pipe hanging off the outside of the barn. I had to force the latch up and yank the door open, pushing hard against the Austin's rust-perforated wing to allow a big enough gap for me to squeeze through.

The room was larger than I had expected, about twenty feet from wooden partition to the barn's end-wall. A single unglazed window, high up, let enough light in once my eyes had adjusted. To the right of the door was a workbench, strewn with long-abandoned tools. A vintage-looking bicycle stood against the far wall, upside down on its saddle and handlebars, with the front wheel propped up next to it. A perished innertube was half out of the tyre, and an open puncture repair-kit tin completed the neglected scene.

One other item was in the room, resting in the far corner. I walked over and stood in front of the radiator of an early Rolls-Royce Silver Ghost. My stomach was doing somersaults, I needed to take a deep breath. The whole chassis was there, complete with engine, gearbox, back axle, and wheels. Everything except the coachwork, although the scuttle between where the windscreen and bonnet would have been, was there, but no gold or tiger's stripes, just filthy black paint. The chassis was as it had left the Rolls-Royce factory in Derby over a hundred years ago. Each rear hub had a pair of wheels; a feature used to take the extra weight of the armoured cars that were designed for use during the First World War. This could be the remains of one such army surplus vehicle. My heart missed a beat as it occurred to me that solid gold coachwork would also be much heavier than the normal aluminium-clad body. Maybe this chassis was a forerunner of the armoured cars. Quite a few saw service in Ireland.

I hurried back to the Defender and pulled my Marauder flashlight from its charger. It was necessary to check the car's all-important chassis number. If this was the remains of an armoured car, or the Tiger's Ghost, then the chassis number would confirm it. I shone the torch around the bulkhead, and there, to the left of the steering column and just above the clutch pedal was the bronze chassis plate, but it was covered in years of dirt, tarnish and settled dust. I looked around the room for something to clean it off: a file, or a piece of sandpaper. The flashlight beam caught the bicycle with its puncture-repair kit. I was in luck, there was a small piece of coarse emery paper for cleaning off the inner tube before sticking on the repair patch. It was brittle, but still abrasive enough to do what I wanted.

Rubbing gently at the chassis-plate, the fragile emery paper started to disintegrate, but not before the part of the plate on which the number was stamped began to shine. I moved the light to one side so that the stamped number would show up against the newly polished bronze. It was 60918: I punched the air. 'Yes!' I shouted, hardly able to believe my luck. I had found the remains of the legendary Tiger's Ghost.

CHAPTER SIX

For a few moments I looked at the car. Its wheels were off the ground, the axles anchored to the tops of concrete blocks and one of the driver's-side rear wheels had been replaced by a large pulley. Next to it lay a wide flat canvas belt that would have driven a generator for the house and outbuildings. That was long gone, but an electrical control board with its dials and brass contact-forks, each below an engraved-ivory label to show its purpose, bore witness to the Silver Ghost's last use.

I scanned the torch-beam over every part of the old Rolls's chassis. Everything seemed to be there, even the instruments. I wondered at the adventures it had taken part in, the loves and losses of its owners, and its downward spiral from brand new, expensive, and revered, to

abandoned derelict, following years of increasing mistreatment and neglect.

But now was not the time for such daydreaming. The legendary Tiger's Ghost chassis was found, but not yet purchased. Some negotiating with Miss Whelan was needed. Leaving the barn I jogged back to the Defender, and its satellite phone that gives me world-wide coverage.

A pre-First World War Silver Ghost chassis, complete but in need of total restoration, is still a valuable car, but I had to find out exactly what it was worth. I called an old acquaintance who has specialised in Rolls-Royce cars for many years. I didn't let on where the car was; all's fair in love, war and exotic car dealing. He confirmed that the value of these Silver Ghosts increases drastically the older they are. I gave a low whistle when he told me what a 1908-built chassis should fetch at auction.

The next call was to wake Mitch in San Francisco to see if he was interested in acquiring the car less its coachwork. After he calmed down and realised that no gold or gems had yet been found he saw the potential for fame in the old-car world even if he owned just the rolling chassis of the Tiger's Ghost.

'How cheap can you get it from the old dame?'

'Mitch, I don't rip people off. I have a reputation in this business, and I hope a rosy future. If I act for you, you'll offer a fair price.'

'But I won't lose money on the deal, right Ross?'

We agreed a price to offer Miss Whelan, which I was tempted to give as a first and final figure to avoid bargaining. As it turned out I didn't have to worry about Miss Whelan's canny negotiating skills. Ringing the doorbell, I let myself in through the front door, this time carrying a contract of sale in my black leather attaché case.

'I'm back, Miss Whelan, shall I come straight in?' I shouted. Tea was being laid out by Mary from the village, a teenager who looked as if she would rather be doing anything else than serving afternoon tea at Clarecourt.

Once Mary had returned to her other duties, I smiled at my hostess and her adviser.

'Good news and bad news Miss Whelan. The bad news is that the Austin is beyond restoration and is therefore only worth a few pounds for some mechanical parts, less than it would cost to move it.' Miss Whelan looked so depressed, I hurried on. 'The good news is there's an old car chassis in the back of the barn, which looks as if it used to power a generator. Do you remember that?'

Miss Whelan's frown turned to a smile. 'Oh yes! I remember now, one of the farm hands would start the engine at dusk and run it until bedtime; early to bed and early to rise for farmers, Mr. Ross. Father always said we would never be in the dark with our Ghost. It was his little joke.'

'Did you know what he meant?'

'At the time, we children thought, that is Michael, God rest his soul, and I thought that ghosts couldn't get us because the lights were on. It was only later that I understood the generator was powered by a Silver Ghost engine. A play on words, do you see?'

'Miss Whelan, did you ever see the car and the generator?' I asked.

'Oh no, we were not allowed in the barn's back room. Father said it was dangerous, what with the engine fan, the pulley belt and the electric. I even think the door was padlocked most of the time. Do you know, in all the years I have lived here, I've never been in that part of the barn. We went onto the mains electric in about 1955, I think it was, so there was no need for the generator.'

'Well, as I said, it's not just an engine, it's a whole car except for its body, and it's quite valuable.'

Miss Whelan looked towards the door, closed to the rain bucket behind. 'Do you think anyone would pay enough for a little work to be done to the roof?'

'Miss Whelan, I would very much like to buy the chassis from you. I think it belonged to Mr. Singh, His Serene Highness the Maharajah Kuldeep Singh of Cooch Sebah, and a client of mine wants that particular car.'

Miss Whelan had an angelic look on her face as she mused, 'A real Maharajah? So, would it be more valuable to your client than anyone else?'

'I imagine it might, Miss Whelan,' I replied, with a fair degree of honesty.

Her angelic look was now tinged with the focused stare of a hard negotiator. 'What would you be offering on behalf of your client?'

Patrick Fogarty leaned forward in his chair.

This negotiation could become tricky. I usually deal with people who have a strong idea of what they want for a car, and it's my task to draw them out on this figure, to establish a starting point for negotiation. I didn't think for a moment that Miss Whelan had a clue as to the value of the Rolls, so, canny as she was, I would have to guide her to a fair deal for both of us. 'How much needs to be spent on the roof?' I asked her.

'Five years ago, Mr. McArdle gave me an estimate of forty thousand euros. He said it would last long after my lifetime.'

'If I told you that my client would be prepared to pay you a quarter of a million pounds sterling, how would you feel about that?'

Miss Whelan's look of surprise was obvious, and she didn't try and hide it, for this figure was beyond her wildest dreams. 'A quarter of a million pounds, for a rusty old engine?' she glanced unbelievingly at Fogarty.

'A not very rusty old complete chassis,' I corrected. I could see the possibilities of the improvement in Miss Whelan's standard of living rushing through her mind.

'And when would I be paid?' she asked, her eyes narrowing a fraction.

'I could have the money transferred to you first thing tomorrow morning.' I could see that she was about to say yes, but I held up a hand to stop her. 'Before you agree to sell the car to me for a quarter of a million, let me tell you that I consider an honest price to pay you is three hundred thousand pounds.'

My phone call earlier had established that the Tiger's Ghost chassis might be worth four hundred thousand pounds at auction. The going rate for a dealer to purchase such a car was seventy per cent of that figure, which in this case was two hundred and eighty thousand pounds. I rounded it up to three hundred thousand as I thought Miss Whelan needed the money more than Mitch, who even after costs and my commission would still be paying a fair price.

Miss Whelan looked at her lawyer. 'I think I should say yes, Patrick. Do you agree?'

Patrick nodded. 'I think Mr. Ross has probably offered you a very fair price.'

'Mr. Ross, if you can transfer three hundred thousand pounds to my bank, we have a deal.'

She made a spitting sound into her hand and held it out for me to shake, which I did.

'Three hundred thousand it is, pounds sterling, and now a little Irish whisky to seal the deal.'

Patrick Fogarty stood up and shook Miss Whelan's hand. 'Not for me, thank you. I must be away to my office now, so goodbye, Caitlin. It seems I was right earlier. There was no need for me to be present.' I received a courteous nod.

I had to smile. This elegant old lady had reminded me that she was the daughter of an Irish farmer and no doubt horse-dealer in his time. Even so, I felt good about paying her the extra twenty thousand of Mitch's money.

Back in the Defender, I used my laptop and satphone to locate a covered trailer and found a livestock transport company just twenty miles away that would hire me one large enough for the Tiger's Ghost. Before setting off to collect it, I called Tegan to tell her the deal had been done. Next I told Mitch that he had to pay twenty thousand more than our target price, and to arrange for the transfer of funds to Miss Whelan's bank account. Crucially, I stressed the importance of him telling no one that we had found the car, until it was finally under his legal ownership as agreed by the British Customs and the Driver and Vehicle Licensing Agency.

It was dusk before the rental trailer was unhitched for the night outside Miss Whelan's barn. At the Bay View Bar, I enjoyed a light meal with two celebratory pints of Guinness. Thankfully, Tegan had secured me a room at a bed and breakfast in the village. It had been a long day, but a good day, one of the best.

CHAPTER SEVEN

The next morning's problem was how to get the chassis out of its resting place of many decades. Luckily, all the equipment needed was either in or on the Defender, and the second barn door proved easier to open than the first. I manoeuvred the Land Rover inside and used its winch to pull the old Austin out of the way of the wooden partition, on the other side of which sat the Tiger's Ghost. I hacked a couple of holes in the partition, looped the winch's steel cable through and, once secured, gently pulled the woodworm-riddled wall down. It came away easily in one piece, falling flat in a cloud of dust, straw and feathers, much to the annoyance of the pigeons. Miss Whelan had readily agreed to this demolition as a necessary evil to attain her new-found wealth.

Unbelievably, after all these years, the Ghost's tyres held air pumped from the Defender's compressor. Undoing the bolts that held the axles on the concrete blocks was all the work needed for the chassis to be free. Using a trolley-jack and ramps I pulled it clear of the blocks and lowered it onto the ground.

By 4:00pm the Tiger's Ghost was loaded in the trailer, and I was ready to leave Clarecourt. Funds had been transferred, and the Tiger's Ghost chassis was mine to take away.

Miss Whelan knew of no documents such as a logbook to prove ownership of the car, so armed only with my standard vendor's bill of sale duly signed by her as the rightful owner, we telephoned Patrick Fogarty and arranged for him to have her swear an affidavit that she had inherited the car along with the house and estate.

Old cars need much paperwork these days for the transference of their ownership from citizens of one country to another, especially if the car has historic significance; it would take some time to achieve this for Mitch. Meanwhile, the car would be safe in a discreet and secure warehouse on the outskirts of Cork, that I had used before. Once the car was tucked safely away, I returned the trailer to the transport company and headed back to the ferry. It was too late to arrange for the night crossing, so I booked a room in a small but comfortable hotel.

Feeling revived after a good night's rest and a fine breakfast, I drove across the ferry ramp in time for the 8:45am sailing that would dock in Pembroke four hours later. Bound for the Club class lounge, I stopped off to buy an English newspaper to while away the time. Having found my seat, with a good view of the Irish Sea, I opened the paper which contained the usual digest of human weakness, greed, and fallibility.

Page six was different; surprise became irritation and then fury in a matter of seconds. The top half of the page featured a grainy photograph taken in 1910 of the Tiger's Ghost with Maharajah Kuldeep Singh standing beside it. The headline above it shouted TITANIC CAR FOUND. A brief description of the Rolls and Kuldeep Singh followed, with comments from the car's discoverer, automotive collector Angelo Mitchelletti of San Francisco.

Thank God Mitch had stolen all the limelight and neither I nor the whereabouts of the car were mentioned. I had warned him, seriously warned him, to keep quiet about our success. Experience has taught me that the car could attract attention from officials and thieves. Also, we could well be pestered by treasure hunters seeking a lead to the gold and gems. In fact, the article only briefly mentioned that it was just the chassis that we had bought; more impact for the newspaper but more potential trouble for us.

I punched my speed-dial button for Mitch. By the time he awoke from his San Francisco sleep I had calmed down enough not to shout at him. 'Mitch, I've just seen the Tiger's Ghost story in an English newspaper. Why didn't you keep quiet like I told you?'

'Hey, all publicity is good publicity, Ross. Someone might call us with a lead to the treasure.'

'Mitch, someone might try and take the car from us, never mind treasure that's probably spread throughout the world by now,' I snapped back.

'Nah, now we got the chassis we can go look for all the jewels and gold and stuff.'

I took a deep breath and waited a second before replying. 'Mitch, I'm a car broker. That means, finding and selling interesting cars. I'm not a treasure hunter and I'm not interested in chasing after long-gone treasure. If you want to do that, that's up to you, but don't involve me.'

'Ross don't be rash. Look how well we work together. A few days and we already found a car lost for over a hundred years. Hey, I'll be back in the UK anyway tomorrow. I'll drive straight from Heathrow down to you, first thing. We can talk about this. Gotta go, see you then.'

I walked out on deck to calm down. The brisk wind felt good, I ambled as far forward as passengers were allowed. The day was bright, and the sea-swell was just the right side of comfortable. The Tiger's Ghost would soon be with Mitch, then he could do what he liked with the car, but if he wanted me to stay involved, he would have to follow my advice. I was prepared to oversee the restoration of the chassis to perfect condition, and order a recreation of the bodywork, just as Kuldeep Singh had commissioned it. The only difference would be that the solid gold body panels would now be gold-plated aluminium, the jewels would be paste and the Tiger's head would be a hollow casting covered with gold leaf.

This way Mitch would own a drivable car and a unique concours d'elegance competitor on the world's top car-show circuit. He would gain kudos from the major players in the old-car world, and another piece in the jigsaw of automotive history would have dropped into place. Of course, all of this would be good for my business and my reputation.

Back in my lounge seat I decided to do my best to dissuade Mitch from chasing the jewels and gold. Surely even he must realise that if the long shot paid off and he actually found anything, then massively expensive legal battles would follow, no doubt with Indian, British, and Irish governments all claiming ownership, never mind interested private claimants who would doubtless appear. Annoying as Mitch was, I couldn't help liking him. He reminded me of an energetic Labrador that wouldn't do as it was told but was always forgiven because of its enthusiastic personality and winning smile.

During the drive home, the blue sky had morphed into scudding cumulus clouds, slowly darkening into the surety of imminent rain. Pulling into the Clock House courtyard, the first drops fell, and I saw Smiler driving the newly running and freshly washed Derby Bentley back into the workshop. I waved at him as I ran across to the office. His only comment, 'Bloody weather.'

CHAPTER EIGHT

Early the next morning after a scalding hot shower and a hurried breakfast, I ground some Tanzanian coffee beans, and took the steaming cup to the office, half expecting Mitch to be sitting in my chair waiting impatiently for my arrival. He wasn't there, but if he was true to form, he would have been in the courtyard sounding his car horn by now. I killed some time at the computer, getting up to date with a trawl through some classic car websites. It only took half an hour, by which time the sun was warming the day. I trotted down the spiral staircase into the garages and pushed the six sets of doors open, Columbus yapping at my heel.

I like to get some fresh air and warmth onto the old metal of my small car collection when possible. Pulling the dust sheets from each of them, I chose my Aston Martin DBR1. A 1959 works reserve competition car, it had a glorious history having been driven by Roy Salvadori to many a victory. If Mitch wasn't here by lunchtime, I would take it to the Carnarvon Arms at Highclere for a ploughman's lunch and a pint of lemonade shandy. If he did show up, I would give him a ride to remember.

Just as I was warming up the engine a police car pulled into the courtyard. A high-viz-jacketed constable and a sergeant heaved themselves out the car.

'Mr. Ross?' The sergeant looked down at his notebook, 'Mr. Benedict Ross?'

'That's me,' I couldn't help my mind racing to find a misdemeanour in my immediate past. Had the Defender been caught speeding or was there trouble already with the Tiger's Ghost importation?

'Sergeant Mbulu and Constable Waters,' he said, nodding at his high-viz mate. 'Do you know a Mr. Angelo Mitchelletti, sir?'

'Yes, I do. In fact, he was supposed to be here first thing this morning for a meeting, but he hasn't shown up yet.'

'So, you've no idea where he might be?'

'Well, he was flying into Heathrow, so maybe his plane was delayed.'

Sergeant Mbulu explained, 'No, it was on time, and he collected a hire car from Avis. A member of the public reported the car abandoned in a lane just off the A4, this side of Newbury.'

'What do you mean, abandoned?' I asked blankly.

'The car was on the grass verge, keys in it and the radio on. That sort of abandoned. We tracked Mr. Mitchelletti to Avis through the registration number. There was no luggage in the car, but your postcode was running as a destination on the satnav, and your business card was on the passenger seat.'

I tried to imagine a reason but could only think he might have had some sort of accident or illness. 'Was the car damaged, have you checked the local hospitals?'

'No damage and the hospitals would notify us under these circumstances. We have checked though, just in case,' said the Sergeant.

'Do you have his mobile number?' I asked.

'Yes sir, from Avis. It's no longer active; either it's switched off or the SIM card has been taken out. In your estimation, do you consider it unlikely behaviour for Mr. Mitchelletti to leave his car and tell no one?'

I thought carefully for a few seconds. 'Mitch is a bit impulsive, bit of a grasshopper mind, but he was coming here for business reasons. I've known him a good while and I'd say he takes business very seriously. So no, I think leaving his car and not getting in touch with me is unlike him. What happens now?'

'That's up to our Control Room Sergeant. He might reckon Mr. Mitchelletti is a missing person, under the circumstances, and the fact you say this is out of character for him.' Mbulu handed me his card. 'Call this number if he contacts you, please. Thank you for your assistance, Mr. Ross.'

'If I learn anything, I'll call you immediately,' I confirmed. 'I'll also call his office in San Francisco, once they're open.'

Constable Waters was back in the car by now, and Sergeant Mbulu nodded his thanks and joined him. They drove off to the squawk of police radio traffic and left me puzzled with the first niggles of serious concern about Mitch. He could be impulsive to say the least, but to walk away from the car with the radio left on and the key in the ignition were not things anyone would do if in control of their situation.

In the evening I called Mitch's San Francisco office. The purring of the American phone ceased after only two bursts.

'This is Graphica Publishing, America's favourite graphic novel and comic book publisher. I'm Christian, Director of First Impressions. How may I help you?'

'My name's Ben Ross. I'm not sure who I should speak to, but is there a co-director of Mr. Mitchelletti's available?' I knew there were three of them, and the usual American plethora of vice-presidents.

'I'm sorry,' said Christian. 'All three of the company's board directors are out of town, but one, Ms. Bassoli, will be back first thing tomorrow morning.'

'Could I have her cell phone number, please?' I asked.

'I'm afraid she's on a meditation retreat and may not to be

contacted under any circumstances, but she'll be back at her desk tomorrow.'

'Thank you Christian, I'll try again tomorrow.'

'I'm looking forward to it, have a nice day, Mr. Ross,' enthused Christian.

The next day I had plenty of work to keep me occupied. At 6:30pm in the evening, it was 10:30am in California, and time to give Mitch's office another call.

Once again Christian answered. He remembered me and who I wished to speak to. The line clicked into a few seconds of appropriate comic-super-hero music before Mitch's co-director spoke to me.

'This is Lucia Bassoli. How may I help you?' Ms. Bassoli sounded efficient almost to the point of being irritating.

'I don't know if Mitch has mentioned me, but my name is Ben Ross, and I have been helping Mitch find a car . . .'

Ms. Bassoli cut me off in mid-sentence. 'Ah, you're in England. Mitch emailed me that you had found the car. Is he with you now, Mr. Ross?'

'No, no he's not with me, and that's really why I'm calling you. Have you heard from Mitch since Saturday?'

'No, but why do you ask?' Lucia Bassoli now had a tinge of alarm in her voice.

'I phoned Mitch from Ireland on Sunday, and we agreed to meet first thing Monday morning at my place. Mitch didn't show up, and later in the day, the police found his hire car abandoned by the roadside. There hasn't been a sign of him since, and his phone isn't live.'

Lucia Bassoli asked the obvious questions: was he at his hotel, had he emailed, had anyone checked the hospitals? I put her mind at rest that all avenues had been investigated, and now that he had been missing for forty-eight hours the police would treat him as a missing person and start searching in earnest.

She then asked a pertinent but unexpected question. 'Do you think the Tiger's Ghost has anything to do with Mitch disappearing?'

I had wondered if his newspaper interview had attracted a criminal gang who thought he now had untold wealth in the form of gold and jewels from the car, but I'd dismissed the thought on balance as being too far-fetched for the real world. There was urgency in Ms. Bassoli's question that made me think she suspected it may be the case. 'No, I can't see any reason why my having found a derelict car chassis would lead to Mitch disappearing, although, against my advice, he did spread it all over the press. You sound worried that Mitch has come to harm. Would you agree that his going missing is unusual, out of character?' I asked.

She answered with a sigh and a slight tremble in her voice. 'Mr. Ross, I cannot imagine any situation where Mitch would be out of touch with this office. I should call the San Francisco Police Department.'

'I don't think you need to do that. The British police are pretty good at this sort of thing, and I'm sure they will contact yours if the need arises. I think we should wait and see what our police come up with in the next few days. Anyway, Mitch will probably reappear with a hangdog look and a totally insincere apology.'

Ms. Bassoli gave a hollow laugh. 'Wow, you got Mitch's number pretty damn quick, didn't you?'

'I've known him a long time, I like him. He just takes a bit of getting used to. Look, I'll email you with any updates and my contact details if you need to speak to me.'

'Okay, that sounds like a plan. I'll take care of things here in San-Fran, Mr. Ross. Thanks for staying with this, I know it's not really your problem,' Ms. Bassoli ended the call.

I didn't know it then, but it was about to be very much my problem.

CHAPTER NINE

It was now a week since Mitch went missing. I had phoned the police right after talking to Lucia Bassoli to let them know that Mitch's office was unaware of his predicament. They took down the contact details for Graphica Publishing and told me investigations were still underway. Mitch was now officially a missing person at risk. Police activity had increased, including a detailed physical search in the area where his hire car had been found. An image flashed through my mind of a line of police officers with long sticks prodding the undergrowth and hedgerows, ending with a shout from one of them indicating a found corpse. I dismissed the thought as quickly as it had come.

Mid-morning another police car pulled into the courtyard. I walked down from the office to meet the occupant, hoping to receive some good news. The car door opened, and the policeman turned out to be a policewoman in civvies, looking more like a trouser-suited business executive than a copper. She looked up from her clipboard, swept back a long, stray strand of blond hair, and gave me a broad grin.

'So, it is you, Lieutenant. I thought there couldn't be too many Benedict Rosses about.'

I recognised her immediately. 'Lieutenant Laing!'

'Detective Inspector now,' Kirstie Laing laughed as we gave each other a long hug. She stepped back, squeezing my arm with her free hand, and shook her head. 'Ben Ross. The blue-eyed handsome pin-up of the Camp Bastion ladies.'

'If only I'd known,' I said.

'What the hell have you been up to since Afghanistan?' She asked.

'How long have you got? Life's not been too bad. Briefly, I buy and sell cars like these, all over the world for rich but shy clients.' I swept my arm around at the Aston and the other cars in my garage.

Kirstie pulled an I'm-impressed face. 'Wife, kids?' she asked.

'No, close once. She decided to return home to New Zealand, and I couldn't see giving up my business to go with her. So, still single,' I smiled and added hastily 'No kids either. And you?'

'I left the army a couple of years after you and went straight into the police. Lived with a guy for a year or two, but we disagreed about my career, so we went our separate ways. I'd love to catch up properly Ben, but I'm here on police business. Let's get that out of the way,' she said, frowning at the papers on her clipboard.

'Come on up to the office, I'll get the coffee on. Is it still double strength Americano?'she nodded that it was, with a shrug and a what-can-I-do?expression.

Columbus greeted her at the door, showing his instant approval of the Detective Inspector, who tickled his ears as she looked around the office, taking in the shabby but comfortable look of the place. 'I can't believe it. We only live about half an hour's drive from each other.'

'We really should have kept in touch,' I replied and meant it. I gave her the coffee and sat down with mine. 'Okay, how can I help?'

'Angelo Mitchelletti. We haven't been able to find out anything new, except for some tyre tracks on the grass verge where the hire car was found. The tyres were most likely fitted to a Ford Transit van, but as we only have camera sightings of Mitchelletti on the M4, and nothing of a Transit van at the scene, it's not much help. Ben, is there anything at all that you can think of that might be a lead?'

'I called your Sergeant Mbulu after I'd spoken to Mitch's office in San Francisco. I've managed to get in touch with a co-director of his, Lucia Bassoli, but she's as much in the dark as we are.

'Nothing else then, however trivial?' asked Kirstie.

Lucia Bassoli's question flashed into my mind. Kirstie saw I had thought of something, by the look on my face. 'What is it, Ben?'

'I can't see that it's relevant myself, but when I first spoke to Bassoli, she rather pointedly asked a strange question. Did I think me finding the Tiger's Ghost was anything to do with Mitch's disappearance?'

'The Tiger's Ghost,' Kirstie shuffled through the papers on her clipboard and held up a photocopy of the newspaper article on Mitch.

I explained about the car's early life in India, the Titanic, the glass plate images, in fact the entire story including my annoyance at Mitch having given the game away.

Kirstie drained her coffee cup and looked at me thoughtfully. 'Ben, with your experience of valuable old cars, do you think there is any possibility at all that your having found the chassis of the Tiger's Ghost could be connected with this case?'

'If Mitch had told the newspaper that he had found the gold and the jewels, or even a clue to their whereabouts then maybe, yes. What I found was a neglected car chassis that had been in a derelict barn for over sixty years. The valuables are long gone, who knows where. I think it much more likely that Mitch has an enemy in his business world of publishing graphic novels and comics. He might have bought a rare edition, and there's some collector who wants it at all costs,' I said, trying to be as resourceful as I could.

'Surely a comic can't be worth a kidnap ransom?' Kirstie said to herself as much as to me.

'Mitch once told me that an early Superman, or something similar could be worth up to three million dollars.'

'Then a ransom could be a possibility. I think it's time for us to call the San Francisco Police.' She stood up and glanced at her watch. 'I haven't got time to catch up right now, Ben. Here's my mobile number, give me a call. Let's make an evening of it.'

Kirstie Laing gave me a kiss on the cheek. 'I'll see myself out,' she said, bounding down the stairs.

As she drove out of the courtyard, the morning post van drove in. I met the postman as he was halfway to the office. He had the usual pile of unsolicited junk mail for me, plus two car magazines and five letters, two of which bore foreign stamps.

The Aston Martin was out again. Tossing the mail on the passenger's seat, I slid behind the wheel and started the engine, with its customary rip-roaring snarl, loud enough to hurt your ears if you stood by the side-exhaust pipes. Once the engine settled at a fast tick-over, I ignored the junk mail, glanced at the magazine covers through their plastic wrappers, but slit open the first of the two foreign letters. The stamp was French, and the contents were from a fellow car dealer, in Angouleme. He wanted to know if I had a buyer for a 1928 Lancia Lambda, one owner and just forty thousand kilometres from new; I thought I just might have.

The second envelope had a Belgian stamp on it, and the letter gave no indication who the writer was, or where he was from. Using an Inkjet printer, on a photocopier-grade sheet of paper was written:

Benedict Ross,

You are now aware that your client, Mr. Angelo Mitchelletti has disappeared. At the moment he is comfortable and well looked after, although he is understandably unhappy about being contained against his will. If you wish to see that Mr. Mitchelletti remains unharmed and in good health, then please use the enclosed ticket to take the Eurostar train to Lille, you have a reservation for a luncheon table at 13:00 hours for two persons at the Restaurant Boniface. Should you fail to turn up, Mr. Ross, then I regret that my next communication will be a parcel which contains a severed finger of Angelo Mitchelletti. The same will hold true if you inform the police or any third party. Further options will be made available to you.

There was no signature, but the return Eurostar ticket was for the train leaving St. Pancras tomorrow, Tuesday at 10:15am.

Part of my army work in Afghanistan had been logistics, the art of moving goods in the most efficient and cost-effective way, where and when they were needed. This had required careful consideration of many factors, not least, how to avoid enemy action interfering with the supply lines. In this case, Mitch was the goods, his captors were the enemy, and I had to analyse the best method for his safe return to either the Clock House or San Francisco.

The obvious thing to do would be to tell the police and let them handle the whole thing. But Mitch's captors had proved themselves efficient and purposeful. He had been taken discreetly, with no worthwhile clues to follow up. I'd bet the Aston Martin that the letter was not going to reveal any fingerprints, or saliva on the self-sealing envelope for forensic databases to compare.

The crime had been committed in England, Mitch was a

United States citizen, the letter had been posted in Belgium, and I was to take a train to the French town of Lille. So, from the start there would be the Thames Valley police, the San Francisco police department, a Belgian and a French police involvement, and doubtless Interpol. That would be at least five police forces from which a leak to the criminals could result in Mitch losing a finger, or worse.

I considered what could I do as a private citizen. More than most, as my logistics work in Afghanistan was also a cover for some more clandestine duties, which is how I had met Kirstie. We had both been undercover officers in the Intelligence Corps.

Revving the Aston's engine for a few seconds to clean the spark plugs, I drove it back into its garage. My mind was made up, I would catch the Eurostar and see what happened in Lille.

CHAPTER TEN

Arriving at St. Pancras there was just enough time to spare for check-in and customs – ideal, as I hate waiting around for trains or planes. Descending the stairs to the platform I trudged along to the first-class coaches, where a smartly uniformed and pretty French girl saw me aboard and into the correct seat, one of a pair facing each other, separated by a table. Compared to the echoing hubbub of the station, the quiet cosiness of the Eurostar carriage made it a pleasant place to sit.

The train gathered speed as it left central London and passed through the suburbs of Surrey and the countryside of Kent. It was goodbye to England as we set off from Ebbsfleet, towards the tunnel under the English Channel, or La Manche as the French would say. It seemed that the seat facing mine, with its reserved sign, would continue to be unused; plenty of room for me to stretch my legs.

No sooner had I done so, than a small, elderly, dapper man entered the carriage and made his way to my table. A grandfatherly smile lit up his face as he compared his ticket with the empty seat's number.

'Ah! My place I think.' He spoke in near-perfect English with just a hint of a foreign accent: German, Swiss perhaps, or even southern Scandinavian.

I nodded and smiled my acknowledgement, dragging my feet back to my side of the table. My new neighbour unbuttoned his fawn raincoat and took off a dog-tooth check trilby hat, complete with a small feather in the band. He wore a white shirt and black knit tie beneath a Lovat green single-breasted suit.

All in all, his outfit and a pair of steel-rimmed glasses made him look as though he had walked straight off the set of a 1960s spy film.

The train entered the tunnel, and our eyes and ears adapted to the carriage lights, and increased air pressure. My companion fumbled to place his tightly furled umbrella against the carriage-side, beneath the table. In so doing he prodded my shoe.

'I apologise, Mr. Ross. I must seem a little clumsy. Please allow me to introduce myself. My name is Heinrich Vogel.'

Vogel had caught me by surprise. I really had not expected a kindly-looking old man to be my contact. Perhaps he wasn't, perhaps by a perverse coincidence some forgotten old boy from the past had recognised me. Vogel must have seen the brief look of bewilderment slip across my face as he continued, with the smile firmly in place.

'Yes, I am the person who you are travelling to meet. Sadly, for me not in the delightful city of Lille, for I must leave you soon at Calais.'

I had not expected to be engaging with my opponent so soon, but the old army training came to the rescue. I decided to play my cards just as I had planned for the expected meeting in Lille. 'What the hell is all this about? What has happened to Angelo Mitchelletti?' I asked, feigning indignant bad temper.

Vogel kept on smiling. 'I am only an emissary from my employer, my principal, shall we say. But I can explain our problem. First, Mr. Mitchelletti is well and unharmed, although he is a little too voluble in complaining of his temporary situation.'

I butted in to keep my indignant facade in place. 'He'd better be all right. And why the hell kidnap him? Are you after money? I certainly can't lay my hands on ready cash.'

Vogel made a calming gesture with the hand that was not keeping his umbrella in place. 'No, no, Mr. Ross. This is not about money.' He leant forward across the table. 'This is about the gold and the jewels that were once part of the Tiger's Ghost.'

For a moment, my cover of irate indignation dropped. It was the look in Vogel's eyes. They were absolutely dead, devoid of all feeling. I knew with certainty that whatever Herr Vogel wanted to achieve was most likely to be successful. Vogel would have noticed my slip, so the only course open to me was to fake a move from indignation to questioning neutrality. 'What's to stop me getting the police at Calais and reporting all that you have said or even wringing your scrawny neck right here and now?' I spoke more with inquiry than malice.

Vogel asked. 'Do you remember in 1978, a Bulgarian diplomat, Georgi Markov? He was terminated by the simple expedient of being stabbed with an umbrella-tip poisoned with a deadly ricin pellet.'

As Vogel spoke, he slid the tip of his own umbrella from my shoe to my ankle. 'Advances have been made since Markov's time, Mr. Ross. Today, a victim would feel no pain at all as a deadly nerve agent was spread onto the skin's surface. Such a person would die within a few seconds. The only outward sign to onlookers would be that he would seem to fall asleep in his seat. Science is a wonderful thing, is it not, Mr. Ross?'

This was a turn of events that I had not envisaged. Vogel really looked the part of a heartless killer when the smile left his eyes, but the whole umbrella thing could be a massive ploy to scare me.

'In answer to your question, I'm afraid informing the police, or to wring my scrawny neck would not help your situation, Mr. Ross, for I am a mere, how do you say, cog in the wheel.

The identity of my principal is unknown to me, and I would be unable to help the police at all.'

The umbrella tip was still against my ankle, and I wondered if I could pull my leg away fast enough to avoid a squirt of the deadly nerve agent if it really existed. Vogel must have had a sixth sense, as no sooner had the thought crossed my mind than he gently increased the pressure against my ankle. I tried to ignore it and take back the initiative. 'How do you communicate then?' I asked.

'There is a foolproof system in place, devised part from the ancient world, part from the Second World War and part from modern electronic communication systems; very complicated, I am told, to develop, but easy to use without trace to either party.'

Vogel continued. 'But, as I was about to say, Mr. Ross, there is a second element for you to consider,' he held up his free hand again. 'And please let me finish without interruption. My principal wishes you to search for the, ah, the valuable components shall we call them, of the Tiger's Ghost, the gold and jewels.'

Despite Vogel's request, I had to interrupt him. 'Vogel, I'm a car broker. I search for, buy, sell, and sometimes restore interesting motor cars for the rich and famous. I wouldn't have a clue how to look for lost treasure, especially treasure that was almost certainly dispersed many years ago.'

Vogel didn't seem to mind me having stopped his flow. 'There you are wrong, Mr. Ross. Your special skills are exactly what is required for this project. Namely your abilities to undertake document research, to draw information from people, and your tenacity in following leads that many others would not even recognise as being important. So, let me continue. Should you feel able to cooperate with us, then Herr, Mr. Mitchelletti will remain safe and be returned to your care. Should you feel unable to help us, then I am afraid he will be terminated.' As he spoke the last sentence the light of his smile left the steely cold grey eyes once more.

'Why now? If the Tiger's Ghost is so important to your boss, why wait until now?'

Vogel gave me a condescending shrug. 'Mr. Ross, you are forgetting. Until Mr. Mitchelletti was kind enough to inform the newspapers of his lucky find, the Tiger's Ghost was thought to be lost in the wreck of the Titanic.

'How did you know I was involved? There was no mention of me in the newspapers.'

'First, it was your business card on the seat of Mr. Mitchelletti's hired car, and upon gentle questioning he explained exactly what your involvement was.'

I had guessed that Mitch was the source of my connection when Vogel's letter had arrived. 'So how long have I got to find these valuable components, as you call them?'

'My principal understands this search may be futile. But it is most important for him to know if they are available, or if not, what happened to them. You have exactly two months from today's date to conclude the search.'

It was now time to move into my third mood, that of greedy interest. 'And if I agree to help, what's in it for me, apart from Mitch living to fight another day?'

'I am sure that Mr. Mitchelletti's safe return is uppermost in both our minds, but my principal is generous.' Vogel took a slim black leather and gold-edged wallet from his inside pocket and slipped out a debit card. He placed it on the table between us. 'As you can see this is a card for a Swiss private bank:

very discreet the Swiss, Mr. Ross. It is in your name. There is one million US dollars in this account and at your disposal to assist your search. Providing your efforts are satisfactory to my principal, then the remainder of the account will be yours to keep.'

'And what constitutes satisfactory efforts in the eyes of your principal, Herr Vogel?' I was now trying to give an impression of greed overcoming honourable intent.

Vogel leaned forward, the smile again sliding from his eyes. 'You will use your best endeavours to ascertain the whereabouts of the gold and jewels that once graced the Tiger's Ghost Rolls-Royce. If you find them, all you must do is let me know. My principal will arrange their acquisition. If you find proof that they are unavailable or lost beyond reasonable expectation of being retrievable, then you will also have done your work.'

'What if I am unable to provide sufficient proof of my efforts?' I asked.

'Then the consequences will be just the same as if you refuse to help, and Mr. Mitchelletti's body will be returned to you. One more thing, should you be successful in finding any or all of the valuable components and decide to keep them for yourself, then you also will be terminated.'

I looked at the debit card, and up at Vogel. His face gave away nothing.

'I don't respond to threats, Herr Vogel, and I don't care that much what happens to Mitch,' I lied as convincingly as I knew how. 'But I am a businessman and am prepared to give it a go. Under one condition,' I added.

'And what is that condition, Mr. Ross?'

'If I'm successful I want the bank facility topped-up back to one million US dollars for me to keep.'

Vogel's recurring smile broadened even wider, as I finally felt the umbrella tip slide from my ankle. 'My principal foresaw this possibility. I am pleased to say that I am empowered to agree to your request.'

We emerged into the French countryside, and the Chef de Train announced that we would soon be in Calais. Vogel stood up, buttoned his raincoat, put on his hat, and picked up his umbrella. 'I shall make my way to the exit now Mr. Ross. Shall I take the bank card, or shall I leave it with you?'

I slid the card to my side of the table, picked it up and tapped it sharply, edge on to the tabletop. I managed the most conspiratorial smile I could muster for the little creep. 'Herr Vogel, it would seem we shall both be working for your principal.' I stood and offered my hand to convince Vogel that I was on board.

Vogel shook it, with no indication at all that he was more or less pleased with me than at any time during our meeting. 'Enjoy your lunch in Lille. You will have time to view the beautiful old city before your return train to London. I shall be in touch at least every week for a progress report, Mr. Ross. Please do not let me down.' Vogel dipped his head in a court bow but stopped short at clicking his heels together.

As he turned for the exit, I asked him quickly. 'Herr Vogel, your umbrella, is it really a lethal weapon?'

He looked down at it, tilted in his hand, and once again the smile widened. 'This old friend, it is exceptionally good at keeping me dry, Mr. Ross, but you know, Markov was the first to die by such a means, he was not the last.' Vogel walked away, leaving me to sit down to contemplate all that had been said, and how near to death I might have been.

CHAPTER ELEVEN

By the time the train pulled into Lille I had decided to take advantage of the restaurant booking that Vogel had made for me. A walk around a new city would be a good place to think through my next moves. The unimaginatively named Lille Europé station is just a spit from the main square, the Opera House, and the old town. There's a mixture of ultra-modern and seventeenth-century architecture, a good deal of which had been recreated after destruction in the First World War.

I found the Restaurant Boniface in the centre of the old town. The Patron showed me to a two-place table, set for just one. The décor was typically French Edwardian. Rich wood panelling and red plush, but the many paintings that hung on each wall were all modern. Somehow the whole thing worked well as a good place to do a business deal, impress a loved one, or in my case work out a plan.

When in France, do as the French do. I ordered foie gras with Melba toast to start, then a sole Veronique with creamed spinach and potato dauphinoise, followed by a dessert of poached pears and almond tart, all washed down with a Petit Chablis. Sitting alone and enjoying the excellent food and wine, I relaxed enough to assess the problem of what to do about gaining Mitch's release.

The bill paid, I took a walk around the locality, and stopped at a small café bar for a coffee and Calvados. The day was by no means warm, but I took a seat at a pavement table, under one of the customary awnings. Just the spot to confirm my earlier thoughts.

My final decision was that it would be too risky to involve the various police forces with what had happened to Mitch, and now me. I had really made my decision when agreeing to help Vogel, I just hadn't admitted it to myself. He at least had faith in my treasure-finding abilities, even if I hadn't.

My allotted time was eight weeks to search out the gold and jewels and find if they were available or not. What Vogel's principal, as he liked to call him, would do to acquire the stuff might require some law-breaking. I just hoped Vogel would keep his word, and not involve me in those antics before he released Mitch.

By then the bank card would be a worthless piece of plastic, as I had every intention of double-crossing Vogel and his principal once I knew Mitch was safe. Swallowing the last of the Calvados, my watch told me I was in good time to catch the train back to London. My worry was, I still didn't really have a clue how to find the treasure, free Mitch and best the enemy, let alone the small matter of doing so in a way that would not get me prodded by a lethal umbrella.

I dozed on the journey home, keen to be in my own bed, where I enjoyed a good night's sleep, perhaps with my subconscious mind working overtime. For in the cold light of dawn, which was in fact a beautiful summer's morning, I started to form a workable plan. I would tell Smiler the complete story as he could be a valuable ally if Vogel came calling, but I wouldn't involve Tegan unless it became absolutely necessary; it would be unfair to put her in danger, however remote.

Smiler said nothing, assembled a roll-up cigarette and lit it, as I paced up and down explaining all. Columbus moved away from the foul-smelling tobacco, giving a very disdainful look for a dog.

Smiler hacked a smoker's cough. 'Look Guv, I don't know this Yank, Mitch. I only saw him once across the courtyard, but if you think he's worth standing up for then I'm in. Don't forget, I didn't just look after army helicopters in Middle Wallop. I was in Serbia and Iraq and got blown up for me trouble,' he spontaneously touched the scarring on the side of his face.

'You sure?'

'Wouldn't have it any other way, Guv,' he said, levering himself from the sofa, spilling roll-up ash down the front of his overalls, and on the carpet. 'I've got work to do.'

The office phone rang. 'This is Lucia. I've just booked into the Crowne Plaza, Kensington, and now I'm in a limo on my way to you.' She sounded none too happy.

CHAPTER TWELVE

A black BMW 7 Series pulled into the courtyard, and a grey-suited chauffeur moved to open a rear door for Lucia Bassoli. I thought it prudent to sprint down the stairs to meet her, expecting a feisty reception judging by her brief phone call. Looking every inch the California executive, she wore a designer trouser-suit, black, over a plain white cotton tee shirt; the jacket's lapel featured a hummingbird brooch studded with clear and green stones. By the sparkle I guessed real diamonds and by the shade of green, tourmaline perhaps, but I'm no expert. I reckoned she was just the other side of forty.

I gave Ms. Bassoli my most welcoming smile. 'Lucia, I hope the jet lag is not too bad. It's always good to put a face to a voice on the phone.'

Lucia frowned slightly as she assimilated my friendly welcome. 'Ah sure, jet lag's fine.' She made no comment about meeting face to face. The chauffeur handed over her briefcase, thanked her and returned to his seat.

'Can we go to your office? I need coffee.'

'Double Americano, I'm guessing, no sugar,' I replied, remembering that was just how Kirstie liked her coffee.

Up until now, Lucia had shown all the expression and body language of a woman on the attack, albeit subtly, but my coffee guess softened her attitude. I noticed that her intensely hazel eyes had flecks of green almost exactly matched by the stones on her broach. Lucia took care in her appearance, although her make-up was a shade too heavy for my taste.

I offered my guest the most comfortable seat, a leather-upholstered chair that normally had a blanket on it to capture Columbus's hair. I always chuck the cover into a cupboard before visitors arrive: a good thing today, as dark clothes and light-coloured dog hairs do not a happy combo make.

Coffee supplied, I decided to ignore Lucia's brittle behaviour and continue as friendly as I could. 'Have you learnt something about Mitch? Is that why you've come over to England?'

Lucia took a heat-sensing sip. 'Your police called ours. They both think Mitch has been abducted for a ransom.' Her aggressive demeanour was now tinted with concern.

I answered clumsily. 'They, I mean your police, they don't think he's come to harm? A personal vendetta or something.'

Lucia looked me straight in the eye. 'You mean is he dead?'

I nodded.

'They consider it a possibility,' she said, sounding dismissive of the fact.

'But you don't think so.'

Lucia took a while to answer. Her combative look melted away as she seemed to slump in the chair. I could see her making up her mind whether to tell me something or not.

'He's not dead. I think he's been taken because of the Tiger's Ghost, and I think it's all my fault.'

Lucia was unknowingly spot on with the kidnapping and the reason, but I couldn't follow why she blamed herself.

'I guess it sounded pretty strange, my saying what happened to Mitch is all my fault.'

'Well, I can't see off-hand why you should blame yourself, unless there's something you haven't told me.'

Lucia's hair fell forward as she lowered her head. 'There is something, Ben,' she said almost on the verge of tears. Taking a deep breath, and raising her head, I could see she was once again in control of her feelings.

I looked at her expectantly. 'Okay,' I encouraged.

'I like to sift through the replies to our regular advertisements for old comic books, in the local newspapers, the San Francisco Chronicle and The Examiner. We buy them to check for story lines we can adapt for today, or if it's something really rare, Mitch will buy it for his personal collection. Well, a couple weeks back, we got a reply from a Mrs. Saparowitz. I called her to arrange for a visit and give a valuation. She said she would only really be comfortable if a woman could come.

'Anyhow, Mrs. Saparowitz lives on Sycamore Street in the Mission district, an old established Jewish part of town. She was a little bird-like lady, maybe eighty, quite nervy, but friendly. She showed me up to her loft ladder, you know one of those concertina-step deals that pull down. Too steep for Mrs. Saparowitz now, but she told me to go ahead and pull the light-switch chain at the top of the steps. The floor was all boarded out and it was well lit. Amongst the usual household junk, were ten boxes, all with comic books from the 40s, 50s and 60s. It took me a couple of hours to go through them. There must have been fifty in each box, so about five hundred in all. There were three really rare issues. Two Superman and one Green Lantern.'

Lucia could see I was having trouble connecting all this to Mitch's whereabouts.

'This is leading somewhere,' she assured me. 'There were five other boxes on the floor. No comic books in them, but old glass photographic plates. All except ten were wedding groups, maybe shot in the 1920s. The ten were old ships. Back down in Mrs. Saparowitz's sitting room we agreed a price for the three rare comic books, and five dollars each for the others. Our writers would check the cheap stuff for out-of-copyright storylines we could reuse, then we'd place them with our graphic novel store to sell on.

'I asked Mrs. Saparowitz about the photo-plates. It seems her husband had died a few months ago, and he had been the comic book collector. He'd lost interest some years back, that's why they were in the loft. Mr. Saparowitz had run a photographic studio, down on Kearny Street, which he'd bought from a Sean Milligan in 1952. Apparently, Milligan was seventy-ish and getting forgetful, so had to sell up.'

'Alzheimer's, maybe?' I suggested.

Lucia shrugged. 'Maybe. Anyway, the photo plates had come with the business stock. Probably just forgotten by the old guy Milligan. I know Mitch is interested in all kinds of transport stuff, not just cars, so I asked Mrs. Saparowitz if the plates were for sale. She told me, no. But I could have them if I wanted, as a gift, because I had offered a much higher price for the comic books than she had expected. So, I loaded up the comics and the ship photo-plates. I sent them down to our computer guys and they scanned positive prints for Mitch. He called me into his office and seemed real excited about a couple of them.'

'The ones showing the Tiger's Ghost.' I suggested.

'Uh ha, and the Titanic,' said Lucia. 'He did a bunch of research and found out all about the car.'

I thought I understood why Lucia felt responsible for Mitch. She obviously saw herself as the catalyst for his disappearance. I decided I couldn't put off telling her about the Belgian letter and my meeting with Vogel on the train. I also told her why I thought it best not to inform the police, but I didn't go into any details about how I was going to handle things. After all, apart from double-crossing Vogel my plans were pretty sparse.

Lucia nodded slowly and pursed her lips. 'You really think

telling the police all this could put Mitch in jeopardy?'

I stressed the point that if Mitch had kept quiet and not told the newspapers about his having found the car, then no one would have known, and he wouldn't have been taken. In my view all this was very much Mitch's own fault, not Lucia's.

'Ben, could I have another coffee and a brandy, a large one please?' She didn't look convinced by my view of her innocence in Mitch's plight.

'Of course, I'll join you.'

'Ben, nobody knows what I'm about to tell you, but I have to trust someone, and you're in this more than I am. You may have guessed from my name that my family originally came from Italy; in fact, my father was Italian. I was born near Modena, where my father was a professor of earth sciences at the University, and my mother was studying her doctorate in physics. In 1998, we moved to San Francisco as Papa became a visiting professor at Berkeley. I transferred there as a student, then I got my Green Card and stayed on. My parents eventually went back to Modena, but both have since passed.'

'I'm sorry about that, Lucia,' I said. 'Did you lose them recently?'

'Oh no, we lost Papa in 2002 and Mama passed just three years later.'

'Do you have family, brothers or sisters?' I asked.

'No, just me. There may be some cousins, probably are, but I don't know for sure.'

'I thought all you Italians had super-close families. Not much chance of cousins getting lost.'

'I'm sure I do have relatives, but not Italian ones. You see, my mother came from the Punjab in Northern India. She was disowned by her family for marrying someone outside the

Hindu religion, and I've never met any of my Indian relations.'

'That seems a bit harsh in this day and age,' I said.

Lucia bit her lip as she decided whether to go on with this explanation. I could see it in her eyes.

'The thing is, Ben, that makes me Eurasian. Until she married, my mother was accepted as Indian, although her great-great-grandmother was English. At the turn of the last century, and even up to the Second World War Eurasians, or Anglos as they were called then, were shunned by both the British and the Indians. They mostly belonged to the middle classes, where the men were engineers, accountants, doctors, and the like. My parents had met in Jaipur when my father was lecturing at the University of Rajasthan. It was love at first sight, and they soon realised they wanted to get away from the prejudice that still held sway, even for their generation. So, my mother was happy to transfer to Modena University, and set up home in Italy.' Lucia took a large sip of her brandy.

'I took you for an American of Italian descent. Bassoli. And when I saw you, your skin said California girl all over.'

Lucia laughed, 'You haven't seen all over.'

'No, no what I meant was . . .' She cut me off in mid-sentence.

'Yea, I know what you meant; I was teasing you. I pass easily for just what you said. An all-American girl of Italian parents, with a California tan. But you know, Ben, I'm just as sensitive about being a Eurasian as my mother was, and I've never even suffered racist abuse.'

The curtain of Lucia's guilty sadness had parted for a few moments, her eyes had sparkled, and a mischievous smile had shown itself for the first time. But now the curtain closed again as she continued her story. 'Thing is, Ben, my triple-great-grandmother's name was Miss Amelia Symington. She was the youngest daughter of Sir Arthur Symington. In 1909 he was the representative of the British Raj in Cooch Sebah.'

'Miss Amelia, not Mrs. ?' I asked.

'Good catch!' said Lucia. 'Miss Amelia, the unmarried daughter, was having an affair with my great-great-grandfather, His Serene Highness the Maharajah Kuldeep Singh of Cooch Sebah.'

CHAPTER THIRTEEN

'What are you going to do now?' I asked. Lucia looked at me with a balance of worry and resolve in her eyes. 'I have to be in London for two more days, and then back to San Francisco, via New York. After that, say in two weeks' time, I can be back here for as long as needed; that is if I can help put things right.'

'I don't know what you can do to help, Lucia, because I haven't decided what I'm going to do yet. But I promise if I need you, I'll ask.'

'I can do some research into my Indian family if that helps,' she replied.

'If you knew you were descended from Kuldeep Singh, did you know anything about the car before Mitch told you what the photographic plates revealed?'

'Yes, yes, I did, but only as a family story. You know the sort of thing. Kuldeep faked his own disappearance with the car, he lived all over the world in disguise, he was a spy for the British Raj. There were a hundred stories, but I know my mother believed the official version of him drowning on the Titanic. I certainly never gave it much serious thought. I mean, it was over a hundred years ago.'

'Did you tell Mitch of your involvement?' I asked.

'I was going to, Ben, honest to God. I admit I kept quiet when he identified the photos and told me they showed the Tiger's Ghost. I could never afford to search for the car, I wouldn't know how to start. Anyway, if anything was found I figured it would be a million-to-one shot that I could prove a rightful claim. So, I thought why not let Mitch do the work for me.

Maybe he'd agree to fund a claim when I told him everything, and we would split any result 50/50. I guess this is the real truth of why I feel so guilty about him. He was kidnapped before I had a chance to say anything.'

Lucia looked close to tears, but I had to know one more thing. 'I can't help thinking it's a bit of a coincidence that you found the images that set this whole ball rolling.'

'Ben, I didn't have them in some secret family hoard and plant them in Mrs. Saparowitz's attic,' Lucia's eyes flashed with fire. 'I'm not in cahoots with the kidnappers if that's what you think. I'd better be going.'

She hurried down to her car, without waiting for me. I caught up as she opened the door. 'I don't think that for a moment. Like I said, it's Mitch's big mouth and the newspapers that's got us in this mess.'

Lucia slid onto the back seat, shut the door, and lowered the window. 'Okay, Ben, I'm sorry. Please find Mitch and get him back unharmed.' As she raised the window, I heard her ask Malik, the driver, to take her to her London hotel. She didn't look back as the car left the courtyard and headed down the drive.

Back upstairs, I sat at my desk. Columbus was my only company, and he was fast asleep, legs twitching in a dreamland rabbit-chase. Somehow Lucia's revelations had made the search for the Tiger's Ghost's remains seem even more hopeless. These negative thoughts didn't last long, as I concluded she might be able to help if there were some clues in her family history to point us in the right direction. Also, I wasn't starting from a hundred years ago. I knew for sure where Kuldeep Singh was when he died for real, and I had the Tiger's Ghost's chassis, so I knew we were looking for the trail of a stash of gold and jewels last seen in Ireland in 1945, not London in 1912.

My heart missed a beat, as I realised with a start that this wasn't true. It was Kuldeep Singh who Miss Whelan had seen in 1945, not the car. The last record of the car and its treasure was the final entry in the Willard's ledger. I checked my desktop database, to find that their gemmologist Mr. Sidelski had taken his last trip to Clarecourt on the 10th of May 1940. Coincidentally that was the day that the German forces invaded France. I had also noted that he had taken a larger amount of jewels from the car than ever before. Twenty-five stones in all, and ten of them were diamonds. The combined weight of these stones was quite something. It looked like Kuldeep Singh was cashing in for the duration. Did that mean he had also stripped the car of all the remaining gold and jewels, squirrelling them away safely until the end of the war? On the balance of probabilities, the complete car must surely have been concealed somewhere on the Clarecourt estate until the redundant chassis took on its new role as the generator's power source.

During my visit to the Goldsmiths' Hall, I had learnt that Sidelski had always taken the replacement paste jewels with him, when relieving the Tiger's Ghost of some of its value. That meant Willard's must have taken an inventory of all the jewels early in the car's life.

These thoughts leapfrogged into others. Were Willard's responsible for fitting the jewels when the car was new? I had no idea who had built the body on the Rolls-Royce chassis. Amazingly, the coachbuilder was not known. I delved deep for an answer on the computer and in my motoring library, but I couldn't find mention of any coachworks that might have built the body. This was strange, rather like a champion racehorse with no one remembering its sire or dam.

I would have to be more inventive to find an answer. Most coachbuilders of the time were based in Europe and America. But India did have some, a few of which were exceptionally good, being capable of handling a discreet commission of that complexity. It seemed unlikely that Kuldeep Singh would have shipped his jewels and gold all the way to England, then have the completed car shipped to Cooch Sebah. More likely a case of hiding the wood in the trees, for it would be much easier for discretion to be maintained with the chassis being shipped directly to an Indian coachbuilder, busy with an established client base of hugely rich Maharajahs and their families.

Stupidly, when I was at Goldsmiths' Hall, it had not occurred to me to see if those Willard's commissions books that dealt with the actual cutting and setting of stones had survived. Might there be records of the creation of paste stones that tallied with the lists of all the original gems? I would have to go back and ask Colonel Levington for another look. A better idea flashed into my mind: Why not ask Lucia to make the visit? After all she was already in London and would be far better at charming the irascible Colonel.

I waited until six in the evening, thinking that would give her plenty of time to reach the hotel, and would be too early for her to have left for an evening meeting or dinner.

'Didn't expect to hear from you so soon,' she said.

'If you have time, I'd like you to visit the Goldsmiths' Company in the City of London.' I explained all, and warned her about Levington, telling her exactly what to look for.

'I could visit with this Levington guy at 3:30pm tomorrow.'

'Thanks, I know he'll appreciate you more than he did me.'

My evening started much better than it finished. I took Columbus for a walk and satisfied a craving for a couple of doorstep-sized cheese sandwiches, washed down by a bottle of Wadsworth's 6X ale. I sat down to watch the day's news as I enjoyed my sandwiches, although I was really thinking more of the Tiger's Ghost and Lucia's search tomorrow, than paying attention to the BBC's finest. The first item of British home news after the day's parliamentary wrangling was of a helicopter crash. Apparently, a privately owned five-seater had plunged into a wood just on the Devon and Dorset border. The two passengers and the pilot had been killed, and the police were withholding the names of the deceased until the relatives had been informed.

As the BBC's man on the spot stood in a field away from the crash site, giving the same details as the studio newsreader, I noticed the glare of car headlights sweep across my sitting room ceiling. I looked out the window and saw a police car. After half a minute or so, no one had got out. I imagined the police were talking on the radio or updating some paperwork. Just as I was about to walk downstairs to let them in, the driver's door opened, and Kirstie looked up at my window. She answered my wave with a small one of her own, but her face looked sad and serious. She was alone, and already at the front door as I opened it.

I buried my sense of foreboding and greeted her with overdone enthusiasm. I had a gut feeling that something nasty had happened to Mitch, and Kirstie was about to tell me all about it.

CHAPTER FOURTEEN

'Come on up. Would you like a drink?' I asked.

'Yes, please. Could I have tea, milk and sugar,' she replied in a slightly shaky voice.

'Go and sit down, I'll bring it in to you.' I was even more convinced that Kirstie had bad news. How the hell was I going to tell Lucia? She'd be devastated. I'd have to go to London and tell her face to face. Not the sort of thing to say on the phone.

I brought the tea tray in, to find Kirstie perched on the edge of the sofa, with her hands clasped tightly between her knees. 'Come and sit down here, Ben,' she said, patting the seat-back beside her.

The lighting was low, but I could see her eyes were glazed with tears. She took my hand in both of hers, and I could feel her trembling slightly. I don't think I'm a cold-hearted person, but I felt her distress was a little over the top. After all, she'd never met Mitch, and she knew I had only a business relationship with him. Upset, yes: devastated, no.

'Ben, I have some bad news for you. Some very bad news, in fact,' she said huskily.

'Mitch is dead, isn't he,' I said more as a statement than a question.

Kirstie looked puzzled, then shocked, then concerned, all in a couple of seconds. 'No Ben, I haven't heard anything about Mitch,' she raised her chin and looked me straight in the eye. 'Ben, there's been an accident, a helicopter crash.'

'Yes, I was watching it on the news when you arrived. What about it?'

'Ben, I have to tell you that the passengers on the helicopter were your father and your stepmother. I'm very, very sorry.'

It took a few seconds to sink in. It was of course a huge shock, but I hadn't spoken to my father for over two years, and Danni his new American wife and I had never hit it off. I think she saw me as a challenge, too much of a reminder of my father's previous life. Memories of my childhood with him flashed through my mind, but no real feelings of warmth and deep sadness were to be found there.

'Has anyone told my grandfather yet?' I said partly to Kirstie and partly to the room.

'The Cornish police have visited him.'

'You know, it'll be much worse for Howly, that's what we all call my grandfather. He never gave up on my father and his difficult nature. I think even Danni, his daughter-in-law, loved him for that.'

Kirstie stirred three spoonsful of sugar into the mug of tea and handed it to me. 'These things are a great shock, Ben. This will help steady you.'

'I don't take sugar,' I said, but took a sip all the same. The hot sweet tea surprisingly tasted good. 'How come you got the short straw to bring the news?' I asked.

'I didn't,' she replied. 'Normally two officers would be given the job. By chance I overheard what had happened. I wanted to be with you when you were told, so there was only one way to do that. When I said you were an old army friend, the duty sergeant allowed me to come alone.' Kirstie leant over and gave me a long hug. Some of my tea spilled on the floor but I did nothing about it.

'Do they know what happened, what caused the crash?' I asked.

'It's got to be confirmed by the air-crash investigators of course, but the pilot's brief Mayday call had the words "tail rotor gone; mechanical failure is most likely at the moment. It seems they were pretty low when it happened, sightseeing maybe, so there wouldn't have been much time to do anything.'

'Well, thanks for coming yourself, Kirstie, it can't be an easy thing to do.'

'Not the best bit of police work. Are you okay?'

I took a deep breath to think about that question. 'Yes, I'm just fine. As I said, I wasn't close to them, but it's still a shock when a parent dies, doesn't matter how old you are, or how distant.'

Columbus had unusually stayed in his basket when Kirstie had come in. Head down on his paws, with eyes looking worried, he had watched us intently. He slowly walked over to me, jumped in my lap, and lay quietly. I swear he sensed our sadness and wanted to help.

'You'll go down to Cornwall to see your grandfather?'

'Truth is, we're not really on speaking terms. We fell out over his acceptance of my father divorcing my late mother for Danni. But yes, I'll phone him tonight and drive down at first light.'

'I'm glad you don't want to go right now. It's better to try and get some sleep after hearing this sort of news. You know, delayed reaction.'

I did know, but I'd be fine. Deep sadness, yes, but uncontrolled sorrow, no. My father had been a self-centred, self-serving bastard, and Danni was a matching spouse. I could even imagine one of their fights having caused the pilot to lose control, but the Mayday evidence was to the contrary.

'I can stay with you if you want, Ben.'

It never crossed my mind that this was an offer of anything more than friendship; to sit and talk or be a guardian angel whilst I slept. But I would be fine alone. 'No, but thanks for the offer. I'll call you when I get back from Cornwall, and I really do appreciate you coming rather than some unknown plod.'

Kirstie smiled, trying to lighten the mood. 'So, does that make me a known plod?'

I smiled back. 'No, you're a very special friend.' I gave her a hug and kissed her cheek. Despite the occasion, the thought of a more romantic kiss sparked in my mind. Just for a split-second, hormones reminding me they were there, that was all.

CHAPTER FIFTEEN

My grandfather General Sir Howel Cador Ross, Howly to the family, had always been pleased to see one of my exotic cars when I visited his Cornish home, that was of course until our falling-out and my visits had become few and far between. Today, though, I chose the Defender, for speed, and its hands-free satphone.

Penhydrock House is a beautiful property, dating in part back to the late 1500s; it was substantially rebuilt in 1885, following a fire, supposedly, caused by an over-zealous mouser chasing its prey, and knocking over a candelabra. The gardens are spectacular, including a tiny sandy beach bordering the Helford River.

I had called Howly to tell him I would set off at first light. He replied that he was going to Dorchester to identify the bodies and would not be back at Penhydrock before mid-afternoon.

I hadn't been to the house for quite some time. My father living there with his new wife, when they were not in their New York apartment, had made visits more than difficult, and something I preferred not to do. I missed Howly, regretting the frosty relationship that had developed.

Before I reached the carved-oak front doors, Farrell, my grandfather's butler of many years, had them open. He and Mrs. Farrell, the cook, were now in their late seventies and undertaking lighter duties with regular help from the village.

'Welcome, Master Benedict, welcome on this saddest of occasions.'

I had been brought up to respect the staff, and having known

Farrell all my life, continued to call him Mr. Farrell. He in his turn had on one occasion addressed me as Mr. Benedict, and that was correctly so on my twenty-first birthday. It made me feel awkward, so I refused that honour of coming of age. 'Yes, very sad,' I nodded in agreement, 'but it's good to see you, Mr. Farrell, and not looking a day over eighty. Is Mrs. Farrell bearing up?'

Farrell smiled at my usual quip of his advancing years. 'Yes, Master Benedict, we are both well. You're in the King's room, and Sir Howel should be back within the hour. He has asked that you join him for tea in the conservatory.'

I thanked Farrell, declining his offer to carry my overnight bag. Houses do have auras, and Penhydrock has one of friendly calm. I was glad to be back among the mixture of oak-panelled walls and highly polished wooden floors, covered in part by ancient rugs, their colours still vibrant in the soft light that seeped through the stone-mullioned lead-paned windows. The furniture is mostly Jacobean, supplemented by the best that the Victorian era had to offer. Ancestral faces looked down on me, beside their companion images depicting fighting ships of the line or English pastoral scenes. I made my way up the wide, creaking staircase, with its massive newel post, carved balusters, and handrails. I flopped down for a powernap on the four-poster bed in the King's room. The story goes that Charles II slept here whilst on a procession around Cornwall, following his return from exile in France. True or not, the room has always been offered to the most important guest at Penhydrock. This was the first time I had been given it. It came to me that now my father was dead, and with no other children, I was the next direct descendant of my grandfather. Would I one day inherit the house, as well as the Baronetcy, and was my use of the

King's room a gentle reminder?

Four o'clock is teatime at Penhydrock, so I made my way down to the conservatory. A tribute to Victorian cast iron and glass, about the size of a tennis court, it housed a collection of rare ferns and orchids. The tepid heat, and scents from the flowers made the room seem in a different part of the world. At one end was a sitting area containing wicker sofas and chairs, with several glass-topped wrought iron tables. Howly was examining an orchid when I entered. Still over six feet tall and in his eighty-seventh year, our recent loss showed in his drawn and grey face.

My greeting was Howly's traditional, but sorely missed, grasping and gentle shake of my upper arms, with the briefest of a smile today. 'Ben, dear boy. How good it is to see you. Come! Sit down and have some tea.'

This was unexpected. I had anticipated Howly's curt nod of welcome, and minimal conversation, the norm since our polarised views of my father's behaviour had caused us to have a blazing row.

Farrell appeared bearing a silver tray with all the paraphernalia for a traditional English afternoon tea, and his wife followed with two large, freshly made cakes.

She beamed at me. 'One is lemon drizzle, and one is death by chocolate. Your favourites, Master Benedict.'

When the Farrells had gone and we each had our cake and tea, Howly spoke about the accident. 'A bad business, Ben, a bad business.' He quietly nibbled a few morsels of the lemon cake before continuing. 'I know you and your father didn't get along, and on reflection I don't blame you. My son was a difficult and selfish man, and his second wife was a gold-digger who didn't care who she upset. Quite the opposite of your mother, God rest her. I think I have been unfair to your point of view, Ben.' Howly held my gaze, with brimming eyes. 'We should never have fallen out. Will you forgive me and attend the funerals, for my sake, if nothing else?'

A flood of relief swept over me, and in my own eyes I felt the smart of tears. Hints of unprecedented emotion for our family. 'There's nothing to forgive, Howly. It was my fault. I'm sorry I was so cross with you, but my admiration and respect for you never faltered, so let's get back to normal. Of course I'll come to the funerals. Whatever happened between us, he was my father. He just didn't have it in him to be a good one.'

Howly was a man of the old school, stiff upper lip at all times, and more than a minimum show of emotion had been revealed. He pulled the paisley handkerchief from his jacket sleeve and blew his nose noisily, replaced the handkerchief, then went back to the business of consuming his cake.

After the unexpected relief of the teatime meeting, during which Howly had kept well away from the subject of the helicopter crash, I returned to the King's room and made a few calls. Tegan told me that all was well at the Clock House, and I had a message to call Lucia.

She answered her mobile after two rings. 'How did you get on at Goldsmiths' Hall?' I asked.

No time-wasting pleasantries from Lucia. 'Ben, I met with your Colonel Levington. Jeez, does that guy need to get a life. Anyhow, I explained what I was hoping to find. I guess he liked me more than he liked you, because he took me right to a bunch of Willard's books, pulled out half a dozen or so and sat me down at a desk. He said if Willard's had been involved with the initial setting of the Rolls-Royce gems, there would certainly be a record of it here.'

'And was there?' I asked hopefully.

'Oh yes, in the second ledger I looked at, I came across some beautiful colour wash drawings of diamonds, rubies, sapphires and emeralds, and some huge pearls, too. The pages were headed H. S. H. Kuldeep Singh. They were drawn in groups with ink lines around them. I would never have guessed what the lines represented.'

'Did you find out?'

'I had no idea, so I asked Levington, and he explained. They were panels as you would find them on an old car. Like the door trims, or the back of the front seats, below the glass division. You know the kind of stuff, and the roof lining, masses inset in the roof,' Lucia added excitedly.

'So, Willard's were definitely responsible for the genuine jewels being set in the interior panels when the body was built.'

'They sure were, but in India, not in the UK; and that's not all. Each and every stone has its dimensions, weight and quality recorded.'

'Can you get a list of it all from Levington?' I asked.

'Already done. Amazing what a wide smile and a toss of the hair can get you. Are you at the Clock House, Ben?'

'No, I'm at my family home, my grandfather's place in Cornwall, but I'll be back at the Clock House late tomorrow.' I didn't go into why I was at Penhydrock.

'Okay then, I'll send the copies of everything over to you by courier. They should be there when you get back. I'm leaving for the States tomorrow but let me know if I can help some more. You take care, Ben.'

I joined Howly for supper, this time in his library. It seemed a lifetime ago that I had been in a similar room at Clarecourt, with Miss Whelan. We sat in a pair of fireside wing chairs, trays on George III side-tables, enjoying poached salmon and new potatoes with some of Mrs. Farrell's homemade Hollandaise sauce. A bottle of Chevalier-Montrachet 2016 did justice to Mrs. Farrell's cooking.

There was nothing more I wanted to say about my father or stepmother, and Howly needed his mind taking off the matter. 'I've got involved in a bit of a problem, and I'm not sure of the best thing to do. Are you up to giving a bit of advice?' I asked.

He immediately lost some of the drawn look in his naturally gaunt face. At the prospect of helping me on a project his eyes regained some of their sparkle and his body language transformed from depressed and forlorn to intrigued and impatient.

'Just what the doctor ordered, Ben. Take my mind off things. Explain the problem, dear boy,' he replied with a semblance of his old enthusiasm for life.

I related the whole story, right up to date.

'That's some tale, Ben. So where are we now?' he asked, already involved enough to use the plural.

'Vogel thinks greed has won me over to his side, a ploy which only you now know. The police are just searching for a missing person, as I haven't told them about the kidnapping yet. My big question is, should I tell the police? If I do, is Vogel likely to find out from one of the international forces that are bound to get involved, then carry out his threat to kill Mitch?' I didn't add that Vogel might well decide to finish me off as well.

Howly walked over to a side-table and grasped a bottle, raising an eyebrow at me. 'No thanks, not for me.' I could see that it was one of his favourite tipples, amoonshine Metaxa. He had acquired a taste for the brandy in the early 1950s, during his time as a military attaché at the British Embassy in Athens.

'Ben, surely you have made your decision already, when you led Vogel to believe you were with him.'

'Yes, but I value your confirmation that I'm right. I don't know exactly what you got up to after you left the army, but we all know . . .' I realised that there was only me left now. I could see in the shadow that crossed Howly's eyes that he thought the same. 'I know there was more to your time at the War Office and the Ministry of Defence than you ever let on. I'm sure you know what the best thing would be to do.'

Howly took a large slug of the Metaxa, neither confirming nor denying my implication. 'There are two things to consider. Firstly, is a leak of confidentiality possible or probable within the law enforcement agencies that would become involved. In my opinion, yes, probably. Secondly how likely is Vogel to have access to this information? You have suggested that he may have once been a member of the old East German Stasi?'

'I don't know for sure. It was the way he talked about Markov and the poison-tipped umbrellas.'

'Let us assume that he is ex-Ministerium fur Staatssicherheit.' Howly smiled at my surprise of his fluent German accent. 'Stasi for short. They are generally considered to have been the most efficient and effective secret police force that the world has ever known.'

'Including the Gestapo?' I asked.

'The Stasi took the Gestapo as their starting point and refined their methods. Of course, many of the founding members were ex-Gestapo, although the Stasi worked closely with the Russian KGB, right up until their demise at the time of German reunification. If Vogel is indeed ex-Stasi and bearing in mind the type of work he is undertaking, I think it safe to assume he has become a, what shall I say, a freelance secret agent. If he is any good, he will have kept up his old Stasi contacts since their disbandment. If this is so, he will be very well placed indeed to know whether you have involved the police or not.'

It was almost unbelievable that Mitch's predicament had roots going back to the cold war. 'Surely, Vogel wouldn't know if the British police mounted an undercover exercise to get Mitch back?' I asked.

'Possible, but not probable,' replied Howly. 'But when the various Continental and American forces become involved, not forgetting Interpol, I think it highly likely that an ex-Stasi operative could find out anything he wanted.'

'So, I made the right decision?'

'You made the right decision.'

CHAPTER SIXTEEN

I was back home around four in the afternoon, having stopped near Exeter to visit a farmer from whom I have been trying to buy a car for over five years. An early Jaguar XK120, it has a racing provenance from its early life. The trouble is the old farmer is convinced that he will one day restore the car, and still flatly refuses to sell it at any price. Meanwhile it slowly rusts to oblivion.

Smiler had taken delivery of a courier's package from Lucia, which he brought up to the office, accompanied by a welcoming Columbus. 'Is your gran'pa doin' okay?' he asked, handing me the package.

'He's just fine, obviously upset, but he's a tough old bird. Thanks for asking, Smiler,' I said, opening the package.

Inside was a Graphica Publishing compliments slip, with just a scribbled L B on it. It was clipped to pages of high-quality photocopies of the Willard's records. Each stone was depicted by a life-size colour-washed drawing of almost photographic quality, as well as a black-ink line-drawing showing the cut facets. Beneath each was a list of the stone's qualities, which meant little to me. I was going to need a crash course in how precious stones were graded and, more importantly, how to tell if they were real or paste gems.

'Do you know what it all means?' asked Smiler, as I showed him the pages.

'No, except there were an awful lot of diamonds, emeralds, rubies, and sapphires on that car. I'd love to know what they're all worth in today's money.'

'As it happens, I can help you there,' said Smiler.

'What, you know all about gems?'

'Not a lot, just what I paid for the wife's engagement ring, but I know a bloke who does.'

'Tell me more.'

'It was when I was working on private aircraft maintenance before I came to you, Guv. I was servicing this twin Apache for a Dutch geezer, Wim de Groot. He was a sightholder in the diamond trade and flew himself between London and Antwerp two or three times a week.'

What's a sightholder?' I interrupted.

'I dunno exactly, but he's on De Beers list as someone they'll sell rough diamonds to. Anyway, I was tightening one of the seat brackets, saw it was cracked, so I took the seat out to weld it. And bugger me, among the sweet wrappers and a couple of coins, was a folded bit of white paper. I was just going to chuck it in the bin, when I realised there was something inside it; six diamonds wrapped in blue tissue paper, as I live and breathe. Well, for a couple of seconds I thought about keeping them. But you know me, Guv, too bloody honest for me own good. So, I phoned up Wim to tell him.'

'That made his day,' I said.

'Too right, not only did he say I was to be the only bloke working on his Apache from then on, but he sent me a five-grand reward. And if ever I wanted a favour, just ask.'

I pointed at the phone on my desk. 'So, ask.'

Smiler fetched his dog-eared and oil-stained address book, all held together with a wide elastic band. Wim seemed to recognise him immediately, despite the years since he had left the aircraft maintenance industry. The Dutchman did most of the talking, after Smiler had explained that a friend wanted a crash course on gem spotting. He grunted the occasional agreement, dropping ash from his roll-up cigarette all over the desk, then scribbled something on a scrap of paper, thanked Wim and put the phone down.

Smiler flicked the now dormant stub of his roll-up into the waste bin and pushed the scrap of paper towards me. On it was a London phone number and a name, Moses Katz. 'He's a dealer in eighteenth- and nineteenth-century jewellery of high quality, and a complete anorak when it comes to the history of exotic gemstones. He knows more about the Crown Jewels than The Queen herself did, God bless her.'

'Thanks. I'll let you know how I get on,' I said, as Smiler coughed his way back to the workshop.

My worry was, should I tell about the Tiger's Ghost jewels?

The simple answer was no. I didn't want anyone joining in the search. I decided to phone Katz and say that I'm writing a book on famous lost gems, and I have a few photos of some putative examples. Could he tell their provenance?

He answered his phone on the first ring. 'Mo Katz.'

I played the part of a researching author perfectly.

'If Wim wants me to help you, then I will do my best, Mr. Ross. Email me images of the gems and I will call you back as soon as I have assessed them.'

Just one hour later the phone rang; unknown caller, it said, so I guessed it was Mo Katz.

There was no mistaking this caller, no need for him to identify himself. 'Mr. Ross,' said Vogel. 'I am telephoning for a progress report. You are making, how do you say, headway, yes?'

I was caught off guard. My mindset had been constantly on how to find enough information to get Mitch released safely, and if any jewels were about, to keep them from Vogel and his principal. Once again though, the old Army Intelligence training came to the rescue, and I became Vogel's henchman.

'Herr Vogel, good to hear from you. I do indeed have some news. Firstly, I have a detailed list of all the individual gems that were fitted to the Tiger's Ghost. I am also consulting an expert who I hope will give us a lead as to the whereabouts of the more important stones.'

Vogel answered guardedly. 'This is indeed progress, Mr. Ross, but is it wise to tell outsiders of our quest? This could put the wellbeing of Mr. Mitchelletti at risk.'

'The expert believes I am collecting information for a forthcoming book on famous lost jewels,' I replied confidently.

'Then proceed with your enquiries. Mr. Ross, but before I go, I have now just placed an email attachment for you. Please look at it.' The phone went dead.

I clicked onto my emails and found one from an unknown and, I would bet my life, untraceable sender. It contained a video clip, and with typical German efficiency, it was of the highest definition. There, sat looking at the camera, was a very cross Mitch. He was wearing the sort of restraints that American prisoners sometimes suffer, ankles and handcuffs chained to a waist chain. He was crumpled and unshaven.

'Ross, do whatever these people want to get me the fuck outta here. They got me chained up like a goddamned murderer or something.' He shook his hands at the camera. 'I haven't had a decent meal since I got here. There's no TV, no radio, I just sit, chained to this goddamned bed all day. I don't know why I'm here. If it's money they want, talk to Lucia Bassoli at Graphica. She'll know what to do.' Mitch's gaze moved to the side of the camera. 'No, wait! I wanna say more.' Then the camera was switched off and some words appeared on the screen. Mr.

Mitchelletti is safe for now, if a little bad-tempered. As you see, he could so easily come to harm. Please continue your good works, Mr. Ross. The screen faded as the email clip finished.

CHAPTER SEVENTEEN

Bright and early as usual, I was on my way with Columbus, this time to St. Albans, to see a pair of headlamps, huge brass affairs powered by acetylene gas. They had been fitted to a 1902 Gladiator, a make long gone, the actual car having been sent for scrap for the war effort in 1941. The owner had kept the lamps, and it was his granddaughter who had placed an advert in, of all places, The Lady magazine. One of the apartment owners in the main house had spotted it and had kindly shown me the advert. A large bunch of flowers for her if a deal was done, and it just had been.

The lamps were safe in bubble wrap and cardboard boxes in the back of the Land Rover, as the satphone rang. It was Smiler.

'Mo Katz just called.'

'Did he find anything?' I asked.

'Yes! More than we wanted. Not about the stones, more about who you are.'

'What the hell happened, Smiler?' I could imagine a future exposé in the press, media reporters battering on the door, and a very upset Heinrich Vogel.

'Katz did his homework and has come up with some answers. He wouldn't tell me anything except he knew the whereabouts of two of the emeralds and one of the diamonds, and he wanted to discuss the matter with you face to face.'

'Did he say why?' I asked.

'Not exactly. He just said he knew where all ten of the stones you'd listed had come from, and what a coincidence it was that you should be researching those very gems for your book. It was the way he said "your book"; he don't believe you.'

'Okay, I'll phone him back.'

I dialled Katz, and after some discussion we agreed to meet at the St. Ermin's Hotel in Westminster, the next day. I know it well, as it's a convenient place to entertain clients in London.

Originally an apartment block, the building was remodelled as a hotel in 1899. The St. Ermin's is famous for its serpentine balconies and plush Victorian decor, now revamped with twenty-first-century brightness. A Houses of Parliament Division Bell is rung to summon MPs to vote in important debates, which curtails their drinking time and scares the hell out of bomb-conscious tourists. The hotel is also famous for being the location where Winston Churchill met and empowered the founding members of the Special Operations Executive, in 1940. An entire floor of the hotel became their headquarters, with MI6 based a couple of floors above.

Our meeting was not to be quite as important to the world, but it was going to concentrate my mind. In the Caxton Bar, Mo Katz was easy to spot, as being a Hasidic Jew, he wore their traditional garb. His unkempt beard was accompanied by the long, never-trimmed sidelocks called payots that curled down each side of his head. Slightly built, he had one of those faces that seemed to have a hint of a smile even when in repose. He was supping a glass of lager.

All I know about the Hasidic branch of Judaism, is that it is based on deep spirituality, and their word is their bond; one reason perhaps why they have been predominant in the European diamond trade in Amsterdam and London for hundreds of years.

I bought a drink for myself at the bar, before going to Mo's table. After introductions, he came straight to the point. 'Mr. Ross, you have sent me a list of rare and valuable gemstones, and you say you are writing a book on them. This I do not believe, nor do I believe in coincidences. In my business coincidence is a flashing red light to the mind.' Mo tapped his head, which caused a payot to bounce up and down.

'What coincidence, Mr. Katz?' I asked, remembering how Smiler had warned me.

'You send me details of gemstones. All belonged to the young Maharajah of Cooch Sebah. They were, shall we say, liberated, by his uncle, Kuldeep Singh, at the end of his days as Prince Regent. All these gems once decorated the fabulous and legendary Tiger's Ghost Rolls-Royce.'

'How on earth did you know that?' I asked.

'Your emailed photocopies, Mr. Ross. The originals are well known to me, through the Willard's records. I make a study of such documents, but of course this was only a matter of history until the discovery that the Tiger's Ghost did not sink on the Titanic.'

Mo had seen through my subterfuge, but he still hadn't explained the coincidence that had made him suspicious. I was about to ask him when he put up his hand.

'The coincidence, you are going to ask me, Mr. Ross. You say you are writing a book, and this, just a couple of weeks after everyone in the gem trade reads in the newspaper that an American car collector has found the chassis of the Tiger's Ghost. So now we know that the car and all those precious stones did not go down on the Titanic. Perhaps the jewels and the gold are hidden somewhere. Perhaps you are looking for them.' Mo smiled at me, taking a deep swallow of his beer, and smacking his lips.

My mind raced, and I took a long drink to give myself time to think. There was only one way through this, and that was to hope I could bring Mo Katz on side, to work with us. My quest for how gemstones were graded would have to wait. I hoped to God that he could keep a secret.

'Mr. Katz, I am in a most difficult position. I am a car broker; I buy and sell exotic cars . . .'

'I know what a car broker is Mr. Ross,' he interrupted.

'I've been commissioned to search for the jewels and the gold that once adorned the Tiger's Ghost, and it's now become a matter of life and death . . .'

Mo Katz interrupted me again. I was beginning to understand he was not rude, but rather had a very quick mind. 'Life and death. A little exaggerated, don't you think, Mr. Ross? Perhaps I should be speaking to your employer, the man who found the car?'

Mo took from his coat a rolled-up copy of the newspaper that I had read on the Irish ferry and placed it in front of me. It was folded open at the report of Mitch and his find.

'I'm afraid that won't be possible. Mr. Mitchelletti has been kidnapped by God knows who and unless I find the whereabouts of the Tiger's Ghost treasure, they have threatened to kill him.'

Mo gave a very Yiddish reply. 'Ei yei yei! Is this true?'

'Mr. Katz, all this is true. The kidnappers are convinced that I am the best person to find the treasure.'

Mo gulped his beer again and once more smacked his lips. 'What do you know of these people?'

I told him of Vogel, and that I was pretending to work with him, for the unknown principal.

Just then my mobile phone vibrated in my pocket. A glance at the screen told me it was Howly. 'Excuse me, Mr. Katz, I must take this call, it's my grandfather.'

'Please, go ahead, family is important.'

I quickly walked out of earshot.

'Ben, dear boy, I've spoken to a chum of mine in London. It seems you were right about Herr Vogel. He was indeed Stasi and quite a formidable character. Last heard of working as a sort of mercenary consultant to rich members of the European criminal classes, but thought to now be retired. In his Stasi days he was a highly regarded psychological interviewer.'

'What exactly is that?' I asked.

'That, dear boy, is what we would call a mental torturer, no physical violence, someone else would do that if he thought it necessary, although he is suspected of having sometimes killed his subjects once all the information he required had been extracted.'

'Well, that sounds a bit like physical violence to me,' I replied.

'Murder, yes, but not violent inasmuch as he was a bit of a dab hand at administering poisons, nerve agents, that sort of thing.'

A rush of adrenaline surged through me as a memory of Vogel and his umbrella flashed into my mind. 'Thanks, Howly, that's another step forward in our knowledge of the enemy.'

'One other thing, Ben, Heinrich Vogel's father was a Waffen SS Sturmbannfuhrer, that's equivalent to a Major. He was hanged as a war criminal at the Nuremberg Trials, for atrocities in the death camps. However, Heinrich's allegiance seems to have been with the Russians, who worked hand in hand with the Stasi. Could be a useful bit of information for you in future negotiations. Bye, my boy, do be careful.'

I walked back to Mo, but I needed time to think. 'Mr. Katz, do you have an idea how much all the gems and gold from the car might be worth?'

'What a question. Who knows how much the gold weighs or how pure it is?'

He took out his phone and tapped it a couple of times. 'In the last year pure gold has been trading at a high of £1,511 and a low of £1,448 an ounce. That's all I can say.'

'I would guess that Kuldeep Singh had the Tiger's Ghost carry as much weight as the chassis could take. I'll have to consult a Rolls-Royce expert about that. Any idea what the jewels weighed?' I said.

Mo's eyes twinkled, and the verge of a smile broadened. 'Just check Willard's records. The weights are all recorded from when they set them in the car.'

'And what of their value?'

Mo gave a shrug and wave of his hands. 'Have they been recut? Are they reset? Will they be sold all at once or fed onto the market? What is their provenance and their history worth to a buyer? All I can say for sure is many millions of pounds.'

I thanked Mo for his help and assured him that if any of the jewels came into my legal possession I would discuss him selling them on my behalf, but then I remembered one last question. 'Mr. Katz, you told Smiler, Wim de Groot's friend, on the phone that you knew of the whereabouts of three of the gems?'

'Ah, yes,' replied Mo, 'Two emeralds of quite exquisite quality and a diamond of impressive size, if not the greatest purity of colour. According to the Willard's records, they were taken from the Tiger's Ghost in 1910. Willard's set them in rose gold as a necklace; quite well done, I must say. The necklace was then sold to an English dealer who had a customer waiting, an Austrian Countess of no real importance. The necklace was next heard of in 2011 when it was recovered by the Italian police in Milan. It, together with other items worth several millions of pounds had been stolen two years earlier by a gang of thieves posing as Arab sheiks. Interestingly, two items, that necklace and a tiara had once been in the possession of the President of Argentina's wife, Eva Perón.'

CHAPTER EIGHTEEN

Driving home from the St. Ermin's Hotel, I wondered how Eva Perón could have ended up with gems from the Tiger's Ghost. Was the necklace sold to her by the Austrian princess or even stolen for her on the orders of her husband, President Juan Perón? My thoughts were interrupted by a call from Kirstie; she wanted to meet up, as soon as possible. I invited her to drive over in the morning for breakfast. She offered to bring her favourite pastries, then we would take Columbus for his morning walk.

Waiting for her to arrive, I filled in the time working at my desk. There were landline phone messages and emails to answer, a small pile of post, mainly old-car auction catalogues and a bill or two.

I had made a good start, when I heard the crunch of tyres on gravel, and there below the office window was a two-seater Morgan sports car, with its top down. Kirstie smiled up at me as she pushed her designer sunglasses up into her hair. She lifted a bakery bag from the passenger seat and shook it at me.

I trotted down to meet her. 'This doesn't look like a duty call,' I said.

'Sort of, but not really. More of a post-duty call,' she answered ambiguously.

Motioning towards the stairs with a theatrical sweep of the arm, I said, 'Well, come on up and tell all, the coffee's on.' A few minutes later I carried our warmed-through breakfast into the office, where Kirstie was paying Columbus far too much attention for his own good.

Once settled, the rug-free armchair for Kirstie and the

slightly worse-for-wear sofa for me, I let my guest blow steam from her mug, an exercise that looked to have as much to do with stalling as thermodynamics. 'So, what have you got to tell me?'

'First things first, Ben. How are you feeling about your dad and everything?'

'I'm fine. I think my grandfather is pretty upset, but he isn't one to show it. Something good's come out of this, Howly and I have put all our ill feelings behind us. We're as close now as we used to be. Nothing like a death to put things into perspective.'

'It makes you think, Ben. Problems, troubles we think are so important, they mostly aren't in the scheme of things. Not when you compare them to something like you've just suffered.'

I nodded my heartfelt agreement, as she took a tentative sip, cleared her throat, and continued. 'As you know, after the army I joined the police. Obviously, they were keen to make use of my intelligence gathering skills, so I ended up being fast-tracked through uniform to the detective side of things. All went pretty well and reaching Detective Inspector rank at the age I did was unusual, so I suppose someone appreciated what I was doing.'

'Not as dangerous as intel gathering in Afghanistan, then?' I asked.

'Well, it has its moments. There's some really nasty people out there. Anyway, I had one of those moments quite recently,' she replied, with an emphasis on the word 'moments'. 'It was really silly. I was on a routine follow up of a burglary. The victim was a single mother with three kids, and I knew they all had different fathers. But our duty is to protect the public, not to judge them. Trouble was, one of the fathers was there and I recognised him as a wanted drug dealer on the run. Standard practice would be to leave the premises as soon as possible without raising the villain's suspicion, then call in for back-up. Maybe he saw in my eyes that I had sussed him. Whatever the reason he pulled a knife and slashed my arm, ripped my radio from my hand, hit me in the face and ran for the door. Blood everywhere and my arm hurt like hell. The girlfriend was in shock, but after I shouted at her a couple of times, she called 999, and I left my colleagues to sort it all out while I was carted off in an ambulance. You should have seen my black eye.'

'God! Kirstie, you were lucky not to have been killed,' I said.

'You know the old saying, a miss is as good as a mile. And here I am, still in one piece,' she said with a shade too much bravado.

'And?' I encouraged.

'And the knife had damaged a nerve in my upper arm and severed a tendon. It's left me with partial numbness in three fingers and restricted arm movement.'

Kirstie raised her left arm to just above head height. 'That's about as far as it wants to go. The upshot of all this is that I have failed my medical check for active service and have been offered a desk job.'

'Which you have refused, knowing you.'

'Which I have refused. So, now I'm out of a job as of midnight last Friday, although there'll be a decent pension that takes a bit of the pressure off financially. It's just that I have to find some work that really interests me, and the pension won't go all that far.'

'Sod the coffee, I know it's early, but do you still drink whisky?' I asked.

'Still only malt,' she said.

'I favour Mortlach at the moment, and luckily a grateful

client gave me six bottles of twenty-year-old.'

Kirstie pulled her I'm-impressed face.

'I managed to find him a perfect '67 Porsche 911R. And along with my commission came this,' I handed her a large tot, clinked glasses and said all I could think of – 'To the future.'

'The future,' she echoed enthusiastically.

'Kirstie, if I told you something that would have an effect on an ongoing police investigation, and I wanted you to keep quiet about it, what would you say?'

'Before Friday I would have said to you as an old friend, only tell me what you want officially reported, otherwise keep quiet. Today, anything can stay between us.'

'I now know more about Mitch's disappearance than I've told the police. Let's take Columbus for his walk and I'll explain everything,' which is what I did, the whole thing: letters, Vogel, Lucia, even Kuldeep Singh's untimely death. I brought her right up to date. Kirstie asked pertinent questions and suggestions, and I was glad that I had taken her incisive mind into my confidence.

After an hour we were back and standing by Kirstie's car. 'I've got to go, Ben. A meeting with my Police Federation rep, and papers to sign about my Industrial Injury award, then that's the last of it for me and the Thin Blue Line.' Kirstie gave me a hug, kissed me on the cheek and said, 'Thanks for listening to my troubles, it's been good to have an old friend to talk to.'

'I'm really glad if it's helped, but it's me who should thank you for listening to the Mitch saga, especially as you've confirmed my thoughts that involving the police at this stage could put Mitch at greater risk.'

Kirstie looked up from her car seat. 'I'm going to give some more thought to what you've said. I'll call you tomorrow,' then with a backward wave from her good arm, she sped off with a squeal from the Morgan's tyres.

CHAPTER NINETEEN

I started the next day with a brisk walk to get the blood pumping, and Columbus happy. It was one of those perfect English summer mornings, not yet hot, but with a light and scent that promised a day of warmth from a cloudless sky.

Mid-morning, I had a young couple coming to view a 1950s twin-cam MGA, which had been restored to show-winning condition by the vendor. It turned out that the husband's father had owned the car when new. This was a pleasing thing for any purveyor of classic cars to hear, as it meant a strong emotional reason to acquire the vehicle.

The MG sold; I finished the office work that had been interrupted by Kirstie's visit yesterday. I also gave some serious thought to what the next step should be to regain Mitch's freedom. Against a background of what we knew for sure, my mind tossed around the possible future outcomes that any actions of mine may trigger. Not least of these possible consequences was the ever-present one that Mitch – and I – could end up dead.

A positive thought sprang to mind: should I offer to employ Kirstie, with her knowledge of intelligence gathering? She was also experienced at living with ever-present danger, however remote or near it may be. I smiled inwardly at the thought that I had already assumed she would agree to join the fight.

I needn't have worried, Kirstie called as she had promised. We agreed to meet at a pub roughly halfway between our homes.

'A pint of Doom Bar for me and …?' I raised a questioning eyebrow at Kirstie.

'Dry white wine, please,' she said to the landlord.

'Well, which dry white wine?' he asked impatiently, 'there's a wine list in front of you, haven't you looked?'

Kirstie quickly pointed at a Pinot Gris. 'That one,' she answered, fixing the surly landlord with a withering stare.

'That's eight pounds fifty pence,' said the landlord, holding out a hand.

'Put it on our tab, we're going to order some food,' I said.

'No! I don't allow tabs, you pay as you buy, and anyway there's no food tonight, the chef's not turned up.'

I paid cash, my change being dumped on the bar, as our charming host turned to the next customers. 'Yes?' was all he said to them.

'Do you want to sit inside or in the garden?' I asked Kirstie. We both looked around the tired and dated décor, made even less inviting by the greenish-white light of old energy-saving bulbs.

We answered in unison. 'Outside.'

The evening air was still warm and sitting at a picnic table in the uncared-for garden was far more preferable to the pub's demoralising interior.

Our meaningful conversation was initiated by Kirstie. 'Okay, who goes first?'

'Probably best if I do, then you can say yea or nay.' My answer caused her to raise an eyebrow and give an intrigued hum.

'Look, I need help with this Mitch problem, someone to bounce ideas off, and seek information for me. If you can't stand the thought of sitting in a police station all day long, how about helping me find what Vogel wants, so we can save Mitch?'

Kirstie took a long sip of her drink and after a few seconds answered. 'I'll help all I can with my thoughts on the matter, but I need to do some paid work to supplement my police pension, at least until my compensation comes through.'

'There's one other point I didn't mention concerning my deal with Vogel and his so-called principal. He's given me a debit card with a ceiling of one million dollars to use in the search. So, I can afford to be as generous as I like, and in your case I like.' I wasn't sure if those last words came out as being generous or flirtatious. By the smile and slight blush on Kirstie's face, neither was she. We both decided to ignore my unintended double meaning. I recovered with a quick suggestion of her salary, expenses, and bonus should we be successful.

'Just like the old days, then,' she answered, with a large grin. 'Except the pay's better than the army.'

Neither of us were about to risk losing our driving licences, so I ordered two flat whites to round off the meeting. Surprisingly, they turned out to be excellent.

'Right, as I see it, and correct me if I'm wrong,' began my new partner, 'we know for sure the Tiger's Ghost didn't go down on the Titanic. We know for sure that the car had lost its gold and bejewelled bodywork by 1945 when Miss Whelan's father bought the estate, and the car sans bodywork was being used to power the generator. So, the gold and jewels disappeared in the thirty-three years between 1912 and 1945.'

'Not 1912,' I corrected. 'Willard's were dealing with the jewels right up until the last entry in their books in May 1940. There's something niggling at the back of my mind about those Willard's records though, but I can't put my finger on it.'

'Do you think another look at them might help?'

'Yes! I think my next move should be back to the Goldsmiths' Hall, and you could go to Clarecourt, speak to Miss Whelan, and see if anyone else is still around who knew anything about Kuldeep Singh. After all, information gathering is your strong point.'

As we walked to the car park, I took a cheap pre-paid phone, commonly known as a burner, from my pocket. 'Here, use this from now on. I'm pretty sure Vogel has got access to my phones and my computers, so let's keep him out the loop. We'll buy new burners every five phone calls.'

Kirstie knew exactly what I was talking about and turned for her Morgan. 'I'll call you from Clarecourt on Thursday or sooner if there's news.'

Neither of us offered or expected a chaste friendship kiss. We were now effectively operational, on a mission, just like the army days.

CHAPTER TWENTY

Colonel Levington was unable to accommodate me at Goldsmiths' Hall until Thursday morning. Once there, I decided to work backwards through the Willard's books, starting on those that ended with the 1945 bombing. On my last visit I hadn't checked in detail all the staff travel and expenses records for Mr. Sidelski. I wished I had because there was the answer staring me in the face. Under the entries for Time Spent were recorded the hours and minutes that he had taken removing the chosen gems and replacing them with paste replicas. But in March of 1939, and thereafter, the entries only recorded gems having been collected, but not replaced with paste.

I also hadn't yet checked the ledgers for the details of newly created pieces. Amongst the listings of every imaginable type of jewellery were items decorated with semi-precious stones and even coloured glass. I noted the items which had the customer's name George. Reference to Sidelski's records showed the paste gems had always been completed a few weeks before his visits to the Emerald Isle. There were no entries in this ledger of paste replicas being made for George after 30th January 1939.

Closing the book with a sharp bang that made the Colonel wince, I thought I'd cheer him up a bit. 'Thank you, Colonel, I shan't need to bother you again.' Relief flooded across his face. He even managed a curt nod.

On the train home, I considered what all this meant. Simply that it was highly probable that in 1939 the Tiger's Ghost had been dismantled to better conceal its gold and jewels. I wondered if Kuldeep Singh had reckoned that a war was coming, and he might need to run for cover if Ireland became involved. If the good Maharajah's death had been accidental, then the treasure might still be concealed at Clarecourt. Or did his so-called trusty servants kill him and make off with part or all of it? Perhaps someone else did exactly that. Fingers crossed that Kirstie would come up with a lead on that little conundrum.

Back at home, I collected Columbus from Smiler in the workshop, and raced him up the stairs to the office, a competition that always had the same winner. I fed the dog and made a cheese sandwich and a cup of tea for me. The sandwich was only half eaten when my burner phone rang; it was Kirstie.

'How did it go, is everything okay?' I asked.

'Oh, yes, well worth the trip. I'll tell all when I see you.'

'Are you on the ferry?' I asked, trying to gauge how long I would have to wait to hear what she had found out.

'No, I'm just up the road, I'll see you in about twenty minutes,' she answered cheerily.

I was still trying to work out how she had managed the trip back so fast, when the Morgan pulled up.

'When did you leave?' I asked, handing her the expected coffee.

'Early this morning, I flew myself: Thruxton to Bantry and back the same route. I've had a private pilot's licence for nearly eight years, and a good friend who lets me fly his Cessna 182 Skylane. Oh, here's the fuel and landing fees receipts for Herr Vogel's debit card. I'm also cooking my friend a thank-you supper tonight, but I won't charge you for that,' she added with a wide smile.

'Having my own pilot sounds very useful. So, what have you found out?' I ignored her supper quip.

Kirstie settled down on the office sofa, with Columbus

beside her, head on lap. 'As you know, I'd telephoned Miss Whelan to arrange the visit before I left. God, Ben you have a real fan there. You can do no wrong in Miss W's eyes. Anyway, after a general chat I asked her if there was anyone else still living who had known Kuldeep Singh, maybe worked for him at the house. Initially she couldn't think of anyone, but then she remembered a lad named Dillon, who'd worked part-time as a gardener's boy. He still lives about half an hour's walk from Clarecourt, in the cottage he was born in, but now with a granddaughter looking after him.

'I expected a tumbled-down hovel, but the little house was immaculate with pink-washed stone walls, slate roof, and flowers around the door. Could have been on a chocolate box or a jigsaw. The granddaughter, Róisin, answered, and once I had explained the reason for my visit, happily showed me in to see her grandfather. She told me he had a seemingly perfect memory for the distant past, but not so much for what happened yesterday.

'I kept my conversation with Dillon about the old days in general to start with, but when I mentioned Kuldeep Singh, he became uncomfortable, which worried his granddaughter a bit. Rather than ask me to leave, she pressed him gently to discuss Kuldeep. They broke into Gaelic for quite a time, with Róisin egging him on, holding his hand. He finally nodded his agreement. She told me her grandfather had quite a story to tell, and it would be best to let him speak in his own time. Róisin then went off to fetch something that she said would interest me.'

'And was the story worth the trip?' I asked.

'Dillon has a soft and gentle Irish brogue with the growl of an old man who's had a hard-working life, so I had to concentrate to take in all he said. The gist of it was that on the night before Kuldeep Singh's body was found, Dillon was out and about poaching rabbits and hares. He was fifteen and it was one of his first times alone, without his father to show him the ropes. He was close to the bay-shore checking his snares, and it was an overcast night, which gave Dillon good cover, but made it difficult for him to see. The result was that he tripped over a concealed rubber boat, crashing onto the wooden seats and paddles. His heart was thumping as he scrambled out and hid back in the undergrowth, intending to wait and see if anyone was about, and if the coast was clear to abandon his poaching and scurry home.'

'So that was it?' I interrupted.

'No, it wasn't it. Eventually his curiosity got the better of him and he crept back to the dinghy as quietly as only a well-taught poacher can. Just then there was a break in the clouds and the moonlight was bright enough for Dillon to see the boat and two similar ones, all concealed in the undergrowth. He heard steps, so he hurried back to his hidey-hole and waited. Three men appeared, dressed in black with blackened faces, guns held at the ready. Dillon was close enough to hear their whispers, but they weren't speaking English or Gaelic.

'One of the men had a torch and flashed it out over the water. Similar flashes appeared out in the bay, and the three men dragged the rubber boats down to the water's edge. One of them quietly whistled, and more of the camouflaged men came into Dillon's sight, each one was carrying an ammunition box with rope handles. There were also four other men, three with their hands tied, who were roughly pushed into one boat each. The fourth, unfettered, was treated more gently, and was guided into the second boat. All three boats were paddled out towards where the flashing light in the bay had been. Dillon finished his story by saying that the four men, not in camouflage, all wore turbans. He knew them by name, as they were Mr. Singh's personal servants.'

'Sounds very much to me as if the crew of a German craft of some sort came ashore, probably with the help of one of Singh's trusted retainers, killed Singh, captured the other servants and made off with boxes of gems,' I said.

'And maybe some of the gold if Kuldeep had melted it down into ingots,' suggested Kirstie.

'I don't think so, an ammo box full of gold would be too heavy for one man.'

Kirstie continued. 'Who knows? Dillon's old and it was a long time ago to remember who carried what, but there's one bit more. Róisin brought in a tin box. She placed it on Dillon's knees. He rummaged around for a bit and pulled out an old tobacco tin: Mick McQuaid Cut Plug it said on the lid. Inside was an old seed packet. Dillon handed it to me and pointed to the pencil marks on the back, saying he wasn't much of a scholar, but that was what was on the side of all three dinghies.'

Kirstie had stopped talking and I was impatient. 'And?' I asked a bit sharply.

'I've got a picture and I think you'll like it,' she took her phone from her jeans pocket and swiped a photo for me. It was the seed packet scribble from 1945. Dillon had written U- Ɛ000. 'The three's back to front,' I said.

'Róisin explained her grandpa was dyslexic and not much of a scholar.'

There was only one obvious conclusion: the crew of a German U-boat had made off with some or all of Kuldeep Singh's treasure.

CHAPTER TWENTY-ONE

Saturday started with an auction near Leominster in Herefordshire, about two and a half hours drive from home. The car of interest was a 1928 Lancia Lambda, an Italian car with a great four-cylinder engine in V formation and sliding-pillar front suspension similar to that still used today on the British-built Morgan. Although the auction estimate was sensible, I discovered that the owner had placed a reserve price that was above my client's top bid. In case the car didn't sell, I left a hopeful offer with the auctioneers and headed for home.

On the journey back, I had plenty of time to think about what I should say to Vogel and when. I hadn't contacted him since emailing a report of my meeting with Mo Katz. Vogel's only reply had been a curt thank-you. I decided to stay out of his way to see if I could find out more about the U-3000, and I knew just who to ask: Silas Brown, a collector for whom I had once found a 1936 Mercedes-Benz model 770. Reputedly, it had been used by Adolf Hitler.

At Cirencester, a quick detour took me to the nearby village of Duntiscombe, on the edge of which is a cluster of redundant farm buildings. Nowadays they contain a mass of British and German wheeled and tracked vehicles from the Second World War. Silas is the man who has lavished much of his considerable fortune, made from dealing in scrap metal, in assembling the collection. If you've seen a British war film that was made in the last thirty years, you are likely to have seen some of his vehicles.

Silas's vast shape lumbered into view, wearing his ever-present smile. Two Alsatian guard dogs trotted at his heels and gave me a salutary sniff. They decided Silas liked me and there was no need for their attentions.

'What brings you to these parts, lad?' he enquired in his strong Gloucester accent.

'Just wanted to see what rare and expensive vehicles you're going to sell me at knock-down prices.'

'I think you've mistaken me for one of your posh friends,' he laughed, giving me a knuckle-crunching handshake.

'I've got a question for you. A pint at the local says you can't answer it.'

'Well, if I can't it'll be the first time, boy.'

Silas has an encyclopaedic and photographic memory for all things military from the Second World War. His interest stretches to things nautical, but the only maritime vessel in his collection is a lifeboat from HMS Exeter, one of the Royal Navy cruisers that was responsible for the scuttling of the German pocket battleship Admiral Graf Spee during the Battle of the River Plate.

'You drive on, boy, I'll see you at the pub, you might as well get'em in and save time. I'll lock up,' he said with a throaty chuckle.

I carried a pint of Severn Cider and a Doom Bar bitter to an alcove table. Fifteen minutes later Silas puffed and wheezed his way to his chair. I waited while he downed half of the cider in one go. 'I would like to know what became of the German U-boat U-3000, after, say, March 1945?'

Silas leant back in his chair and closed his eyes. 'Ah well now, U-3000 you say. She was a type XXI. The last design of Hitler's super-submarines. One hundred and eighteen were recorded as being completed, but only two saw active service,' eyes now open, Silas emptied his glass and pushed it across the table. 'Worth another one, boy?'

Cider replenished, Silas continued. 'Some say a hundred and nineteen were built, and there's a bit of hearsay proof that U-3000 was the extra boat.'

'Go on, Silas,' I encouraged.

'After the war when German records were being scrutinised, there was no build record for U-3000, although the number was in sequence. Nearly all the XXIs were destroyed by bombing in their construction docks or home bases, but the two boats with active roles have been credited with all sorts of clandestine sorties; torpedo raids in New York harbour, carrying stolen art, treasure and even Adolf Hitler to South America. Of course, most of these stories are complete bollocks.'

'I thought some Nazis like Adolf Eichmann escaped to South America in submarines,' I said.

'No, boy. Those buggers got there on surface ships using false names and documents. But there were at least two known submarines that made it to Argentina: U-530 in July 1945 and U-977 in the August, but no solid records of high-ranking Nazis or treasure were on either of them. Just the crews trying for asylum.'

'So, what's all that got to do with U-3000?' I asked.

'Maybe nothing, boy. But a submarine calling itself U-3000 was come across by a Royal Navy corvette, HMS Stokesay Castle. Those XXI class subs were prone to problems despite their super specifications, mainly due to sub-standard materials and rushed detail design at war's end. Anyway, there she was on the surface, just sitting there when Stokesay's radar spotted her, steamed at best speed, and opened fire. Lucky hits maybe or perhaps the sub was sinking anyway. So, she puts up a white flag and signals Stokesay, asking for a boarding party, just one officer, though.'

'Is that usual?' I asked.

'No boy, it's not usual. Usual was battle to the death or a full boarding party, officers, and men. Anyway, the poor old third officer gets the job of being rowed across to the sub, where the captain invites him up to the conning tower. They go below, and after about an hour up they come and signal to the corvette that the sub captain and his crew are surrendering and claiming asylum. They say they're bound for Argentina, as they're scared if they go home and the Russians get them, they'll all be shot. So, arrangements are made for the sub's entire crew of five officers and fifty-two men to be taken prisoner aboard the Stokesay. Last off is Kapitan Hans Valentiner, just in time as U-3000 is sinking fast, stern first. By the time he reaches the Stokesay, the sub is just a frothing mess of air bubbles on the surface. All the Krauts are treated well as prisoners of war, and arrangements are made for Stokesay Castle to rendezvous with her refuelling tanker. With both ships steaming towards one another it'll be a few hours 'til they can transfer the prisoners, who are all so windy, none of them will take off their life jackets, including their Captain.' Silas looked as if he was reliving an event that he had actually taken part in.

'Where did all this happen?' I asked.

'In relatively shallow water for the Azores, but too deep for souvenir hunters today. No professional wreck companies have bothered to look for it as there was nothing of great value on board. It's not a designated war grave, as all the crew made it on to the Stokesay Castle.'

'And when did it happen?'

'As neither the submarine's nor the Stokesay Castle's log

survived, we only have the survivor's recollections, but they agreed it was about 08:30 hours on the twenty-ninth of April.'

'How on earth do you know all this stuff, Silas?' I asked, incredulous as ever at his knowledge.

'Well, boy, truth is there's a book, more a large pamphlet really, on what happened to Stokesay Castle, written by the third officer, Sub-Lieutenant Harold Tyler. I've got a copy. I'll lend it to you before you go. Anyway, back to the story. They're about three hours from meeting up with the tanker, when there's a chance in a thousand; another U-boat, and this one sees the Stokesay through its periscope. But these Krauts of course don't know what's happened and who's on board. All they see is an enemy ship, and a submarine hunter at that, so they line up on the old Stokesay before it spots them. They shoot off two torpedoes, and for whatever reasons no one on the corvette sees them until it's too late. One explodes in the magazine just aft of the forward deck-gun and one tears into the aft boiler room. Two almighty explosions blow the ship to smithereens, and she goes down in seconds. The sub never even surfaced to see if there were any survivors.'

'How many were there?' I asked.

'Like the mighty Hood sunk by the Bismarck, just three; two seamen who had been manning the RADAR room above the deck, and third officer Tyler. Some of the crew were blown overboard dead and some drowned in the blazing oil slick, but most went down with the ship, as did all the Krauts, except the U-boat's commander. He'd been the guest of the Stokesay's captain on the bridge. Tyler was also there on duty. By a strange quirk of fate, he survived the explosions and managed to avoid the burning oil slick. He found Kapitan Valentiner's body floating next to him. As no one was expecting an attack, Tyler didn't have a life jacket on, so he took the dead Kraut's off and used it himself. He wrote that the German life jacket had certainly saved his life.'

'No mention that the U-3000 was carrying any special passengers or maybe works of art or gold?' I asked nonchalantly.

'No mention of anything like that, just scared sailors who'd lost faith in their Führer and the Nazi regime.'

'I guess I won't find out much more about the U-3000, then,' I mused dejectedly.

'That's just where you may be wrong, boy. I wrote to Harold Tyler a few times about the submarine that torpedoed his ship and he always replied. Got his address through his publisher, see. Harold Tyler was alive and kicking a year ago.'

CHAPTER TWENTY-TWO

I had spent most of Sunday dealing with my mainstream business, which included taking on a new client from the state of Oman. A seriously rich businessman with connections to the ruling Royal family, he wanted to start a collection of rare cars with interesting provenances within the Middle East. The plan was for them to become the prime exhibits in Oman's National Motor Museum.

Of more immediate interest, with Silas's help and a few phone calls, I had managed to track down Sub-Lieutenant Harold Tyler. The warden at his sheltered accommodation knew his life story. Harold had left the Royal Navy in 1946 and returned to his peacetime trade of teaching German and French at a minor public school for boys in his home county of Yorkshire. Retiring in 1993, and never having married, he had moved to Robin Hood's Bay just south of Whitby; perhaps the sea had remained in his blood. Harold had fended for himself up until five years ago, when just six days after his ninety-fifth birthday he had fallen in the street, broken his hip, and become seriously concussed. During his recovery in hospital, he had agreed with his carers to sell up his cottage and move into sheltered housing. Lastly, the warden told me that Harold was now in a nursing home, and unlikely to return to the sheltered accommodation.

Just after 2:00pm on Monday, I turned the Defender into the car park at Saint Bosa's nursing home, near Whitby. Well-manicured grounds with wheelchair-friendly paths amongst mature trees surrounded a typical 1970s-built single-storey building. The reception was unattended, and its ring-for-staff bell stayed unanswered. After wandering along a few corridors, I found a helpful east-European woman whose name badge told me she was Sophia. She took me back to reception to wait while she looked for the matron, whom I had spoken to before setting out this morning. I had time to read a brass plaque that told me St. Bosa had been schooled at Whitby Monastery, became a monk there and eventually Bishop of York. He died in 705. The home had been opened in 1976 by the then Archbishop of York.

Eventually, Matron Pamela Warner showed me to her office, and a seat across from her desk. She looked friendly if a little guarded. 'So, Mr. Ross, what do you want with our Captain Tyler?'

I knew for sure that he had never risen above the rank of a wartime Sub-Lieutenant but saw no point in spoiling the old boy's grandeur. 'I'm researching some naval history from the Second World War, and as I'm sure you know, the chances of speaking to people with first-hand experience, those who actually took part, are becoming fewer and fewer. I only found out yesterday that the captain was here, and no longer living in sheltered accommodation.'

'Mr. Ross, I have to tell you that it's very unlikely that Harold will leave St. Bosa's before his passing. He's now in his hundredth year, and although he's surprisingly agile of mind, his body is failing fast; imminent multiple organ failure, which will probably be complicated by pneumonia in the not-too-distant future. I'm sad to say, Mr. Ross, that had you delayed your visit just a few days, it is not certain at all that you would have been in time.'

I finished my tea, and looking suitably sorrowful, thanked the matron for her forthright description of Harold's situation. 'Do you think I could see him, without causing distress?' I asked.

'Oh, yes, a visitor would be good for him, on condition that if he falls asleep you leave quietly without waking him. There's a bellpush by his pillow if you need a nurse, but I shall leave you to enjoy a private conversation.' She ushered me from her office and took me to Harold's room.

A printed slip on the door stated 'Captain Harold Tyler RN (rtd.)'. The matron knocked lightly and after a short pause we entered the bright and pleasant room. He was lying propped on a bank of pillows. Slightly built, he looked emaciated, with waxy, sallow skin.

Harold opened his eyes when the matron gently squeezed his hand and smiled. 'You have a visitor, Captain; would you like to chat to him?'

'A visitor, now there's a turn for the better,' said Harold, whose pale blue eyes had focused sharply on me.

'I'll leave you two alone then, Captain. Tea will come round as usual in about half an hour,' she said, as she gently closed the door.

The room had warm but institutional decor and furniture. Harold waved weakly at an upright armchair. 'Pull the chair to the bed, can't hear so well these days.'

I did so.

Harold peered at me with piercing but watery eyes. 'Did I teach you at school, I don't remember the look of you, what's your name?'

'My name's Benedict Ross, Ben, and no, you didn't teach me. I'm doing some research into Royal Navy corvettes during the Second World War. A good friend of mine, Silas Brown, who I know you have corresponded with, gave me your name. We had been discussing the Stokesay Castle and the U-3000.'

Harold's head sank back onto the pillows as he gave a sigh so deep, I thought it was a death rattle; I moved to press the emergency bell, but before I did, Harold gave a bitter little laugh, and once again looked at me.

'Why don't you tell me first what you know about the U-3000 incident,' he said.

I relayed all that I had learned from Silas Brown, and Harold's own book, plus a shortened version of what Dillon had told Kirstie in Ireland. I shared the thought there was a good chance the submarine had been carrying a fortune in stolen gems.

Once again Harold's head rested back on his pillows, but this time there was no deep sigh, just a growly-hum of decision making. He didn't speak for at least half a minute.

'So, you know I'm not really a Captain? I'd rather you didn't mention that to anyone.'

'It says Captain on your door, so Captain it is.'

Harold nodded his thanks. 'I can remember as clearly as if it was yesterday everything that happened on the Stokesay from the minute we spotted the U-3000, until we were rescued. When I boarded her, we went through the official rigmarole of the surrender of an enemy vessel. Captain Valentiner gave me his ceremonial dagger. It had an eagle and swastika on the ivory and gold banded handle. I gave it up to our captain, of course. Valentiner had destroyed his boat's log, which I expected. There were no coding devices that I could find, you know, the Enigma machines. I searched the boat as best I could, but as she was already sinking there wasn't much time to do so. No signs of hidden jewels anywhere, but there's plenty of places to stash secrets on a large submarine of unknown design.'

'So, you did search for contraband, hidden valuables?'

'I was suspicious. Why was I the only person allowed to

board, and why was a U-boat heading towards the South Atlantic and the Americas if there wasn't something or someone to conceal? Back on the Stokesay we all accepted Valentiner's explanation that they were running from the Russians and certain death at their hands if Germany surrendered. Anyway, we knew the crew were in for serious interrogation when they got to England, in case any were high-ranking Nazis on the run.'

'Do you think there was any chance there could have been some gems concealed on board?' I asked again.

Tell me, Mr. Ross, why is the fate of the U-3000 of such interest to you? Could you be a treasure hunter, a desecrator of war graves rather than a naval historian?' He spoke with a new-found strength in his voice.

I made an instant decision to tell him the truth about Mitch and the Tiger's Ghost, but in an abbreviated version. There was no point in correcting him that the sub was not a war grave.

Harold closed his eyes for long enough for me to remember the matron's warning to let him sleep and not to awaken him, but just as I decided to leave as requested, he opened his eyes and nodded towards his wardrobe.

'In there, on the floor, my deed box; bring it to me.'

I placed it on the bed beside him. 'Is there a key?' I asked.

Harold smiled. 'What's the one thing that always comes to hospital with you and no one steals? A wash-kit.' He said, pointing to his on the bedside cabinet.

'There's a removable base, easy to keep clean, you see. Pull it up, the key's underneath. Open the box for me.'

Inside were some official-looking papers, deeds, certificates, and the like. Also a few old photos, including a shot of Harold in his Sub-Lieutenant's uniform, looking far too fresh-faced for the job. Much of the deed box was taken up by an old cardboard shoebox, with broken corners and crumbling edges. Harold flipped the lid aside and told me to take out the contents. It was a Thermos flask-sized gas cylinder of some kind, chipped and rusty with the remains of some letters and numbers in the archaic Germanic typeface that was used by the Nazis. It was heavier than it looked. Harold weakly cleared his throat, with a crackle that came deep from his lungs.

'Mr. Ross, what I wrote of the sinking of the Stokesay Castle in my little book left out one important aspect and contained one lie. The sinking of our ship was just as I wrote, fast and furious and totally without warning. Why three of us were spared, God only knows but that's what happened, except there was a fourth person who survived the actual sinking: Capitan Valentiner. He wasn't dead when I found myself next to him in the water, but he was badly injured. Oil in the lungs, I think, and burns. A burning oil slick was coming towards us, so I grabbed him to pull him away to clear water. When we were safe from the flames, he was almost finished, and he knew it. He thanked me on behalf of his men and himself for being treated well on the Stokesay. He said he had never been a Nazi but was fiercely patriotic for the Fatherland. He told me to take his life jacket and keep it safe, for it would be my fortune. I of course thought he meant because of its designed purpose. His last words were that all his crew had been wearing theirs. He died a minute or two later. I took the life jacket off his body, as I was tiring and needed it badly. We had been on our way to meet our bunkering tanker, and I knew we would be in the water for some hours at best before they found us; I didn't know how many of us had survived, of course.'

Holding up the gas cylinder, I asked 'Is this from the sub, Captain?'

'Yes, it was part of the German Kriegsmarine life jacket, a compressed-air cylinder. But it's been altered: look, there's a join near the top. Unscrew it, Mr. Ross, it's a left-hand thread.'

It took some doing, but once moving, the fine threads turned easily. As I eased the top off, the contents spilled out onto Harold's bed. They were a selection of diamonds, rubies, emeralds, and sapphires of assorted sizes, but all large. I looked at Harold, speechless.

'I had not the slightest clue where Valentiner had found them, until you told me just now of the U-3000 and the Maharajah in Ireland,' said Harold.

'Valentiner said the jacket would be your fortune, but it wasn't. You never cashed the jewels in. Why did you keep them, and why show them to me now?'

'Initially I had so many plans for them, but as time went by, I became frightened to do anything. I knew nothing of the criminal world, where to sell them discreetly. If the authorities found out they would take them, and probably throw me in prison. So, I kept them. In a funny sort of way, the possibilities they held for me were as good as realising that potential. Every now and then I would take them out, dust them off and hold each one up to the light, just to admire them.'

'But why show me?' I repeated.

'Mr. Ross, I shall very soon die. I have no family, and all my friends have passed on before me. The jewels would end up God knows where, causing God knows what arguments and strife. From what you have told me, they will save your Mr. Mitchell's life.'

'Mitchelletti,' I corrected him.

'Yes, Mitchelletti. Good karma, you see. Valentiner saved me, and now I can save someone else: so unexpected this late in my life. Take the cylinder and its contents and do some good for me as well, Mr. Ross.'

I scooped up the gems and put them all back in the cylinder, screwing the halves together firmly. Should I take them? If he left them to the nursing home, would they ever get the benefit? I could imagine years of legal wrangling about rightful ownership; a case of twenty-first-century Jarndyce versus Jarndyce. The immediate possibility of saving Mitch won the day. I decided to accept Harold's offer, an offer that would also give him peace of mind in his dying days.

Standing up, I thanked him profusely and gently shook his hand. 'Goodbye, Captain Tyler. I hope all goes as well as it can for you.'

'I think it will be preferable to drowning in flaming fuel oil,' he said with a smile and a weak squeeze of my hand.

As I opened the door, a thought flashed into my mind. 'You said Valentiner told you all his crew had their life jackets. Does that mean their air bottles had also been doctored?'

'Mr. Ross, your guess is as good as mine, but mine is yes, they are all crammed with jewels, at least five thousand feet down in the Atlantic Ocean, at a site that could be anywhere in a hundred square miles. But don't forget all those lads who died on the Stokesay Castle, British and German. They deserve to be left in peace.'

CHAPTER TWENTY-THREE

The trip home took me about five hours. Plenty of time to consider what Harold had said and done. I really liked the old boy, and wished he was going to be around long enough to know him better. Matron Pamela had agreed to phone me when he died and give me the details of the funeral. I promised myself I would attend, especially as there probably wouldn't be many mourners for a centenarian with no living relatives.

The next morning, when Kirstie had arrived at the Clock House, I called Smiler on the intercom to join us in the office. They both had a right to know what had taken place in Harold Tyler's room. I told them all, up to the point when Harold had shown me the oxygen bottle. Taking it from my desk, I handed it to Smiler.

'This is what he gave me. What do you make of it?'

He turned it over in his oily hands and squinted at the German lettering. 'It's a German compressed air bottle, see here,' he pointed to the chipped remains of the words Atmungsaktive Druckluft. 'It's bloody heavy though, must be thick metal for high pressures.'

'Let me see,' said Kirstie, reaching over for the cylinder. She shook it carefully and heard it rattle. 'There's something in it, or a lot of rust.'

'Give it back to Smiler and see what he can find,' I said, grinning wide enough for them to know something interesting lay ahead.

He pinched out his cigarette, putting the remains behind his ear. Squinting at the bottle and running a grimy fingernail all over it, he snicked the near-perfect join of the threads and gave an obvious twist to the left to undo it, with of course no result.

'No, turn it the other way, it's left-handed,' I told him.

As Smiler unscrewed the container, Kirstie sat on the edge of the sofa, and bit her lip excitedly, her eyes darting from the cylinder to me and back.

Smiler peered inside. 'Fuck me!' he said as he tipped the contents onto the coffee table.

There was enough light in the office to make the gems sparkle to life. Kirstie gave a gasp and a loud 'Shit, Ross!'

I finished off the story, as they cascaded the gems through their fingers.

Smiler asked, 'What do we do now, Guv?'

'Well, we have something to give Vogel and we can tell him that the rest of the jewels are just waiting for him in the U-3000. I don't want to let him know they're probably on the Stokesay Castle just in case he manages to locate it and arrange a search and salvage operation. I just hope this is enough for him to release Mitch.'

'He's going to want the gold as well, though,' added Kirstie.

'That's my main worry,' I said. 'I reckon from Dillon's account that no heavy gold sheets or even melted down bullion was taken by the sub's crew, but Vogel doesn't know this. Suppose we tell him that Kuldeep Singh had melted down the Tiger's Ghost's body panels into bars and they also are on the sub.'

'Won't Vogel check all this out?' suggested Smiler as he drew deeply on his re-lit cigarette.

'He'll probably want to check with Harold Tyler, and he, bless him, according to Matron Warner, will soon no longer be with us, so I'll delay telling Vogel where to find Harold as long as I can. That will leave Dillon, and he has no idea what was in the boxes he saw being loaded into the dinghies. I just have to be very persuasive, and let's face it, the gems we do have are worth God knows how much, but millions. He may be satisfied.' This I said with more conviction than I felt. 'So, what do you think?' I added.

'I think it's worth a try. Either he'll bite or he won't,' said Smiler.

'If he doesn't, do you think he'll harm Mitch to keep you at it?' added Kirstie.

'On balance, I think with the gems we are giving him, and with Harold's booklet version of the Stokesay Castle and the U-3000, I might pull it off. If he has reservations about the gold, I reckon I can back-track quickly enough to keep him on side. Kirstie, important job for you, see if you can get details of the Stokesay Castle from the National Archives at Kew, while I get in touch with Vogel.'

Kirstie looked at her watch. 'Yes,' she answered hesitatingly. 'But I have to be away by lunchtime. I'm flying to Le Touquet with the owner of the Cessna that I use, we're meeting some French pals of his for dinner tonight.'

'Flying back in the dark, then?' suggested Smiler mischievously.

'No, we're staying over, at the Westminster Hotel,' replied a blushing Kirstie.

Smiler and I looked at her but said nothing.

She broke the silence. 'No dammit, separate rooms, I made that quite clear to Quentin.'

'Quentin!' Smiler and I shouted together.

'What sort of name's that for a bloke?' asked Smiler.

Kirstie couldn't suppress a wide grin. 'I've a good mind to

scoop up the gems and run off with them. Now sod off, you two, and let me try and get the Stokesay information.'

And sod off we did. Smiler back to the workshop and me to my desk. Vogel's email address was contactable but as expected untraceable. I used it to say progress made. We need to meet. I didn't know whether he yet trusted me enough to arrange a rendezvous, or if he would just show up somewhere as he had done on the Eurostar.

Thirty minutes later, there was a reply. Tomorrow 5:00pm. Piccadilly Station. Bakerloo Line. Northbound. Wait in centre of platform. Rush-hour, I thought, giving him plenty of escape opportunities if he sensed a trap.

The next day, I delayed even thinking about the evening's meet with Vogel until after lunch. I had plenty of work, arranging the delivery of a low-chassis Invicta from its private vendor near Northampton to its purchaser in Chichester.

To meet Vogel, I would catch a train to Paddington where I could jump on the tube to Piccadilly Circus. I had decided not to take all the gems in their cylinder for reasons of security, and more importantly it would leave me with a bargaining position to secure Mitch's release. I envisaged a future exchange, gems for Mitch rather like a spy film or a TV drama. Selecting the largest diamond to show Vogel, I wrapped it in a yellow duster and zipped it up in an inside pocket of my driving-coat.

Just before 5:00pm a train arrived as I waited at the rear of the platform, halfway down as Vogel had instructed. The place was heaving with commuters, just as many getting off the train as were getting on. A quarter of an hour passed, along with four more trains. I decided Vogel wasn't coming and the entire journey was a waste of time. As the breeze was pushed in front of the next train coming along the tunnel, I decided to take it back to Paddington and go home. I shuffled forward to the platform's edge, the train screeching to a halt. The doors opened and spewed out the Piccadilly-bound travellers. The last one out was Heinrich Vogel. He saw me immediately, grabbed my arm in a surprisingly vice-like grip for a man of his age and pulled me aboard. We stood in the crush, pushed to the doors on the other side of the carriage. It was time for me to become Ben the Vogel-henchman once again.

As I spoke he held a finger to his lips. 'Not here Mr. Ross. Just stay by me.'

We got off two stops later at Regent's Park. Vogel hurried me around the corner to Park Crescent where an electric black cab was waiting. The driver jumped out and opened the door for us, a courtesy that along with his blond crew-cut and Teutonic looks made me think he was on Vogel's payroll, and not your run-of-the-mill London cabby.

'So, Mr Ross, what is this information you have for me that is important enough to bring me from my home in Germany?'

I thought he was going to slip up and tell me where he lived. I didn't answer but checked the cab's little red light that tells you if the driver's intercom is on or off. The light was off. Vogel saw my look.

'Do not worry about Conrad, he is most discreet and loyal, but you are right, the intercom is off.'

I unzipped the inside pocket of my coat and took out the yellow duster, held it towards Vogel and poured the contents onto his hand. The diamond slipped into his lap. His comment was easy to understand. 'Mein Gott'.

As the taxi turned into Marylebone Road, Vogel held the pear-shaped stone up to the window, between thumb and forefinger. He turned it slowly to let the facets catch the light. I don't know what it weighed but it was nearly two centimetres from top to bottom.

'Mr. Ross is this the only stone you have so far found or is it a sample of what you have for me?' asked Vogel, as he slipped the diamond into his pocket.

'It's a sample. There are forty gems in total, diamonds, rubies, sapphires, and emeralds. About ten are of this size, one bigger but all significantly large, and of differing shapes. Here, you can see them all on my phone, I took photos for you.'

'This is most impressive, Mr. Ross, but I do not think these stones are all that were contained in the Tiger's Ghost, and you have not yet mentioned the gold.' Vogel spoke in his quietly threatening manner.

I told him of the Stokesay Castle, and how I had come by the gems. Of course, I added the fictitious fact that according to Kapitan Valentiner the gold was also on the seabed, but inside the U-3000 with the rest of the jewels. Vogel looked disappointed, as I told him I would soon have the Naval records for the Stokesay Castle, but that no mention of the gems or the gold would have been recorded as being on the submarine, because only Harold Tyler knew of them.

Vogel was silent for maybe two minutes as driver Conrad weaved around the side streets between the Marylebone Road and Oxford Street. 'Tell me more of this gold; you say it is bullion inside the U-boat,' he finally said.

I knew I had to be careful here – one hint that I was lying could be the end for Mitch, and probably me, at Conrad's deft ministrations. 'Maharajah Kuldeep Singh dismantled the Tiger's Ghost at some stage. We know that for sure, as Miss Whelan remembered the engine was powering the generator when her father bought Clarecourt in 1945. I'm only guessing here but suppose Kuldeep Singh foresaw the coming of war and decided his treasure should be made more easily transportable and concealable. The gems would be easy to carry, but the gold panels from the car's body were cumbersome and each would be extremely heavy. So, melt them down into manageable bars.'

'You have not yet told me how you came to know of the involvement of the U-3000,' said Vogel.

I told the tale of Dillon and his night of poaching, adding pairs of men heaving very heavy boxes aboard the rubber boats, hoping Vogel's mind would leap to the conclusion that they contained both gems and bullion. I thought if I showed a bit of personal greed it might take his mind off the details.

'Herr Vogel, I think I have done what you have asked of me. I know it's disappointing for you and your principal that most of the treasure is lost thousands of feet down in the sea, but as Mitch is no further use to you, I think it's time for you to release him, and let me have the agreed one million dollars on the debit card.'

Vogel snapped his head around and fixed me with that ice-cold, dangerous stare that showed no human feeling at all. 'Mr Ross, my principal shall decide when Mitchelletti is released, and exactly how much of the debit card funds you will keep.'

'But we agreed you would top up the card to a million dollars.' I replied indignantly.

'That was only if you were successful in retrieving the entire treasure, Mr. Ross, not a minor portion.'

'Look, Vogel, the deal was to get you the jewels and gold or find their whereabouts and whether or not they are retrievable, and that's exactly what I've done.'

'We shall see, Mr. Ross, but first I need more proof. One of my associates will speak to this Harold Tyler and the Irishman,

Dillon, I think you called him. If I am satisfied that all you have said is true, then Mr. Mitchelletti will be sent back to you in exchange for the gems that you have found, unharmed if a little disgrundelled, is that the word?'

'Close enough,' I said. 'But what about my money?' I wanted to keep the image of the greedy and unprincipled Ben alive and well.

'We shall see, Mr. Ross, we shall see. Now please leave my taxi, send me the history of the Stokesay Castle and the addresses of Tyler and the Dillon man. Goodbye, Mr. Ross.'

With that he pressed the intercom button and told Conrad to pull over and let me out. We were in Eastcastle Street, just a stone's throw from Oxford Circus underground station, so I was able to make my way back to Paddington quite easily. It was no surprise that I was returning home with an empty yellow duster.

Just as the train swept through Southall station, famous for its castle-like water tower, once used to refill steam engines, my burner phone rang. 'Mr. Ross, this is Matron Warner at Saint Bosa's Hospice. I'm afraid I have some sad news for you. Captain Tyler passed away in the early hours of this morning.'

'Was it a peaceful end?' I asked.

'Yes, it was. He slipped into a coma around midnight and just stopped breathing at ten minutes past three this morning.'

I thanked Matron Pamela for letting me know and reminded her to email me details of the funeral. Guiltily, I couldn't help feeling relieved that Vogel now had only one line of questioning that he could follow.

The catering trolley came past, pulled by a cheerful East European lad. He sold me a miniature bottle of whisky. I needed to raise a glass to Harold Tyler.

CHAPTER TWENTY-FOUR

For another two days I delayed emailing Vogel the sad news of Harold Tyler's passing, nor had I yet given him Dillon's phone number. Meanwhile Kirstie had arranged for a copy of the Stokesay Castle's war history to be emailed to me. Vogel would already have read it, but I forwarded him the promised copy to maintain the illusion that I was unaware of his ability to snoop in my computer.

This left the major problem of how to stop Vogel's henchman from probing deep enough into Dillon's memory to surmise that none of the gold from the car had been loaded onto the submarine.

I phoned Róisin to warn her someone unwelcome would be calling. I was planning to tell her that the visitor would neither do me, nor Miss Whelan's interests any good, and to hope that she would sympathise with my point of view, but I needn't have worried.

Róisin replied, 'Mr. Ross, is the man any friend of yours or Miss Whelan?'

'No, he is not. He works for a person who for financial reasons would like to stop me from researching what happened to Mr. Singh. If Dillon tells the visitor only the barest of details, then that would be good for both me and Miss Whelan.'

'Leave it with me, Mr. Ross, your man will find Dillon only has the Gaelic. I shall translate for him; I know just what to do,' Róisin replied.

'That's kind of you, Róisin, please pass on my thanks to Dillon.'

There was no word from Vogel for another three days. At

last, he phoned, while Smiler was in the office, so I put the call on the speaker.

'Mr. Ross, a great shame that Captain Tyler has died, and all his knowledge and maybe secrets with him. However, my associate has visited Mr. Dillon O'Brien and his charming but watchful granddaughter. I have spoken to my principal, and it is agreed that you seem to be in possession of all the artefacts that are likely to be available to us in the foreseeable future. We are therefore pleased to release Mr. Mitchelletti once the jewels are in our safe keeping.'

'And how do you propose we do that, Herr Vogel?' I asked.

'I will email you the location and time to meet, and ah, how do you say, the conditions: precautions you understand.'

'And my money?' I asked.

'I have discussed this with my principal, who thinks it fair under the circumstances that you should retain $100,000. A generous offer I think as it is one-tenth of the one million we spoke of for all the gems and gold, and what you are about to give us is nowhere near one-tenth of the Tiger's Ghost's value. You may transpose this amount from your Swiss debit card to any account you wish, once our transaction is complete.

'That was not our agreement, but I suppose I don't have a choice if I want Mitch back in one piece,' I said with what I hoped sounded like frustrated resignation. Vogel ended the call with no further comment.

Kirstie arrived within an hour, desperate to know if Vogel had been satisfied with what I had told him. She looked dressed for action, in red cargo pants and a white tee-shirt with 'ACTION' over a clenched fist emblazoned on it.

'I see you've dressed in camouflage,' I said. No reply was forthcoming, just a raised eyebrow and a 'hmm!' through pursed lips.

'You look great!' seemed a wise reply, and a truthful one.

We sat outside by the office stairway, in a couple of folding director's chairs, taking advantage of the warm sunshine in a cloudless sky. Smiler was working away, with Columbus laid out flat in the workshop entrance. Bringing Kirstie right up to date, I could see that her mind was in serious army-trained mode.

'Okay,' she said. 'It seems he swallowed the story that the rest of the jewels and all the gold are on the seabed, the retrieval of which, if they could be found, would cost a fortune and be impossible to keep secret. So, do you really think he'll swap Mitch for the gems that we have?'

'I think the check he made with Dillon and granddaughter confirmed what I'd told him. We're just waiting for Vogel to get back to me with the exchange plans. Meanwhile, I'd better bring Lucia up to speed.'

Kirstie sat back in her chair and folded her arms. She didn't say, but the almost imperceptible change in her tone of voice showed she was not a great fan of Lucia Bassoli. 'I'm sure she'll be relieved to get Mitch back unharmed, but she's going to be none too pleased that her family fortune is beyond her grasp,' she said.

'Don't forget about all the gold. We know it wasn't taken by the Nazis; as soon as Mitch is released, we'll start looking for it ourselves,' I said.

'You've changed your mind, then, about looking for the gold?'

'I know the last time I spoke to Mitch I told him I wasn't a treasure hunter and wouldn't take on that task, but situations change.'

'What's changed?' Kirstie asked.

'Vogel! I want the bastard, and the gold will be the bait.'

Kirstie held up her hand. 'You said before, that after you'd found the chassis Mitch was going to try and persuade you to take on the gold and gems search. That implies a new agreement.'

'Well, yes!' I agreed.

'Then if you did find the remaining gold, without a further agreement with Mitch, he would have no legal claim on it.'

'No, but it wouldn't do my reputation much good to pull the rug from under him, and don't forget, there's two other possible claimants. Lucia, as a direct descendant of Kuldeep Singh, and Miss Whelan. At some stage this is probably going to land up on a lawyer's desk.'

Kirstie snapped her fingers. 'Ah! Then shouldn't you also negotiate a finder's fee with Lucia and Miss Whelan, separately of course.'

I knew it had been a good day's work when I brought Kirstie on board. She was dead right. 'I'll try and sort something with Lucia, and would you phone Miss Whelan and make an appointment for me to visit? I think a face to face is best,' I replied.

As Kirstie pulled her burner phone from her pocket, and started dialling, I sprinted upstairs to use my landline, so that Vogel could listen in. He would expect me to bring Mitch's concerned co-director up to date.

'Lucia, Ben,' I started, but gave nothing away to a probable eavesdropping Vogel. I ended with the news that I was waiting for Vogel to get back to me.

'Is he really happy that the gems you have are the only part of the Tiger's Ghost that can be retrieved?' she asked worriedly.

I winced at the question. 'He'll have to be, Lucia, because it's the truth. I'm as sure as I can be that everything else is on the seabed. If he doesn't accept this, then I'm afraid there's no more we can do to get Mitch released.' I didn't like giving her such brutally honest news tinged with a lie, but it was necessary to bolster Vogel's belief in what I had told him.

'When you know exactly how Vogel wants to make the switch, let me know and I'll come right over to look after Mitch,' said Lucia, as we ended the call.

Kirstie came into the office and stood by my desk. 'Ben, I couldn't get hold of Miss Whelan, but eventually the sulky girl that works at the house, Maria, Mary or whatever her name is, she answered. She told me Miss Whelan had a stroke a week ago. She's in the Bantry General hospital at Carrignagat.'

CHAPTER TWENTY-FIVE

It was 8:00am and I was sitting next to Kirstie, looking down the grass runway 07 at Thruxton aerodrome. She had just gained clearance for us to take off, replying with our call-sign of Golf Whisky Kilo. As the airspeed indicator touched seventy-five knots, she gently pulled back on the control column and the Cessna leapt willingly into the air. We landed at Kerry airport at 10:12am. Paperwork cleared, we were in a taxi to the Bantry General Hospital three-quarters of an hour later.

I was more than a little depressed, being back in a hospital so soon after visiting Harold Tyler. We were shown into a private room, which could have been the twin of the one at St. Bosa's hospice, except here there was a lot more monitoring equipment by Miss Whelan's bed.

The nurse spoke quietly to her. 'Orla, there's a grand couple of people to see you. Would you like that?'

Miss Whelan took a few seconds to focus on us, but she nodded yes, with a lop-sided smile. Her right arm was lying on a couple of pillows for support, which her nurse adjusted for comfort.

'Miss Whelan,' I said. 'It's very good to see you again, but what have you been up to?'

She replied with slow and slurred speech. 'Oh! Just look at the state of me, will you. It's the old age has caught up with me. Did I tell you the same thing happened to my mother, but she was only seventy-two at the time?'

Miss Whelan held a large white paper handkerchief in her left hand, which she dabbed at the right-side of her mouth.

'Now you and Kirstie pull up two chairs and take note of what I have to say.'

We fetched the chairs. 'Miss Whelan, we'll do anything we can till you're back on your feet again,' said Kirstie.

'Oh, I don't think that is going to happen, but that's why I wanted to see you, and you've come so quickly.'

Kirstie and I glanced at each other because we had not heard that Miss Whelan wanted to see us.

I backed up what Kirstie had just said. 'Tell us what we can do for you.'

'The doctors say at best I shall be here for a good while and even then, I shall be unable to go back to Clarecourt. I think the time has come for me to go into a nursing home, and I can afford a fine one with the money from the Rolls-Royce motor car.'

Frail as she looked and slurred as her speech was, her steely resolve showed through. This was not the time for platitudes about being as right as rain in a few weeks. Miss Whelan was compos mentis and quite able to face the truth of her predicament, so we remained quiet and nodded our understanding.

'It's about the house, Mr. Ross. I want to sell it and give the proceeds for the good of the village, just as Mr Singh did all those years ago.' Miss Whelan broke off and gestured towards the water glass and jug by the bed. I poured half a glass, which she took a little shakily in her good hand. After a few sips she gave the glass back to me, and with another dab of her handkerchief, she continued. 'I don't trust estate agents to do the best they can for me, and I may just not have the time to see Clarecourt sold. Mr. Ross, you were honest and speedy with the buying of the motor car, and so I'm asking if you will see to a quick sale of Clarecourt for me, and that the proceeds are used as I wish.'

Kirstie and I exchanged a quick glance, and she placed her hand on my forearm. A gentle hint to be careful. I didn't need the hint.

'Miss Whelan, I, Kirstie, and I would love to help you, but it may be difficult. You see, when relative strangers agree to do something for a person in your situation, some people may think you were persuaded against your will, that you've been taken advantage of when you are not at your best.'

'You mean not of sound mind,' said Miss Whelan. 'I know a stroke like this can make a person unsure of themselves, confused. But the doctors have given me tests and it seems my troubles are physical, not mental at all, except I get very tired, so easily.'

Kirstie reached out and held Miss Whelan's sound hand. 'Are you feeling tired now, should we come back later, after you've had a rest?'

'No, this is playing on my mind, and I shan't be able to rest until it's settled.'

Kirstie answered her. 'I know how to comply with your wishes. I've been through a similar situation with a great-uncle. Do you have a solicitor, Miss Whelan?'

'Yes, Patrick Fogarty. He was with me when Mr. Ross came to buy the car.'

'Do you remember the name of the firm of solicitors he works for?' Kirstie continued.

'Oh! Yes! Downey, Neeson and Fogarty. His grandfather was the original Fogarty. They are in Waterford, where my family is from.'

'You'll need to have Mr. Fogarty come here and have your doctor say you are of sound mind. Then tell the solicitor that you want Ben, Mr. Ross here, to act on your behalf in the sale of Clarecourt. Mr. Fogarty will then draw up a document and have you and the doctor sign it. All will then be legal and above board.'

Miss Whelan looked downcast. 'Won't all this take a long time?'

'No,' I said. 'I'll speak to Mr. Fogarty and expedite matters. In the circumstances I think he will visit you as soon as he can.'

Miss Whelan seemed to relax into her pillows a little and a lopsided smile lit her face. 'As soon as we can then, Mr. Ross. I think that would be grand.'

'There's one more thing, Miss Whelan. It's the reason why we wanted to see you.' I told a short version of the Dillon, U-3000, Stokesay Castle, and Harold Tyler story. I didn't mention the gems that Harold had saved, and given to me, as I didn't want any leaks about them until we had exchanged them for Mitch. 'So, the gold may still be at Clarecourt, or maybe it's hidden somewhere miles away, or in a bank vault, or taken by thieves. We really don't know. We just wanted to be fair and say you may be the legal owner of a lot of gold.'

Miss Whelan was silent for a while. 'Mr. Ross, it seems to me to be very unlikely that all this gold is hidden at Clarecourt, and if it were, then I think many people would put in a claim as rightful owners. The whole thing would be too stressful for me just now, but I'll tell you what would give me real peace of mind, especially considering what you have just said about the gold. I would like you to buy the house and all the contents, except for a few things I shall want at my nursing home; but not the books. I wish to donate the entire library at Clarecourt to The National Library of Ireland, in Dublin. They've been interested for years, they'll be very pleased. I know I wanted them to stay at the house, but once I've gone, they could be sold anywhere. This way they will stay together, as they've been for over two hundred years. There's a catalogue listing them all. It's on the little round table just by the library door.'

'But just supposing the gold is at the house?' I asked.

'Then that will be your good luck, but I wouldn't retire just yet if I were you. Do we have a deal, Mr. Ross?'

My mind was racing; I was taken completely by surprise at Miss Whelan's suggestion. I had no idea what a house like Clarecourt would be worth. I guessed not a lot in its dilapidated state. I have a good relationship with my bank, as I sometimes need to fund the purchase of cars on behalf of my customers. I thought to get three estate agents' valuations, take the average, and offer that to Miss Whelan. That should also satisfy my bank, and Patrick Fogarty. When all this was done, and on the million to one chance that there was any gold at Clarecourt, it would be mine. That is if Mitch, or Lucia, or the British, Irish, and Indian governments didn't win a claim to it. If things did go that way, there would still be a substantial finder's fee, making it worth the punt. No gold anywhere and I would sell Clarecourt and possibly take a loss on the deal. 'He Who Dares', as half the motto goes.

My silent thoughts had taken long enough for Kirstie to nudge me for a response. 'Ben,' she said softly.

'Sorry, yes, yes, Miss Whelan, we have a deal.' This time I made a spitting noise into my hand and gently squeezed Miss Whelan's on its pillow.

CHAPTER TWENTY-SIX

While Kirstie filed her flight plan and completed the navigational tasks for the flight home, I arranged for three estate agents to value Clarecourt. One the next day and two the day after. They all seemed keen to have a grand Georgian house on their books, no matter how dilapidated. I hadn't told them it would only be a valuation fee.

After an irritating conversation with a difficult and none-too-bright receptionist, I eventually managed to speak to Solicitor Fogarty. He was prepared to visit Miss Whelan and her doctor the following day. If he was satisfied that she was of sound mind he would comply with her wishes and draw up the contract of sale as a matter of urgency. My own solicitor needed some persuasion that the purchase of Clarecourt was a wise decision, but she too agreed to expedite matters.

Safely landed at Thruxton, Kirstie immediately booked a ferry back to Ireland, to oversee the estate agents and arrange for twenty-four-hour security at the house. I wasn't going to risk tinkers or unscrupulous builders ripping out the architectural features or stealing the books if the house was left unguarded.

We drove back to the Clock House, but just as soon as I arrived, so did an email; it was from Vogel.

Mr. Ross,

I have completed the arrangements to exchange Mr. Mitchelletti for the gems. Please drive alone to the GPS location reference 50. 51'19. 65N, 1. 28'59. 83W on your satellite navigation system. Be there at 06:30am tomorrow morning. You and I, Mr. Ross, are not in a relationship of blackmail so there is no future value in my keeping of Mr. Mitchelletti once I have the gems. Please be informed that he has no idea where he has been, shall we say as a guest, and he has no idea where you will find him tomorrow. He also has not been able to identify any of my colleagues who have been caring for him. If you comply with these instructions, then we shall have no future contact.

I ran down to the Defender and punched in the coordinates; it was a parking area by a lane close to Beaulieu Road station in the New Forest. It should take about an hour to get there at that time of the morning.

I called Kirstie on the burner phone and read out the email word for word.

'Bloody hell,' she said. 'Are you going to do it?'

'I don't see why not. I think Vogel trusts me, and as he says, there's no advantage in killing Mitch or keeping him for any other reason.'

'What about the gold?'

'If he had any doubts that it wasn't on the submarine, he would have told me in no uncertain terms.'

'I think Vogel's got the upper hand in keeping the police out,' said Kirstie, 'If we did involve them in a trap, he'd surely kill Mitch for revenge. You could take Smiler to keep an eye on you in case there's trouble.'

'No point. Vogel wants the gems, no trouble, no fuss. He didn't say it, but he knows if he did renege on the deal and top Mitch, I would go after him with the help of all the involved police forces. No, I'll do what he says,' I added emphatically.

'Just be careful, Ben, and call me as soon as you get Mitch.'

It was almost three weeks past the summer solstice, but at 5:15am the sun was up, and traffic sparse to say the least. I knew the route to Beaulieu Road station well, as it was on the way to the National Motor Museum by Beaulieu village. The whole area was deserted, no vehicles, joggers, or cyclists: just a few New Forest ponies warming their backs in the rising sun.

Scanning the numerous stands of trees, interspersed with heathland and larger forested areas, there was not a sign of Vogel. I poured a cup of coffee from my Thermos and stood by the Defender, enjoying the fresh morning air, and like the ponies, the sunshine. Columbus was with me, and he scurried around the wheels, sniffing the new scents with relish, all the while eyeing the ponies with more caution than bravado. Suddenly he stood stock-still with ears pricked, looking across a densely wooded stand of trees, the rumble of a growl gave warning.

I checked my watch for the third time, and it said 6:29am. If Vogel was not going to be late some sort of vehicle should be in sight. It wasn't, but a buzzing sound broke the silence. I whistled Columbus back into the car, as over the trees came a drone, travelling straight towards me. I moved to the back of the Defender for safety, as the nearby ponies trotted and cantered away. The drone hovered a couple of feet from the ground and about ten feet from the front of the car. There was a central squarish body with four arms in an X shape, each with a helicopter-like rotary wing at the end. Attached to the body was a camera lens, and an aerial. Beneath the main body was a box. The hovering drone descended, gently released the box and settled on the ground beside it. Inside the clear-plastic container I could see an envelope. I took it out and read the contents. Doing so, I could see the drone's camera lens follow me; Vogel was obviously watching. Within the safety of the vehicle, Columbus became brave and loudly barked his aggression.

The instructions were simple: Place all the gems from the German life jacket into the box, reattach it to the drone and stand clear. Within an hour, if the jewels were confirmed as genuine, the whereabouts of Mitch would be sent to my mobile phone.

Control was very much in Vogel's hands, so I tipped all the gems into the plastic box, followed the instructions on how to attach it back under the drone, and stood clear. The blades spun into life and the drone once again hovered, now at head height in front of me. It tilted towards me rather like a veteran Harrier jump-jet saluting at an air show, did an about-face and shot up and away, back over the trees.

I had to smile. Vogel had chosen the perfect spot. He could be anywhere within radio range of my location and able to watch me through the camera. I couldn't even race after the drone, as the cross-country heathland was protected from vehicles by ditches and logs alongside the roads and tracks. There was only one thing to do, drive home and wait for Vogel's message.

A stop for breakfast in Lyndhurst helped while away the time, and it wasn't until 8:30am that the phone finally rang; by then I was nearly home, but it wasn't Vogel, it was Smiler.

'You comin' home, Guv?' he asked.

'About ten minutes, why, what's up?'

'That Mitch bloke, he's here!'

CHAPTER TWENTY-SEVEN

The final ten minutes' drive took me only five. The workshop doors were closed, but the Judas gate was open. Sliding to a halt, I leapt out of the Defender, and ducked into the workshop. There was Smiler standing over a seated Mitch. He was unshaven, unkempt and in the same clothes he had been wearing when the emailed video had been sent, nearly a fortnight ago. His sports coat had been torn at one elbow, and both knees of his trousers were ripped through.

'Mitch, are you okay?'

'Do I look okay? I feel like shit, but I guess I'm free of the bastards,' he snapped back.

'How did he get here, Smiler?'

'I arrived usual time at half eight, came inside and was about to unlock the main doors, then heard what I thought was you coming back. I came out just in time to see a Ford Transit van do a 180-degree turn. Without it even stopping, the rear doors were flung open, and Mitch was thrown out onto the ground, trussed up like a bleeding turkey he was. By the time I reached him, the van had disappeared.'

Mitch's face was red and sore-looking where his eyes and mouth had been taped. 'Let's get him up to the office,' I said.

'Do you think you can walk, Mitch?' I asked.

'Yeah! Gimme a hand, damn sonsabitches.'

He managed the stairs using his right leg first for each step. I eased him down on the sofa, with his back propped against a cushioned armrest, then checked his gravel rashes, cleaned them, and bandaged his elbow, which was more damaged than his knees, but nothing looked as if it warranted a hospital visit.

Mitch eyed his crumpled, torn, and dirty sports coat. 'Jeez, will you look at that. It cost me $700 from Nordstrom.'

'Are you up to telling us what happened?' I asked, handing him a large mug of coffee with a good slug of brandy in it.

'Who knows what the hell happened. I was driving down for our meet, nearly here when a girl by a van with the hood up waves me down. She's cute, so what the heck. Hey, it's her lucky day, I know cars, right? So, I take a look at the engine and wham! I'm nearly knocked unconscious. I kinda feel myself being manhandled into the back of the van. When I come to fully, I'm blindfolded, gagged, and tied up for crissake. I figure out there's a guy driving, the broad's in the front and another guy keeping a check on me in back.'

'How long was the drive?'

'Maybe a couple of hours. About halfway through, the van stops, I can hear money being counted and the girl gets out. She says thanks and the driver says this never happened, right? The door shuts and we're off again. Maybe another hour and we turn onto a real rough dirt track for another three minutes or so. We stop and I'm dragged out. We cross a hard surface, concrete maybe and into a building. It sounds and feels old and large, like from the echo of our footsteps. I'm half pushed, half dragged up a wooden staircase, wide and no carpet. Along an equally bare corridor, through another doorway and up some steeper, narrower stairs. They push me into a room, and chain me up like you saw in the video.'

He said all this with a deep frown and his eyes closed, as if reliving the kidnap.

Mitch finished his coffee and brandy. 'So, they take off my blindfold and untape my mouth and hands. I let them know that

I am far from happy with the situation, but they say nothing, the tall one just points to a bucket for me to piss in, then he points at a bathroom. Taps his watch and holds up one finger, then two. I figure I got an opportunity to take a dump twice a day.' Mitch shot us an apologetic look. 'Excuse my crudeness.'

'Were there any clues as to where you were?' I asked.

'Naa, all I could tell was that after the first hour in the van the road was flat, no up and down hills that I could sense. My room was in an old house, and I was on the top floor, under the eaves. The chain stopped me from getting to the small window, but I guess I was in the country. No traffic noises, sirens, car horns, planes.'

'Do you know how long you were there?' asked Smiler.

'Oh yeah. Every morning when I woke up, I scratched a line with my chain on the bed head. I had twenty-eight marks the day before I was bought back here.'

'Well, you're free now Mitch, so well done.'

I was surprised how calm Mitch was and how well he'd handled the situation. 'Did they tell you why you were being held?'

'No one spoke at all, ever, the whole time. Just took me to the john or brought me my meals, and a fresh bottle of water. Same stuff every day. Oatmeal for breakfast, a cheese and pickle sandwich for lunch and a bowl of soup with a hunk of bread in the evening. I guess I lost some weight,' he said, sticking his thumbs in his waistband and pulling at the belt.

We all smiled. 'Look, why don't you take a shower and a shave and have a good sleep. Smiler can go into Newbury and buy you some new clothes.'

Mitch told him his sizes and what he'd like.

As this was happening, I called Kirstie as promised, and

then Lucia to give her the good news. She said she would fly over right away to collect him.

It was past 4:00pm when a clean and reinvigorated Mitch appeared, now in pale blue chinos, a short-sleeved blue and white striped shirt, and a camel cashmere sweater draped across his shoulders. Smiler was back at work reconditioning some upholstery in a Jaguar XK140, and I was at my desk, catching up on the never-ending paperwork.

'Okay, how much money did they want for my ransom?' asked Mitch.

'It wasn't about a ransom. You were a lever to make me search for the gold and gems from the Tiger's Ghost.'

It took fully forty-five minutes to explain exactly what had transpired, and what we had all done to get him back. At first, he was peeved we hadn't involved the police forces of the world, and given pleading TV interviews, but as I explained why we hadn't, he calmed down.

Mitch being Mitch, his thanks lasted only a few minutes. He then became more and more annoyed that his kidnappers had made away with the only treasure they thought was to be had.

'Mitch don't forget you now own the chassis of the Tiger's Ghost. Recreate the look of the bodywork and you will have a hugely valuable car that will be the star of the international classic car show circuit.'

I was ready for him to persuade, inveigle and insist that I continue the search for the gold, which he was sure to feel was rightfully his, but he didn't.

'I don't care about the frickin' gold. I'm not risking another kidnapping or worse. I'm outta here as soon as I get a flight back to San Fran. I've had enough of merrie England. You can keep it.'

I patted Mitch's arm. 'I understand. I'll let our police know you are safe, and that you'll make a full statement to the San Francisco boys in blue. I'll book you a seat. Business class?'

'Shit no! I think I've earned a first-class seat,' he said loudly, holding out a Delta Airlines Platinum card.

Damn it! I'd forgotten all about Lucia; she had emailed her flight details, and would be arriving at Heathrow, 12:15pm tomorrow. Working out the time differences, she wouldn't have left for the airport yet, so I called her mobile number which she answered in a few seconds.

'Lucia, Ben. Look, is it too late to cancel your flight? Mitch is just fine, a little battered and bruised as I said earlier, but he's adamant he wants to fly back home as soon as possible. He's rather taken against England and doesn't even want to wait for you. I've just booked him on the 10:40am Delta flight, so you'll miss each other by a couple of hours.'

'Okay, if that's what he wants to do,' sighed Lucia. 'I was planning to come over in a couple of days anyway to try and put a deal together with your Inksmile Publishing company. I have to keep the appointment, so maybe we can meet up Thursday sometime. Send Mitch my best wishes and tell him what I'm doing.'

'Sounds like a plan, I'll wait to hear from you. Have a good flight.'

As Mitch wanted to be rid of us all as soon as possible, I suggested he stay at the Hilton Garden Inn at Heathrow. It was closest to Terminal Two, which Delta uses. I offered to drive him there, but he wanted a chauffeur-driven car, a limo as he called it.

His limo arrived, and I helped him as he limped down the stairs. 'I'm sorry about how things have worked out, Mitch. I'll get the Tiger's Ghost shipped directly to San Francisco instead of here.'

'I guess none of this was your fault, but I've been thinking about getting into classic power-boat racing. They do that up at Lake Tahoe. Maybe I'll let someone else recreate the Tiger's Ghost. Someone'll buy it in the States.'

As I waved him off, I couldn't help thinking of the anti-hero in Kenneth Grahame's most famous novel: The Wind in the Willows.

CHAPTER TWENTY-EIGHT

It was just after ten in the evening when Lucia called me. 'Hi Ben, I'm at the Marlborough Hotel, on Welbeck Street. I've had my meeting at Inksmile Publishing moved to tomorrow morning, and it could last all day. So how about dinner afterwards in London? I've booked you a room here, so we can enjoy a drink or two. My treat.'

A free night in London sounded fine, so I agreed to meet her in the bar at 6:30pm. It would be the ideal opportunity to let her know the truth about the gold, and my own involvement as the new owner of Clarecourt.

The day of my dinner with Lucia, was also a day for Tegan to be in the office, so I brought her up to date with all that had transpired, especially Miss Whelan's wishes for the Clarecourt library.

'Then someone needs to check all the library books against the catalogue, before sending them to Dublin,' she said, with a very enthusiastic look on her face.

'Any idea who could do that for me?'

'I'd love to do it,' she said excitedly, 'I really miss my work at the V&A, and who knows, I might just find a rare and important volume.'

As soon as the Clarecourt purchase is completed, you can go over. Either stay in the house or the local B&B that I use.'

'I know Kirstie's arranging security at the house, but I'd rather stay in the B&B. Meanwhile, I'd better get on with this office work so I can go to Ireland with a clear conscience. I'll ask my sister to come and look after Gwyn while I'm away, just in case he has a bad asthma attack.'

It was time for me to take stock of the whole situation. Truth to tell, I felt infuriated over Vogel getting what he wanted, without me handing him over to the police. Okay, Mitch was returned safe and sound-ish, and Vogel thought he had all the treasure that was recoverable, so I suppose not capturing him was more about my personal pride than anything else. Plus, I was a hundred thousand dollars to the good from him, and I would soon have my commission from Mitch for finding the car in the first place. But the more I thought about it, the more I had a gut feeling that more trouble was to come.

I phoned my grandfather to let him know how things stood but didn't mention my forebodings. He was of course pleased for me, but he had his own news.

'I'm afraid the CAA have nothing to say on the likely release of the bodies for burial. Post-mortems have been completed and all died from the results of catastrophic impact. We have to wait until the cause of the crash is verified,' he said.

'Let me know as soon as you hear anything, Howly. I'll come down as much as I can. Changing the subject, do you think there's any chance we'll find out who Vogel was working for, his principal, as he called him?'

'I can't help you much there I'm afraid, Ben. If I did still have any contacts in certain government departments, and I was asking questions, I'm sure they wouldn't share information with an old buffer like me, out to grass years ago.'

'No, I suppose they wouldn't. Just thought I'd ask your opinion. Speak soon.' I had to smile. Howly was telling me that he was asking questions, and he still had serious connections who held him in high esteem.

I drove to London early, as I had a car to see at a Rolls-Royce and Bentley specialist in Leinster Mews, just north of

Kensington Gardens. I had known the owner, Bill, for many years, and he was happy to let me leave the Defender overnight to save on London's criminal parking charges. The car in question was a 1938 V12 Lagonda, a beautiful beast that Bill had been asked to sell for a client. I made a strong offer as I knew who I could immediately sell it on to.

A short taxi ride took me to the Marlborough Hotel, close to the Wallace Collection and Wigmore Hall, ideal for lovers of the arts. Both the hotel's public rooms and the bedrooms are up-to-the-minute interpretations of plush 1940s, with a dash of Japanese-style architecture.

I had time for an hour's snooze, before my 6:30pm rendezvous in the bar with Lucia. I was five minutes early, and the bar was only about two-thirds full. I easily found an alcove table for us. A waiter arrived in seconds, from whom I ordered a bottle of Perrier-Jouët and two glasses. As he moved away, Lucia appeared, looking the proverbial million dollars. She wore a little black dress, except it was a vibrant peacock blue that changed hue with the light. A gold necklace with what had to be a paste emerald, judging by its size, rested happily in her perfectly defined cleavage. Peeping out through her shining hair were earrings to match the necklace.

As I stood to greet her, my effort at a hello kiss on her cheek was waylaid by a turn of her head that landed the kiss on the corner of her mouth; Lucia must be in a good mood.

Our hellos and compliments over, the waiter returned with glasses, fizz, and ice bucket on a stand. A practised flourish of opening the bottle by him, and a taste of the wine by me completed, Lucia held up her glass as the froth receded. I matched her action.

'Champagne, Mr. Ross! What are we celebrating?' she asked

with a radiant smile.

'Someone once said champagne should be drunk to celebrate and drunk to commiserate, may have been Churchill or perhaps Napoleon, someone like that. So, we are celebrating getting Mitch back safely and commiserating having to give up the gems to Vogel.'

Glasses clinked and champagne sipped, Lucia spoke next. 'I've talked to Mitch, and he seems fine now that he's on home turf. I expect he'll give everyone at Graphica a hard time for a couple of days, but that won't last long. Now, tell me all about the handover of the gems, was it really necessary to give them up?' I noticed Lucia's voice had a brittle edge when she asked about the jewels.

I gave a full account of what I had told her briefly on the phone but saving the truth about the gold until we were seated for our dinner. Chitchat slipped into flirtation by the time the Perrier-Jouët bottle was upside down in its ice bucket.

Lucia glanced at her watch. 'Time to hit the restaurant, it's a short cab ride.'

I really wasn't sure if I was on a date, with a friend, or at a business meeting. The old enemies were squaring up, brain versus hormones. Brain had our short but friendly business relationship on its side. Hormones had Lucia's flirtatiousness, and the little black dress that wasn't. The winner would be decided by Lucia's manner once it was time to say goodnight: or not.

We hailed a taxi. 'Gymkhana, on Albermarle Street,' instructed Lucia, with the brashness that Americans accept as perfectly good manners.

Spread over two floors, Lucia had booked us a table on the lower, the decoration of which was apparently typical of the

North of India, all peach and chilli-red colours.

'I know you Brits are fond of your Indian food, so I thought I'd show you just how good the dishes from my heritage can be,' said Lucia.

When the menus came, I read that Gymkhana had a Michelin star. I know my way around an Indian menu pretty well, but I asked Lucia to choose for me. The proof of great Indian food can be judged by however many constituent dishes are on your plate; they all have their own flavours that complement each other. Gymkhana was top of the class in that.

At meal's end, with coffee served, I decided it was time to get back to the Tiger's Ghost. 'There's something I haven't mentioned yet. Something that will please you I think.'

Lucia smiled at me, leaning forward with chin on hand and elbow on table. 'Go ahead, Ben, do please me.'

'The gold, none of it was taken by the Nazis. It's not on the submarine, so there's still a chance it could be found.'

I expected her eyes to light up with excitement, but they flashed anger like laser beams.

Lucia sat back up in her chair and pushed one side of her hair behind her ear, her face a mask of aggression. 'You lied to me on the phone.'

'I couldn't tell you then, I know Vogel has tapped into my computer and phones; I couldn't risk it. I didn't mention it earlier this evening because we were getting on so well, I didn't want to change the mood by dwelling on the car and Mitch.'

Eyes still blazing, Lucia almost spat the words at me. 'What are you planning to do, keep the gold for yourself, cut me out? It's mine by rights. Well, screw you, you bastard.'

Within seconds the attractive and flirtatious Lucia turned into a spiteful and venomous aggressor. She stood, pushing her chair back so hard, it fell over. Grabbing her bag, she stabbed a finger at me. 'Fuck you!Don't even try looking for the gold, or you'll be sorry, and I mean real sorry. Don't ever try and contact me again: I'm warning you. Just stay out of this.'

The room was silent with all eyes on us. The only sound was the staccato click of her heels as she hurried from the restaurant.

CHAPTER TWENTY-NINE

I wanted to drive home immediately after Lucia's restaurant outburst, but I had drunk far too much to risk my licence, or worse. The staff at Gymkhana must have witnessed scenes of discord before, as Lucia had hardly left the restaurant before the bill arrived alongside a dish of cardamom seeds, both on a silver tray. I paid up and left, saying to all the onlookers, 'Sorry, everyone, the lady's contesting a family will.'

I paid for my hotel room on my return, not wanting to be beholden to Lucia Bassoli for anything. On reflection I was glad that a night of lustful passion with her had not materialised. For no logical reason I felt it would have been disloyal to Kirstie.

Up and out of the room by seven, I hailed an early taxi to Bill's garage, above which are his living quarters. He told me the Lagonda owner had agreed to my offer, so I arranged for the car to be delivered to the Clock House. On the way home I called my prospective buyer, and he wanted to test-drive it in a week's time. Long enough for Smiler to check and rectify any minor niggles with the car.

Back at base Columbus greeted me with his usual enthusiasm, knowing a good walk was in the offing. A change of clothes and messages checked, I was just about to whistle for the expectant hound, when my burner phone rang; it was Kirstie. I couldn't think of a reason why she would need to use a secure line now that Vogel had gone on his way; perhaps she was just using the remaining money before dumping it.

'How are things going?' I asked her.

She sounded quite excited for a simple status report. 'Well, the three estate agents have now valued the house. Two were within ten thousand of each other, and one was fifty grand higher. Don't like him, I got the feeling he was over-valuing just to get the sale, hoping we would be greedy. I'll email you the figures.'

'How about the security for the house?'

'I asked Mr O'Shea, you know, the guy who runs the B&B, if he could recommend a local company. He said not, but he knew of a suitable man who would take on the job. Would you believe it, he's only Dillon's grandson, Róisin's brother. It turns out that he's just left the Irish army, and he and another ex-soldier are setting up together as security guards.'

'What are they charging?' I asked.

'A good deal less than a large security company would; I've checked. They'll take it in turns to have at least one of them on site at all times. I've put the details and a copy of their contract in the email that I'm about to send you.'

'You coming back now?' I asked.

She answered with even more excitement in her voice. 'No, I'm not! You're coming over here, as soon as you can, and if I were you, it would be today.'

'What the hell's gone wrong, Kirstie?'

'Nothing, quite the opposite. There's something you'll want to see for yourself.'

'Not a bad thing?'

'A good thing, an intriguing thing,' she answered.

I knew Kirstie well enough not to try and badger her into telling more, and on reflection it wouldn't be a bad idea to have a really good look around the house that was soon to be mine. 'Okay, I'll get a flight tomorrow and email you the arrival time.'

'Bye, Ben,' she said with a mixture of excitement and

humour.

Luckily the flight I wanted from Heathrow was available. I eyed Columbus at my feet. 'Come on then, let's go for this walk.'

Kirstie was waiting for me at the Shannon arrival's gate. She drove with her usual panache, and we were soon nearing Clarecourt, but our destination turned out to be Dillon and Róisin's pretty little cottage on the outskirts of the village.

'Are we going to see Dillon?'

'Yes,' replied Kirstie, 'I realised I hadn't asked him if he remembered the Tiger's Ghost, so I came here yesterday to ask him about it. He looked very sheepish, and after a few exchanges with him in Gaelic, Róisin said her grandfather was worried that he was in trouble for stealing.'

'What are you saying? Don't tell me he pinched some jewels or a gold bar.'

Kirstie turned off the engine, propped her sunglasses into her hair and smiled at me. 'Come on.'

Róisin greeted us warmly, and the elderly Dillon less so, with a little apprehension it seemed to me.

'Can I show Ben, please Róisin?' asked Kirstie.

'Go through, I'll make us all some tea.'

Kirstie led me into the tiny kitchen, and out into a surprisingly large garden. There was a perfectly manicured lawn. About three-quarters of the way down was a dividing beech hedge, which arched over the path, leading to a well-tended vegetable and flower garden. Kirstie ducked through and turned to me, striking a pose like a stage-magician's assistant.

'Voila!' she said.

I followed her through the arch, turning to look where she was directing my attention. It took a couple of seconds for me to understand what I was looking at. Head on, it was a homemade wooden garden seat with a canopy over it. Attached to the back of the seat was a glazed garden shed, painted lawn-mower green, except it wasn't a shed at all, it was the major part of an ancient limousine car body.

'This is the body of the Tiger's Ghost,' said an excited Kirstie.

I tapped one of the green panels. 'It can't be, Kirstie, it's aluminium, not gold.'

Kirstie moved to the back of the body, which was tight against some hedging. 'Look here!' she said, rubbing at the flaking green paint. Underneath was the faint but unmistakable look of a tiger-like stripe, on a gold-leaf background.

Pacing back to take a critical look at the side of the body, I tried to remember the details of the Tiger's Ghost from old photos. Everything matched as far as I could remember; general shape, wrought iron roof rack, rear door window, and a side window behind the door. Also curved glass on the corner, running into the glazed back of the front compartment, where chauffeur and bodyguard would have sat, but now made into a garden seat. Door handles, bevelled glass and mouldings all looked right.

I opened the rear door and peered inside. All the interior had gone, just the bare framing and wood backing for the trim remained, no sign of precious stones or their mountings. I pulled out the various tools, pots, and general garden clutter, to get a better look. The rear seat back and armrests had gone. All the upholstery was of course missing but the wooden seat-base was there, now a hinged lid. I tried to open it, but it objected to my first efforts. Squatting adjacent to it, and using both hands, I heaved upwards. The problem was not one of rusted hinges, but the sheer weight of the lid. Underneath the wood, was a quarter-inch thick iron sheet. Finally open, I could see that the seat base was in fact the lid of a solid iron box, built into the frame of the body on massive supports.

A call from the kitchen told us our tea was ready, so I clambered out, replaced the garden clutter, and shut the car door. After all these years, neglected in the open air, it still closed with the ease and reassuring clunk of a Victorian railway carriage.

Over tea and shortbread biscuits, Dillon told us how the Tiger's Ghost body had ended up in his garden. We assured him that we would tell no one, and anyway there was nobody alive who would charge him with theft.

'It was just before the start of the war, well before Mr. Singh had died. We had no idea that there was a Rolls-Royce motor car hidden away in the big house. Just one day, the Indian servants pushed the chassis into the barn, and left the body from it on the front drive. Mr. Singh told us to take it away and burn it, as it was no longer needed. It seemed a terrible shame as it was such a beautiful thing, all gold paint and tiger's stripes on the outside, but the inside was all bare.'

'Were any of the outer panels missing?' I asked Dillon.

'No, none at all, t'was just as you see it in my garden, but of course the paint was like new back then.'

'Sorry, Dillon, I interrupted you, please go on.'

'We loaded it onto a cart and took it to where we had the bonfires, a place away from the house and the barns, for safety. you see. Raining it was, so the head gardener, Mr. McMahon decided to wait for dry weather before setting it on fire. When I came home that evening, here to the cottage, I told me Da about the car. The next morning it was still raining, so Da came up to

Clarecourt with me to see Mr. McMahon. A deal was struck, a bottle of whisky changed hands, and instead of the body being burnt we brought it here on one of the farm carts. We all carried it round to the back and put it just where you see it today. Da painted it green, as he said the original colours would attract unwanted attention.'

'Do you know anything about the iron box under the back seat?' I asked.

'No, t'was empty when we took the body, and has been empty ever since. I think it's time to get rid of it now, I need a proper shed that's easier to get in and out of. Old bones it is I have now, Mr. Ross.'

Kirstie moved her attention from Dillon to me in a flash. We were thinking the very same thing.

'Dillon, how would it be if I bought the body from you, and paid for a new shed to replace it?'

'That would be grand, but why would you want that old thing?'

'The truth is, I own the chassis that it came off, the one that was pushed into the barn. It would be worth more to me than anyone else, as I could restore the body and put it back on the chassis.'

Róisin joined the conversation. 'How much would it be worth to you Mr. Ross?

'If I didn't own the chassis, it would only be worth five hundred euros or so, but as I do have the chassis, I will give you ten thousand euros and a new garden shed.'

Dillon leaned forward in his chair. 'Did you say a thousand euros, Mr. Ross, for that old thing?'

'No, Dillon,' I spoke louder, 'I said ten thousand euros.'

He replied in Gaelic; whatever he said, Róisin blushed

slightly. 'Daddo, watch your language. I'm sorry, Kirstie,' she said.

Dillon spat on his hand, a little more forcefully than Miss Whelan had done in the library at Clarecourt and held it out towards me. I glanced at Róisín and nodded briefly for her assent. She nodded back, and I shook the hand of the man who had saved the remains of the coachwork that had graced the legendary Tiger's Ghost.

CHAPTER THIRTY

Kirstie and I drove the short journey to Clarecourt in silence, both thinking over the implications of what we had learnt, and how it might affect our future plans. She had collected a set of keys for the house, and after a few tries found the right one for the front doors. 'Dillon's grandson Oisin is coming to see the house at five this evening. I've got a spare set of keys for him, so the place will be secure from today,' she said.

'Before I forget, here's his copy of the security guard contract, I've signed it,' I said.

Miss Whelan had not been gone from the house long enough for her aura to have left. I fully expected her to emerge from the library, warning us to mind the water-catching buckets. We settled down in a couple of the library chairs and Kirstie poured us some coffee she had brought in a vacuum flask.

'I would never have guessed in a million years we would discover the car's coachwork, albeit stripped out. But to find it never had solid gold panels is unbelievable. Every book, newspaper and record of the car says solid gold bodywork. God knows how Kuldeep kept the myth going. You'd think someone would have leaked the truth. Or perhaps the rumoured solid gold panels did exist at some time,' I mused.

'Could be, but worth coming over for, wasn't it?' asked Kirstie with one of her irrepressible smiles. 'What happens now?'

I didn't answer her immediately. She was sitting in a shaft of sunlight with dust motes dancing in the air. The scene could be an artist's dream pose, with not an iota of artistic flattery needed. Kirstie's looks match her personality, and I couldn't fault that pairing.

'Ben!'

'Sorry, miles away. Yes, well worth coming over. I was just thinking about reuniting the body with the chassis while it's awaiting customs clearance for shipping.'

Kirstie sipped her coffee and casually asked, 'And how did your evening go with the luscious Lucia?'

I'd heard a similar casual question from a woman before. Then it had been the precursor to a jealous row, but this time it gave me a fleeting thrill that Kirstie could be interested in me more than as an old friend and boss. 'Let's just say, we both know where we stand. I doubt we'll see anything more of her, and we don't have to consider her interests in the gold. If we do find any, she can claim it in court.'

'She didn't fall for your charms then?'

'Quite the opposite. Come on, let's go for a walk in the grounds and see what I'm buying, we can walk and talk.' Right now, thoughts of romance with Kirstie were best left for the future, but once we had taken the Tiger's Ghost search as far as we could, who knows?

Miss Whelan's previous lack of capital showed sadly in the gardens. Derelict, ivy-clad statues, and an overgrown pond with a dry fountain stood amongst roughly topped grass and unkempt topiary. The flower beds were long gone, except one, that must have been all Miss Whelan could manage herself. We made our way to the barn where I had found the chassis, and back in a loop around the other side of the house.

'Kirstie, would you go back to Dillon's tomorrow and have one more try to see if he remembers anything more about the Tiger's Ghost. Then come home as soon as you can. I've got to fly back first thing tomorrow for a car auction. Meanwhile we can both think about how we might try and track down what happened to the gold, that is if there really was any. At the moment I haven't the faintest idea how to do that.'

'Me neither,' she said pensively.

We spent the rest of the afternoon checking the layout at Clarecourt. All the reception rooms could be described as distressed grandeur. The fixtures and fittings were of the highest quality, but years of wear and tear were beginning to show. Carpets were bordering on threadbare in parts, curtains needed a serious dry clean, and much of the furniture had been already sold off, judging by its sparsity. There were still a few pieces left that even I could tell were examples of the best of Irish Georgian furniture makers. On all the walls, less-faded patches were witnesses to long-gone paintings.

Much of the upper floors were empty and looked as if they had been so for a good few years. The attics contained the expected household junk. One bathroom and three of the bedrooms were in good order, one having the bed still made up for Miss Whelan, complete with a seriously love-worn bear; from her own youth, I would guess. I'd make a point of taking it to her.

Kirstie and I both spent a comfortable night at the B&B, having eaten at the local bar. As it was too early for us to come up with a meaningful plan about the gold search, our conversation slipped easily into army days, old comrades, and more catching up about our lives since that time. A goodnight hug and cheek-kisses came naturally, but we held each other's gaze for a few seconds longer than we needed. It took a while for me to get to sleep.

Right after breakfast we were back in the hire car, heading

for Shannon. I pride myself on being a good driver, but once in a while I have to admit the driver I am with is one of those rare people who have a magic touch at the wheel. Kirstie is one such person, Sir Lewis Hamilton on the public highway, in female form.

A normal journey time would be about three hours. We did it in two hours and thirty-eight minutes. Double parked by the departures entrance, I leapt out, taking my bag. 'You'd better get off before any parking wardens appear.'

She selected first gear, and looked up at me, smiling. 'See you at the ol' homestead.'

Checked in and sitting down at the gate, I viewed my phone. There was a message to call Howly.

'Ah, Ben, dear boy, I don't want to interrupt your Tiger's Ghost search, but there's something you will want to know. I've just heard from the CAA. It seems the reason for the helicopter crashing was a gearbox failure to the rear rotor, caused by a leaking oil-seal. The bodies can now be released to us as soon as we wish.'

I had been pushing the thoughts of the crash and my family to the back of my mind. In truth, using the car search to keep the enormity of it at bay. Despite my dislike of my father and his new wife, Howly's news shattered that delay of grief. It descended on me like a physical weight. It must have shown, as an elderly couple sitting opposite looked at me with concern.

'Would you prefer me to arrange the release?' I asked, with a lump in my throat.

'No, I've already spoken to our local undertakers; everything is in hand. Your father is to be buried here at the local church. Danni left instructions for her body to be cremated at a non-religious service, with just a celebrant. Her ashes are to be sent back to her family in Rhode Island. The services will be a week today; the church at eleven in the morning, and the crematorium at three.'

'Danni never was really part of our family.' I said.

Howly was quiet for a few seconds. I could feel his distress down the phone. Eventually he spoke. 'Tell me how you're getting on with the Tiger's Ghost.'

I walked to where I couldn't be overheard. Despite his sad mood Howly sounded genuinely pleased to hear what we had found.

'The next problem is to find out if there was ever a gold body, and if so, where's the bullion cast from it,' I said.

'I'll think about it, Ben. It'll occupy me until the funeral. You'll be staying of course, and we can discuss it then. Goodbye, dear boy.'

'Don't worry, Howly, we'll get through this together.'

I spent the flight reminiscing over my childhood, and my times as an adult with my father, my much-loved late mother and then the awful Danni. They say you shouldn't speak ill of the dead, but are you allowed to think ill of them? On refection I didn't, I felt disconnected, sad for them, that both my father and Danni had led lives of self-obsession, and meaningless acquisitions.

The Clock House was deserted when I arrived. Smiler was taking a rare day off, and Tegan was back home having already brought Columbus over to greet me. The dog fulfilled the role of perfect host, welcoming me with unbounded enthusiasm. No doubt the prospect of a walk and some food coloured his attitude. Nevertheless, home seemed cold and empty. I was looking forward to Kirstie's return, life was beginning to feel less happy without her.

After attending to Columbus's needs, I wandered down to my personal car collection, and pulled the dust sheets from each of the six cars. I sat on the workbench stool and took a swig of my beer as I admired them all. There was only one that was suitable to drive to a funeral; the 1962 Bentley Continental. It was my sole black car.

CHAPTER THIRTY-ONE

The week passed quickly. There was an auction to attend at the Bicester Heritage Centre where the two cars I was interested in both sold for more money than I was commissioned to offer. And another day was spent with Kirstie and Tegan, the three of us trying to think how to progress the search for the gold bullion, but we failed to come up with a credible answer.

I wanted to drive to Penhydrock the day before the funeral, but that wasn't possible. My Lagonda client was coming to see the V12 in the morning, and in the afternoon my solicitor would be ready for me to sign the legal papers for Clarecourt. The car sold at a modest but quick profit, and my solicitor congratulated me on becoming the proud owner of an estate in Ireland.

Late in the evening, I received an email from the matron at Harold Tyler's nursing home. She apologised for not telling me sooner that Harold's cremation would be the next day. I called her back to explain why I could not be there and wondered if there had been anyone to give specific instructions about his ashes. Apparently not. She agreed to keep them for me, as I had strong feelings about what should be done with them.

I left the Clock House at 4:30am on the day of the funerals, needing an early start to be down at Howly's by 9:00am. That would give me some time with him before my father's hearse and the limousines arrived.

Farrell welcomed me. 'A sad day, Master Benedict.'

I squeezed his arm. 'Thank you, Mr. Farrell, is Mrs. Farrell bearing up?'

'A bit tearful, but she will be stoic at the church.'

Neither Howly nor I ate much breakfast, just some toast and coffee. Howly kept checking the time, taking a gold pocket watch from his waistcoat pocket. It had been his grandfather's, then his father's. I hoped it would be a long time before it was mine.

'The funeral cortege will be here at half-past ten, Ben. I'll come back down when it arrives,' Howly said, as he slowly made his way upstairs. It was the first time that I had seen him look his age, and more.

Farrell found me in the conservatory and quietly told me that the cortege had arrived. Howly came down as the hall clock struck the half-hour. The first limousine was just for us. The Farrells had a second one to themselves, as all the other mourners would be at the church. Riding in a funeral procession isolates one from all other realities. Thoughts of the outside world are suspended, as memories ebb and flow, of times spent, and opportunities missed with those whose funerals you are attending.

'Why was he so, so' – I couldn't find the right word, and settled for difficult – 'difficult?' I asked Howly of my father.

'Ben, my boy, I really don't know. From a small child he was that way, sly and deceitful. Maybe your grandmother and I should have been more modern in the way we brought him up, or perhaps it was just his nature to be the way he was.'

'Well, Danni and he suited each other perfectly.'

Howly nodded, took the paisley handkerchief from his sleeve and wiped his eyes, as we stopped behind the hearse at the lychgate. The church was full, mostly local people and a few business colleagues of my father's. I suspected the locals were here out of respect for Howly and not out of affection for the deceased.

The cremation of Danni could not have been more different from the morning's church burial. Obvious differences apart, the only mourners were Howly, me and the Farrells. The celebrant did her best, but no one shed tears for Danni.

Back at Penhydrock, Howly told the Farrells they should take the night off and we would eat a cold supper. They would hear none of it and we enjoyed a beautifully prepared three-course meal. It was their way of showing their support for us. We went to our beds early, Howly suggesting we meet in his study at 10:00am, to discuss the problem of the Maharajah's gold.

It had been agreed that the day of the funerals was not the time to discuss any aspects of the Tiger's Ghost, so by the next morning I was intrigued to find out what Howly wanted to say or ask me. My hope was that he would have some tips on how best to take on the search.

Knocking lightly on the study door, I looked in. Howly was on the phone, seated at his vast antique partners' desk, a piece of furniture that fitted in perfectly with the luxurious but business-like room. He waved me to the seat opposite to his. His only contributions to the phone call were confirmatory murmurs, and the occasional 'yes' with a final 'thank you' and 'I thought that may be the case'.

'This gold you wish to find, Ben. I'm afraid there's no point in you searching for it,' Howly said, gesturing at the phone.

I must have looked puzzled, as he continued. 'I'll start at the beginning, always the best place. History tells us that His Serene Highness Maharajah Kuldeep Singh used the ploy of a gold-bodied and jewel-encrusted Rolls-Royce car to legitimately leave his Indian state of Cooch Sebah, of which he was the Prince Regent until the coming of age of his nephew.'

'Correct,' I said.

'But you have discovered that the coachwork of the car was not in fact solid gold. It was just finished to look like it, beneath the decorative tiger-like stripes.'

I nodded my agreement.

'I have spoken to some old friends of mine in Whitehall, and this is not to be repeated outside these four walls. In fact, what I am about to tell you was covered by the Official Secrets Act until 2009, a hundred years after what transpired.'

' So, it's been in the public domain for over twelve years,' I reflected.

'Not so, dear boy. A further notice was placed upon the affair, owing to the political situation in India in 2009, a situation that concerns British interests. The notice continues today. Do you understand, Ben?'

'Yes, I do.'

Howly nodded and continued. 'In 1909, when Kuldeep Singh left Cooch Sebah, he had negotiated with the British Raj permission to reside in England. He would have to be self-supporting, which with the valuable Tiger's Ghost would not have been a problem. However, whilst he made the nine-week voyage, the new Maharajah, his nephew, and his council were incandescent with rage when they found out how much had been taken from the Cooch Sebah treasury. Not only the gems, but some bullion and a host of gold artefacts that Kuldeep Singh had melted down into more bullion bars.

'Small as Cooch Sebah is, it is strategically placed as a buffer zone between surrounding states that could easily have erupted into warring factions, unless the pro-British support of the Cooch Sebah ruler continued. In short, they wanted the Tiger's Ghost back, and that was their price for continuing their support of the British Raj.'

'But we know they didn't get it. Kuldeep Singh lived off the jewels and maybe the gold for years,' I said.

'The gems, yes, but not the gold. When his ship docked, Kuldeep Singh was ceremoniously escorted to a London house that had been allocated to him and his modest retinue, not forgetting the Tiger's Ghost itself. The pomp and circumstance was actually a cover for the fact Kuldeep Singh was, unbeknown to him, under house-arrest until the issue of the treasure could be solved. We can only imagine the negotiations that took place between the Secretary of State for India on behalf of the India Office, and the ex-Maharajah.'

'Do you know what the end result was, Howly?'

'It seems the gold that Kuldeep Singh had taken was concealed in the iron chest beneath the car's rear seat. There were three boxes, about a cubic foot each in size that were full of bullion. They would have weighed about three thousand six hundred pounds and be worth in today's money . . .' Howly tapped the keys of his mechanical desk-top calculator and pulled the handle. 'About forty-eight million pounds. It was this gold that was returned to Cooch Sebah and enabled the status quo to be maintained.

'Was the coachwork ever real gold? No,' said Howly. 'Most probably Kuldeep Singh thought the story would conceal the existence of the gold bars, knowing them to be more attractive to thieves.'

'How did Kuldeep take the seizing of his gold?' I asked.

'Badly, as one might expect, but he had been placated with a government offer of a grace and favour London town house and a small estate in Suffolk. He was, as we know, allowed to keep the car with all the jewels attached. It was made quite clear to him that should he tell what had happened, or make a fuss in any way, then his right to stay in Great Britain would be forfeited.'

'Then why did he up-sticks and say he was going to America in 1912, if everything was settled?'

'Because he broke his word and told a visiting Indian Maharajah of how the British had robbed him, as he put it. This was following a minor disagreement with his India Office contact about who should pay for extra running costs for his houses. Our government has a long memory, and his right to stay was rescinded. The United States was ostensibly his country of choice.'

I was silent for a while. 'That's it, then. The gems have gone, the coachwork was aluminium, and the bullion went back to Cooch Sebah. But all of Ireland was under British rule at that time, so how come he was allowed to stay?

'Initially, of course, he was thought to have drowned on the Titanic, and if his survival and whereabouts did become known to the British Government, they most likely decided to let sleeping dogs lie; providing he remained incognito.'

I had mixed emotions as I left Howly's study; relief that I could get back to my work as a car broker, and depressed that I had only achieved partial success for Mitch and myself. Worst of all, I had a worrying thought that I had missed something.

Howly walked with me to my Bentley, and the Farrells waved from the front door. Thanking him, I promised to come back soon. Driving off, I glanced in the rear-view mirror. I caught sight of my grandfather. He had the paisley handkerchief out from his sleeve.

CHAPTER THIRTY-TWO

Two days later I collected Kirstie from Heathrow. Tegan had driven her over to Clarecourt to show her the ropes before she began work cataloguing the library. I brought her up to date on the fate of the gold bullion.

She nodded thoughtfully but changed the subject. 'How were the funerals, Ben? Silly question, I'm sorry.'

'No don't be. All went as planned, and as well as such occasions can. My grandfather showed the stoicism you'd expect, but I doubt he'll ever get completely over it. He won't let it show though.'

'What about you?'

I really wasn't sure how I felt. Kirstie had to make do with a less than helpful reply. 'I'm fine.'

As we steamed down the M4, Kirstie said, 'The local paper in Bantry found out you'd bought Clarecourt, and they did a piece on you and Miss Whelan. I hope it won't cause trouble like the Daily Mail's Mitch interview.'

'Probably not, it's just a local paper. Very unlikely that Vogel and his boss would still be keeping an eye on us. They think they have everything that they can get their hands on.'

We drove in silence for a couple of miles. A silver Range Rover entered the motorway, baulked by lorries in the slow lane. As we edged past him, also held up by a line of slow traffic, I saw a small mascot on the bonnet, near the windscreen. It was a little silver galloping racehorse and jockey. The rider's silks were painted red and blue, most likely the racing-colours of the Range Rover's owner.

Looking back at the road ahead, a thought flashed into my mind. The sort of thought that causes the hairs on the back of the neck to stand up, and a lightning-like jolt to the stomach.

'Shit.'

'Ben, what's wrong?' Kirstie looked across at me in alarm.

'Did you see the mascot on the Range Rover, the racehorse?'

'Yes, I thought he might pull out in front of us, why?'

'I don't know how I could have forgotten, not checked. Select Gerry in the satnav's phone book for me please, Kirstie.'

It was the number of the warehouse company near Cork who were looking after the Tiger's Ghost chassis, now reunited with its body. I asked for the owner and was put through immediately. 'Gerry, Ben. Do me a favour. Go and look at the Rolls chassis for me and check the frame that supports the scuttle and windscreen. I need to know its construction.'

Gerry agreed to call me back as soon as he'd checked.

'What on earth is all that about, Ben?' asked a perplexed Kirstie.

I gave her a crash course in coachbuilt car-body design, basically the fact that the coachwork was normally aluminium panels fixed to an ash wood skeletal frame; very light.

'And?' she asked a little impatiently.

'Wait until Gerry has phoned back, and I'll explain.'

We spent another few miles in silence, until Gerry called back.

'I've had a good look, seems a bit strange. Maybe all old cars are like it. The body that you just sent has a wooden frame, except for the bit between the bonnet and the windscreen, which is still fixed to the chassis. What did you call it again, Ben?'

'The scuttle, or the Yanks call it a cowl,' I replied.

'Well, the scuttle is supported by a massive iron structure, looks like the Forth Bridge. It's all riveted to the chassis, not bolted like the main body would be. Oh, and the scuttle's steel, not ali like the rest.'

'Gerry, I owe you a bottle of Ireland's best, and I don't mean Guinness.'

I ended the call. 'Okay, Kirstie, what do you remember about the Tiger's Ghost, the look of it?'

She closed her eyes and tilted her head back in thought. I imagined her mind scanning the few photos I had shown her, and the descriptive words from various conversations. She recalled the general shape, the gold and black tiger stripes, the bejewelled interior, and then she shouted, 'The head, the Tiger's Head in front of the windscreen, just like that horse and jockey but a bloody sight bigger.'

'Exactly,' I replied. 'I'd forgotten all about the Tiger's Head. We know it wasn't melted down with the bullion, as we have a photo of it on the car being off-loaded from the Titanic in 1912. We know it didn't get taken by the U-3000 crew as it was far too heavy. But was it a fake like the gold body? No! It was real or why else would the scuttle frame have been so massive? The solid gold head would weigh close to half a ton.'

Kirstie tapped away at her phone. 'Ben, if the head is gold and weighs half a ton, today it would be worth at least twenty million pounds.'

CHAPTER THIRTY-THREE

Back at the Clock House, Kirstie was welcomed with a nod from Smiler and unbounded enthusiasm from Columbus. He knew which side his bread was buttered. We told Smiler of the journey's revelation.

'So, the search is still on then, Guv,' he said.

'It is if we can figure out where to look.'

'Before you both get too involved, a woman called in. Her father-in-law died, left her and her old man everything, including a house near Burbage, its contents, and a garage with two vintage cars and a '60s Maserati in it.'

'Did she say what the other two cars were?'

'Nah, she had no idea, apparently horses are her thing, not cars. Here, Guv, she jotted down her address and phone number.'

Up in the office I dialled the woman's mobile. She answered with the unmistakable English of a born and bred Aussie.

'Noreen White. Can I help you?' she said.

Mrs. White, Ben Ross, you called earlier to talk about …' She interrupted me.

'Ah, yeah, Mr. Ross. Did the old guy I spoke to tell you what it's about?'

Yes, he did. I imagine you'd like me to come …' Again she interrupted.

'Yeah, can you come this evening? Eddie and I are flying back to Oz tomorrow. We've got the sale of the house tied up, and auctioneers for all the stuff in it, but there's been some legal hassle over the ownership of the cars, and we only heard yesterday that they're legally ours to sell. We'd really like to settle something before we go.'

This had all the makings of my being able to strike a profitable deal. 'As it happens, this evening would suit me well, Mrs. White.'

'You've got the postcode for Fir Tree Cottage; can you be here around eight? The garage has plenty of lights, to see what you're buying.'

'See you then, Mrs. White,' I said and hung up.

I told Kirstie what the call was about.

'Ben, I'd love to come with you one day and see what it's like to discover an exciting old car.'

'Come tonight, then,' I said.

'Can't tonight, but soon, I hope.'

That agreed, I went back to the subject of the Tiger's Head.

'I want to tell you everything that my grandfather told me about the gold and where it is, but international politics are involved. Stuff covered by the Official Secrets Act, even now. I've given my word to Howly that I would not repeat what he told me. What I can say is that the gold is not hidden waiting to be found, so we can forget it completely. I know why Kuldeep Singh became a recluse, and why he pretended to have planned a life in America. The sinking of the Titanic was a godsend to him personally, as it's easier to forge a new identity when everyone thinks you've drowned.'

Kirstie nodded her understanding. As a former soldier she was well acquainted with the need-to-know basis. We tossed some ideas around, and the best we could come up with was to research Kuldeep Singh's London and Suffolk properties, and re-visit Clarecourt, of course. Kirstie suggested we try and find the firm of solicitors, if any, who acted for Kuldeep Singh during his life in Ireland. By the time we reached these conclusions, Kirstie had to leave, and I had to check on Smiler's progress with tuning a 1964 E-Type Jaguar.

Smiler had road-tested the Jag after his ministrations, but I thought it a perfect evening for a fast test drive myself. The pillar-box red car had black leather upholstery, so no harm would come from having a small well-behaved dog sitting in the rear. I set off in time to be at Mrs. White's cottage for eight o'clock. The address turned out to be on the edge of the Savernake Forest, rather than Burbage itself.

There was an estate agent's For Sale board half a mile down a single-track road, and a wooden sign saying Fir Tree Cottage. A strange choice of name for a house in a forest purporting to have one of the largest collections of ancient oak trees in Europe. The gravel drive was about a hundred yards long, opening out to a formidable house, far too grand to be called a cottage. A good-looking example of 1920s Arts and Crafts design.

I parked in front of the garage. Set apart from the house, it would easily hold three or four cars. Its style was in keeping with the residence. The dense woodland bordered the site, but the touch of human hands could be seen in the cultivation all around the gardens.

Much to his disappointment, I told Columbus to wait in the car. The garage and house showed no sign of life, so having rung the bell and knocked on the door with no answer, I peered through a couple of windows only to see the rooms were completely bare. For some reason I had it in my head that the auctioneers had yet to transport everything to their rooms, and the Whites would be staying at their newly acquired house.

We'd agreed 8:00pm, and it was only five-to, so I really couldn't complain if they had to drive here from wherever they were staying. Just as I decided to look around the back of the house to see the gardens, the lights came on in the garage; it seems the Whites were not tardy at all.

The main door was shut, so I walked around to the small door at the rear. To my surprise the place was entirely empty, just the obligatory oil stains on the concrete floor. No Mr. and Mrs. White, or cars under dust sheets. Maybe there was another garage in the grounds somewhere, but why did the light come on here? I jumped as the metallic thunder of the up-and-over door being raised revealed two men. My heart leapt, adrenalin shooting through my arteries. One had the head of Edvard Munch's painting The Scream, and the other that of a manic Halloween clown.

After the initial shock, disbelief and intrigue were the headings for my thoughts, not fear or concern which would have been much more appropriate. In a second, Scream tilted his head to one side and raised his hands to ape the famous painting. A split-second later clown hit me hard in the solar plexus. I crumpled to the floor, unable to gasp a breath. Clown stood over me, yanking me from my foetal position and lifting me by my jacket lapels so his mouth was right by my ear. 'This is your last warning. Do not try and find the gold. Do not go back to Ireland.'

He dropped me to the ground and both he and Scream gave me a serious kicking. The combination of military training and natural instincts had me curled in a ball, but with a vicious kick to my head from Scream I slipped into unconsciousness.

When I came round, it was fully dark, but with enough moonlight to see the world in monochrome through the open door. Before trying to sit up I tested my hands, feet, arms, and legs. Everything seemed to work as it should, providing I ignored the all-enveloping stiffness and pain. I sat up slowly and was rewarded with a dizziness that almost forced me back down, quickly turning to nausea and finally vomiting, which did no good at all to my bruised, battered ribs and stomach muscles.

I staggered my way out of the garage, towards the E-Type. Close up I could see that all the windows and lights had been smashed. I groped my way around the car, seeing and feeling that every body-panel had been dented; badly enough to have been rammed from every direction by another vehicle, and a big one at that. To cap it, all four tyres had been slashed.

I just about had the strength to force open the deformed driver's door and look for my phone. I found it in the floor-well amongst the fragments of windscreen glass. Bending down caused another wave of nausea, but no following upchuck, thankfully. My aches and pains receded as a more dominant thought took over. Where was Columbus? 'Columbus, here boy, come on here!' I croaked and whistled, thinking he must have jumped out when all the windows were smashed.

I always take an emergency tool kit with me when driving old cars, and there's a powerful torch in it. I'd put the kit on the rear deck of the E-Type. Reaching through the now gaping hole of the rear screen to feel for the tool-bag, I let out a muffled grunt, and leapt backwards, fast enough to trip over my battered legs. In place of the leather tool-bag I'd found a soft and furry body. I scrambled back onto my feet, leaned in and scooped up the dead weight of Columbus. I half-ran, half-stumbled back into the garage, fearing the worst, found the light switch, and thankfully saw he was still breathing. I could smell the sickly sweetness of chloroform on him. He'd been knocked out, otherwise he was unharmed, by the look of things.

CHAPTER THIRTY-FOUR

Englishmen don't cry, soldiers don't cry, hard-as-nails classic car dealers don't cry, but my eyes briefly brimmed with tears and fell like summer-storm raindrops onto Columbus's fur. I wrapped him in my torn and bloodied jacket and carefully put him back in the rear of the car.

My watch had been smashed during the beating, but the phone showed that it was nearly two in the morning, so I must have been unconscious for nearly five hours. I'd always thought unconsciousness from concussion lasted just a few minutes, but I'm no expert, and my thought processes seemed normal, just my body was screaming for a rest.

I pressed three on the phone's speed dial, it rang for a good thirty seconds. 'Do you know what bleedin' time it is?' said a sleep-laden Smiler.

'It's me, serious trouble, Smiler, I need your help right away. Get the Defender and the covered trailer and come to this address.'

I heard a hacking smoker's cough the other end of the phone, ending with a serious clearing of the throat. 'Hang on Guv, let me get a pen.'

When he came back online, I gave him the postcode and what to look out for. 'Quick as you can, Smiler, things aren't too good here.'

'I'm on it, Guv,' he said, putting down his phone without further ado.

For all his good-humoured grumbling and dour looks, Smiler could be relied on one hundred percent, and I had no doubt he was wide awake and moving as soon as our call had ended. I guessed he would suspect the newly tuned Jag had caused some catastrophe, but he hadn't wasted a moment asking.

Exactly one and a quarter hours later, I saw lights coming down the drive. I hid in the trees until I knew it was Smiler. He parked with the E-Type bathed in the Defender's lights.

Smiler got out, put the roll-up behind his ear and said, 'Fuck me, Guv. What did you do, tap dance all over the bleedin' car?'

I walked into the headlight beams, and Smiler's jaw dropped as he saw the state of me. He apologised for his sarcastic remark. 'Sorry, Guv. What the hell happened?'

I told him all and lifted Columbus from the wreck. He was awake now, but groggy as hell, so I gently placed him in the back of the Defender.

'Someone, someone is going to pay for this,' Smiler said with chilling authority.

By now the sky was showing a pre-dawn lightening, and I wanted us to be back home before the sun was up and traffic about, and we were.

The E-Type was left in the trailer, and I laid Columbus on his bed in Smiler's workshop, exchanging my jacket for his blanket.

I asked Smiler to phone Kirstie, while I took a long and ridiculously hot shower. By the time I was drying off, my concern had moved from Columbus and the entire episode to how to bring down justice on the heads of those responsible.

'Ben where are you?' called Kirstie, as she ran from the office to my sitting room. I was just leaving the bathroom, with only a towel around my waist, but I came to meet her. She stopped in her tracks when she saw the state of my face and torso.

'Oh, Ben! What did they do to you?' she said tearfully.

She rushed towards me and hugged me gently before stepping back and sweeping her eyes across the cuts and bruises. She frowned and touched the crook of my left arm, peering closer before again looking at my battered face, the left eye now swollen and closed.

'That's a needle mark on your arm. I've seen plenty of those. How long were you unconscious?'

'About five hours, I think. They kicked me into oblivion.'

'Not for that long without brain damage,' she said. You were drugged with an injection.'

I rubbed the little red mark. 'Better than brain damage then,' I half-joked.

'God, Ben, you could have been killed,' she snapped, 'you've got a spare bedroom, I'm going to stay and keep an eye on you, just in case.'

I could see by the tilt of her chin that there was no point in arguing. I willingly nodded my acceptance.

CHAPTER THIRTY-FIVE

Despite my injuries, the next morning the three of us were in the workshop, a therapeutic outing ordered by Kirstie. Smiler at his grubby and parts-strewn desk, a stool on castors for Kirstie and an old car seat for me. Columbus was looking sorry for himself and moving around very slowly. If dogs suffer from hangovers, this one surely was. No one needed to mention the change in mood, for each in our own way was a professional at not letting emotions get in the way of task resolution.

I cleared my throat. 'Look, this is my battle, and I've no right to put either of you in danger, but . . .'

Kirstie interrupted me. 'Ben, look at the state of you, left to your own devices. Smiler and I have discussed it, and we're agreed, you need our help and we're both in.'

'Yeah, and if you get yerself killed, who's going to pay me wages?' added Smiler.

'Well, I guess you two can take care of yourselves, even if I obviously can't. So, thanks, both of you.'

'Right! now that's all settled, any ideas, Ben?' asked Kirstie.

'The first thing is to let Tegan and Oisin know what's happened and ask him to take precautions to stop any armed intruders and attacks at Clarecourt. Kirstie, will you phone Oisin, as you've been dealing with him and see if he is willing to help, and I'll call Tegan.'

Tegan answered on the third ring. I explained about my nocturnal attackers but did not mention Columbus. I suggested she come home right away.

'I'm getting on really well with the cataloguing. All the

books are in good condition, no tears on either binding or paper: a few have foxing, not unusual in nineteenth-century books. Overall, the Dublin Library is going to be incredibly pleased. So, I really would rather carry on and do the packing myself, then personally take them to Dublin.'

'How long will it take to finish?' I asked her.

'I should think I'll need to be here for eight, maybe ten days to do the job properly. I feel quite safe with Oisin and his pal to look after things.'

'Okay! But if you become at all worried just leave everything and come back, promise?'

'I won't, but I will, if you know what I mean, Ben. I'd better get on,' said Tegan.

Kirstie had walked out to the courtyard to phone Oisin. She came back, saying goodbye to him as I finished my call.

'I think we've hit gold dust with our Oisin. He grasped the situation right away. Asked all the right questions and said he would have a team made up of his ex-army mates by tomorrow morning. Meantime he and his oppo will stay at Clarecourt together. One in the grounds, one in the house at all times.'

'What did he say when you mentioned armed intruders?' I asked.

Kirstie giggled. 'All he said was that they wouldn't have the only guns in Ireland, and then something in Gaelic I didn't understand.'

Smiler handed around a mug of tea each. We sat quietly having a few sips of the hot brew, always strong enough to strip paint when made by Smiler.

I broke the silence. 'I've been thinking about the attack on me, the whole plan and what the thugs said, which wasn't much.'

'What did they say?' asked Smiler.

'The one with the clown mask said nothing, and the Scream-masked one only said it was my final warning. That's all I remember hearing.'

'Are we all thinking that Vogel must be behind this? I mean, who else would know enough to get involved now?' asked Kirstie.

'And if Scream said this is your final warning, they must be working for someone whose warned you off before,' said Smiler.

'That's not the case, Vogel has always thought I was working with him. He even paid me the hundred thou for finding the Harold Tyler jewels. I agree this sounded like a warning being reinforced, but there just hasn't been one.'

I must have turned white, looked shocked or something, as a thought hit me.

'Ben, what is it?' asked Kirstie, with a worried frown.

'Guv?' Smiler asked simultaneously.

'I have had a warning, from a very bitter woman. The last thing Lucia Bassoli said to me in the Indian restaurant was to stay away from her and not to look for the gold.'

Smiler's phone rang. He listened quietly, only giving a confirming 'yeah' now and again. 'Thanks, Lenny, I owe you one,' he said, ending the call. We both looked at him.

'I've got five brothers and two sisters. That was Lenny, the youngest. Thing is, Guv, they've all taken after the old man. Gone into the family business as it was. They've all done time in the nick for thieving. Nothing bad, no drugs, no girls, no robbery, just honest burglary.'

Kirstie caught my eye as she looked down to hide her grin.

Smiler carried on. 'All retired now, except Lenny and

Shirley, but we're still a family with respect in the East End. So, Lenny puts the word about to see if anyone had been hired to, er, to explain things to you, Guv.'

'Any luck?' asked Kirstie.

'Yeah, word is that some expensive muscle was hired from south of the river. People who are capable of giving you a serious pasting, but no lasting damage if ordered; experts who knew what they were doing. The point is they were approached and paid by a Kraut. No name though, but a big bloke with crew-cut blond hair.'

'Conrad, Vogel's cab driver,' I blurted out.

'So, the thugs were employed by a German, their contact looked like Vogel's driver, and Lucia is the only person who has threatened you,' said Kirstie.

'That's about the sum of it. Looks like Vogel's so-called principal is none other than Lucia Bassoli.'

CHAPTER THIRTY-SIX

Twenty-four hours later, I was feeling more bruised and battered, even though I had spent much of the previous day sleeping or just resting. Thankfully, Columbus was back to his old self, as if nothing at all had happened to him. I did call Noreen White, but of course that phone was no longer in service, and the estate agent as advertised at Fir Tree Cottage knew nothing of her.

During the afternoon I took a couple of short walks followed by steaming hot showers to loosen up painful muscles. My bruises, of course, looked worse as they matured, but I could now open both eyes. I suspected a cracked rib or two, as deep breaths were painful, but necessary to avoid lung problems. Ice packs administered by Kirstie helped and by the next day I was feeling well enough to have her drive us in the Land Rover to the ferry and Clarecourt. The journey wasa good opportunity to tell her all about the impending Pebble Beach Concours, and why it was such an important event in the old car world, but it took a while for me to convince her that I was fit and well enough to spend a week in California.

Oisin was waiting at the front door to greet us, using a walkie-talkie as we drew to a halt.

'Quinlan watched you arrive!' he exclaimed, gesturing with the radio towards the trees.

The three of us went straight to the library, where Tegan was hard at work, surrounded by packing boxes.

'I'd like to thank you on behalf of my crew and myself for being so generous with the financial arrangements. Miss Laing tells me you were both lieutenants in the British army, served together in Afghanistan, so you'll understand what I've planned here,' said Oisin.

'Yes, but I'm afraid Mrs. Jones here wasn't, so civilian-speak would be best,' I said.

'Well, I've pulled together a small team to look after you. Two teams of four each. Eight hours on, eight off, around the clock. Three will be in the grounds and I guarantee none of you will ever hear them or see them on duty. One will be in the house, who you may see from time to time. Off duty we'll be bunking on the top floor; good lines of sight, you see, if we're needed. All will be in place by dusk this evening. Any questions?'

'If there is any trouble, how will you protect yourselves?' asked Kirstie.

Oisin glanced at Tegan who was now looking a little apprehensive for the first time. 'We have what's needed, but last resorts if we have to.'

'What do you mean, last resorts?' asked Tegan nervously.

'He means that if any of us are in danger, Oisin and his team members will put themselves at risk to protect us,' I explained.

Oisin caught my eye and gave a slight nod, as he picked up that I didn't want any mention of guns in front of Tegan.

'Oisin, Kirstie is going to stay here until Tegan has finished the cataloguing and packing of the books, but I'm leaving tomorrow.'

He flashed a far too attractive smile at Kirstie. 'It seems my teams may have an honorary member if lieutenant Laing is staying,' he said.

The following morning Kirstie drove me to the airport. She assured me she felt in safe hands with Oisin to look after Tegan and herself. I grunted my agreement, which only served to increase her telling of the Irishman's charm and manliness, and his undoubted ability to look after two poor defenceless women.

On parting, Kirstie took on a serious tone. 'Ben, you be careful. Vogel's men could come after you again if they know you've been back to Ireland. If they catch you, the next beating's bound to be worse.'

'I'm only going to be home for a day before I'm off to Pebble Beach. I'll be ready for any trouble from now on, believe me. I'll be as careful as if I were back in Afghanistan.'

She nodded her acceptance and gave me a long hug. 'Go on, get out of here, you'll miss your plane,' she said, pushing me out the car and driving off quickly.

There was no trouble at all during the few hours at home, and the following day Smiler drove me back to Heathrow. I have a rule that if a flight is longer than eight hours, I travel in Business Class. So, it was a pleasant and restful trip. I had a window seat and couldn't help but smile as we descended into San Francisco and flew past the industrial building with the misleading words 'Welcome to Chicago' on its roof.

Locating my reserved hire car, I punched in the destination of Carmel, some hundred and twenty miles south along the coast, where I always stayed at the same B&B run by a charming couple who were natural hosts.

The annual Pebble Beach classic car week, held at the Pebble Beach Golf Links, is the most important and prestigious event of its kind, situated just two miles from Carmel. It's the perfect event to meet and greet established clients and hopefully gain a few new ones. Every conceivable type of veteran, vintage and classic car is eligible in the competitions to find the most original, or best restored example in each class. The Pebble

Beach venue is perfect, with its lawns running to the water's edge, attractive buildings, and easy access to the plethora of marquees erected in the Concours Village for auctions, book sales, spare parts, clothing and just about anything with a connection to the hobby of enjoying old cars. Events spill over into the town of Carmel, with bars and restaurants hosting book signings and lecture evenings.

On the third day, I was walking from the Concours show area to one of the auction marquees, when I felt my arm grasped from behind. My subconscious was now alert to Vogel's henchmen catching up with me, so I swung around, breaking the grasp from my arm. I stepped back ready to repel an attack, only to see the smiling, friendly face atop the six-foot, six-inch-tall frame of Yuri Propopenkov.

CHAPTER THIRTY-SEVEN

I hadn't seen or heard from Yuri for over five years, not since he left working at the Russian embassy in London. Ostensibly he was something to do with cultural exchanges, although I suspected that this was a cover for more clandestine activities in the best tradition of spy stories. We became good friends and had done some amateur rallying together. It worked well, as he is a much better navigator than driver, and I am the opposite.

Yuri had been put in touch with me through a client of mine in the British Diplomatic Service. He wanted me to find him a vintage car to enjoy in England, then take back home when his tour of duty finished. Something with Russian connections and 'a grand car, a car with presence', as he put it. He was ecstatic when I had found him a 1917 Hispano-Suiza that a member of the Romanov family had driven into exile, after the execution of the Russian royal family. Yuri had sworn undying brotherhood and kissed me on both cheeks when I had shown him the car that would be his.

'Yuri, how are you, what have you been up to?'

'Benedict, I am well, very well and still enjoying much my beautiful Hispano-Suiza. Putin is very jealous of me; he hints that he should like my car.'

'Are you still working for the KGB?' I teased him.

'Benedict, there is no longer KGB, now there is FSB. I still have a little work to do when requested, but for the most I run the family company. We are now the biggest producer of paper in Russia. Government and overseas contracts are good to me, Benedict. Maybe it is time for another beautiful car. Let us discuss that tonight. I have a table booked at Aubergine. Be there at seven,' he said, leaving no room for a rejection.

'That's very kind of you, Yuri. I shall be delighted to come.' I had expected my usual KGB quip to be answered with mock indignation, not casual confirmation.

'Good, but I am concerned, Benedict. You seemed nervous just now when I approached you, dare I say a little fearful and you look as if you have been in a fight.'

'Yuri, it's a long story. I'll tell you tonight.'

'I will not be happy until I know your problems, Benedict. Maybe I can help you. Now I go.'

At the Aubergine, Yuri was far too excited about me finding him another car to listen to my woes, so it wasn't until our main course of steak fillet mignon had been washed down by a bottle of 2013 Opus One that he broached the subject.

'So, my friend, tell me this long story of yours?'

I did, most of it, but I didn't mention my hopes of finding the gold Tiger's Head. I also left out the facts that Howly had sworn me not to reveal.

'This Vogel, you need him off your back, as the English say, and you think the American woman Lucia may be involved?'

'Vogel yes, Lucia probably.'

'You say you contact this Vogel by an untraceable email address, yes?'

'Yes'.

'I don't suppose you have a photograph of the man?'

I smiled and took out my phone, selecting a file from the photo gallery. It was a half-minute movie that I had discreetly filmed in the cab after I had shown Vogel the diamond, and the photos of the other gems. About ten seconds showed clear images of Vogel. 'I thought it might be useful if I ever managed to bring him to the attention of the police.'

'Ha! Benedict you should be working for the FSB, not selling old cars – please transfer this movie to my phone, here.'

'That's some phone case, Yuri. Puts my scuffed old leather one to shame.'

Yuri tapped his phone with a forefinger. 'Ben, this is a replica of a cigarette case designed by Fabergé in 1900, made to his exacting standards and of the same materials, dimensions are changed to fit the phone, of course.'

He handed it to me; its tactility demanded attention. 'What's it made of, Yuri?'

'Translucent purple enamel over a guilloche, that is an engine-turned silver base, with gold edging and a sapphire mounted clasp. Press the jewel and the case is open.'

I transferred the film clip and handed the phone back. 'A beautiful thing to own, Yuri,' I said.

'You say his name is Heinrich Vogel? I shall see what I can do to help you, my friend. Now what shall we have for our dessert? And a little Tokaj wine, I think.'

Talk went back to Yuri's dream cars and tales of his epic drives. We finally parted company after midnight, a parting that involved a bear-hug from Yuri that did my healing ribs no good at all.

I spent another three days at Pebble Beach, and it was on my last afternoon that Yuri called me to arrange a meeting. We sat at a pop-up-bar table, overlooking the Concours car displays and the bay beyond.

'Benedict, my friend, I have a gift for you.'

It was a kid-leather pouch. The contents slid out into my hand: another Fabergé inspired phone case. 'Here is a case that will fit your phone and last you a lifetime, Benedict. I have them made for my business colleagues. A little appreciation for favours done.'

I peeled off my old leather case, and gently snapped on the new one. Where Yuri's was translucent purple, mine was translucent red, and the clasp on mine was an emerald.

'Thank you, Yuri, I shall treasure this always,' I said sincerely.

Yuri dismissed my appreciation with a smile and a twist of his hand. 'To business, Benedict. My government colleagues have been unable to catch Herr Vogel through his email address. He has been sophisticated in his internet hiding. We of course have tried to trace everything, but his system will never allow us to catch him at a keyboard.'

'That's disappointing. Was the video of him any use?'

'Yes, most helpful, Benedict. The images were good enough for facial recognition software to identify Herr Vogel. He is known to us as Heinrich Richter, and my colleagues in Moscow would be most happy to speak to Herr Richter.'

'What has he done?'

'Many years ago, during his time as a Stasi agent, he abused his position for personal gain. Not an unusual pastime you understand, but he became a little too careless in his choice of victims, so, how shall I say, in Russia we do not forget.'

'Yuri, are you saying you can catch him for me?'

'No, I am saying you can catch him for us, and maybe find proof of this Lucia's involvement.'

'And how am I to do that, Yuri?'

'You have told me that you are sure the gold is no longer available, but Richter, let us call him by his new name of Vogel, does not know this and neither does Lucia. So, the shoe is on the other foot, I think you say.'

'As far as I know, Vogel still thinks the gold is on the seabed, but I told Lucia that was not the case. So, if she is his boss, then he'll also think there's still some gold to be had.'

'All the better, my dear Benedict, for now you are the one calling the shots. You can afford to be brash, to be forceful and tell Vogel how things will be. You will cast your line, and the irresistible bait will be the fictitious gold. Together we will catch Herr Vogel and his principal.'

CHAPTER THIRTY-EIGHT

Kirstie had phoned every day to report on how things were going at Clarecourt. There had been no trouble at all, except a very startled and embarrassed young couple from the village, whose lovemaking in the woods had been disturbed by one of Oisin's team.

With Smiler driving me home from Heathrow, I called Kirstie to let her know I would be coming to Clarecourt on the ferry the following day. She in turn told me that Tegan had finished the cataloguing and packing of the books, and so they were both ready to return home themselves. She also said that she had told Tegan about Columbus.

'In that case, there's no need for me to come over. Tell Oisin to keep his team in place for the time being. I'll explain when you and Tegan get back.'

'We've got something to show you. Tegan found an anomaly. It may be something or nothing; we'll bring it. See you tomorrow, late I expect.'

I'd said nothing about Yuri and the plan, as I thought it best to be back on guard against hacked phones and computers. I still had some chuck-away burner phones, so I would give Kirstie one of them again. I hadn't yet decided whether to let Tegan know what I was planning or keep her in the dark on the principle that the less she was involved, the safer she would be.

It was just after midnight when Kirstie and Tegan pulled into the courtyard. Each gave me a big hug and a kiss on the cheek.

'Kirstie told me about Columbus, I'm glad he's fully recovered,' said Tegan, as the dog made an enthusiastic fuss over the late-night arrivals.

We decided it was too late to tell each other what we had been up to. Tegan walked over to her apartment, and Kirstie decided to go home in her own car and return the next day, with fresh clothes, washing done and homely duties attended to. Two o'clock was the agreed time for us all to meet.

Warm, sunny afternoon that it was, I'd put three director's chairs out in the courtyard by the office staircase entrance. Settled with cooling soft drinks all around, it was time to ask Tegan what she had found at Clarecourt.

'It maybe something or nothing. As you know, Miss Whelan had kept the original catalogue of the library contents on the little table by the door leading into the hall. The beautiful copperplate handwritten entries were easy to read and reference the books on the shelves. Three of the books are unaccounted for, but I found out they are of no special interest or value. Not bad for a two-hundred-year-old library,' she said.

'Surely books have been added over the years?' I asked.

'Oh yes,' replied Tegan, 'but none since 1895. That's the beauty of a handwritten catalogue. New additions can be entered into the system as they come, but then I suppose it's even easier on a computer. Just not as beautiful to look at.'

'Aren't books classified by the Dewey Decimal system, or something?' asked Kirstie.

'They often are nowadays, but it wasn't in use until 1876. Before then, small private libraries like Clarecourt's usually used a system devised by the librarian of the day. That's what Miss Whelan and the Maharajah before her inherited,' explained Tegan.

I looked at Kirstie. 'Is this relevant to our problem?'

'I think so, let Tegan finish. As she said, it may be something or nothing.'

'So, the Clarecourt system is simple and effective. The library shelves are ten high and wide enough for twenty or thirty books each, depending on their size of course. There's a lovely set of Georgian library steps. Anyway, each shelf has a little ivory label. Starting with 1 at the bottom of the column of shelves to the left of the entrance, and of course 10 on the top shelf of that column. Do you see, Ben?'

'Yes, I've got that. Go on.'

'The next column has shelf 11 at the bottom and shelf 19 one from the top, and that's where I found the only book that isn't recorded in the catalogue.'

I must have looked more impatient than intrigued, as Tegan told me to hang on.

'The catalogue cross-references the books by subject, title and author, along with its shelf number, and position on shelf. So, this mystery book was on shelf nineteen in the fourteenth position, in place of one of the three missing books.'

Kirstie had obviously been through all this before with Tegan, and her look told me that there was a connection here for me to make.

'What is this important mystery book?' I asked.

'It's William Blake's Songs of Innocence and of Experience. A first edition from 1794, no less.'

Tegan reached into her shoulder-bag and took out the book. It was in a bubble-wrap envelope. The condition was perfect to my untutored eye. 'Is it valuable?' I asked.

'If it were complete, you could have five thousand pounds' worth of book here, maybe,' said Tegan.

I took it with care and gently turned a few pages.

'You'd better keep it from now on, Ben, it'll be more secure in your office safe than my flat.'

'I give in, Tegan. What makes you think this is linked to the Tiger's Ghost?'

'There's a missing page in the book, I checked, it's the page for the poem The Tyger. You know, Tyger Tyger, burning bright, and so on.'

'Intriguing,' I said, 'but it could be a coincidence. Look, supposing you wanted to leave a clue about hidden treasure, you'd need a tip-off where to look. I just don't think a random check of a library catalogue would be a realistic pointer.'

Kirstie and Tegan both had wide grins as they looked at me.

'Describe what you remember about the entrance hall at Clarecourt,' said Kirstie.

'Right, you go through the front doors. It's a large oblong space with the stairs against the far wall. They split to the left and right giving access to the landing which runs around three sides of the room. You can look down through open archways to the floor below. There're some marble sills each side of the staircase, six in all, I think. The floor is black and white marble in an Indian geometric pattern, which I happen to know represents the lotus leaf. That's about it apart from the buckets to catch water from the leaking roof.'

Think hard about the lotus pattern, Ben,' said Kirstie.

I closed my eyes and tried to imagine standing on the floor and looking down. 'Oh, yes, the lotus pattern is contained within two concentric rings, with various squiggles all the way around them. Maybe Hindi words.'

'Well done!' laughed both my inquisitors.

'You see, he's not as dim as he looks,' chortled Kirstie.

'In fact, the squiggles as you call them are ancient Sanskrit numbers. They're repeated all around the circles. Nineteen, fourteen, five and four,' said Tegan.

'How do you know that?' I asked.

'My speciality at the V&A was South Asian art.'

'Coincidence it may be, but we're looking for a tiger's head, and two of the Sanskrit numbers match the location of a mystery book, that turns out to have the 'Tyger' poem torn from its pages. If this had been something to do with the Taliban back in Afghan, we bloody well wouldn't have shrugged it off as a coincidence,' said Kirstie.

'Good point. I didn't mean to be flippant, just playing devil's advocate,' I added as a bit of a face-saver. 'Any thoughts on the other two numbers?' I asked them both.

'It may be way off, but supposing the numbers five and four refer to words, lines or verses in the poem. Maybe it's homing in on the clues,' replied Tegan.

'Does anything sound possible?' I asked.

Tegan answered. 'The fourth and fifth words, bright and In don't make sense. The fourth and fifth lines are better, Could frame thy fearful symmetry? and In what distant deeps or skies?'

'The fourth line we know refers to a tiger, so does the fifth mean it's buried at sea or concealed high up somewhere, maybe the roof structure at Clarecourt?' I suggested.

'Possibly,' replied Tegan, 'but listen to the fifth verse, especially the fourth line:

When the stars threw down their spears

And water'd heaven with their tears

Did he smile his work to see?

Did he who made the Lamb make thee?

If ever the stars threw down their spears, and if ever they watered heaven with their tears, it was during the Great War, which started in 1914: the date that matches the book's position on the shelf.'

I cottoned on fast to her thinking. 'And the last line could mean we must look for a Lamb to find the Tiger's Head.'

CHAPTER THIRTY-NINE

'Tegan, I've got a good feeling that your research is going to lead somewhere. If not the Tiger's Head itself, then at least to another clue. Look, I've got to bring Kirstie and Smiler up to date on my time at Pebble Beach. I know you want to get away now, but I think we'll need your views on the treasure hunt, when we start.'

'Thanks, Ben,' she said. 'I'm really interested in this now, I'd hate to be left out of the loop. I'll ask Smiler to come over, on my way.'

'One more thing you could do, Tegan: Give Oisin a call from your landline at home, and see if he can find any images, reliefs, statues or pictures of lambs, sheep or rams. Could be in the house, outbuildings, or the grounds. Anything depicting a sheep of some kind.'

When Smiler was settled next to Kirstie, I told them about the chance meeting with Yuri at Pebble Beach, and the positive outcome.

'So how you going to set the trap for Vogel and Lucia?' asked Smiler.

'Originally, I told Vogel the gold had gone down on the submarine, but later I told Lucia that wasn't the case. That's when she stormed out of the restaurant, never wanting me to darken her doorstep again.'

'And told you to stay away from the gold,' added Kirstie.

'Yes! Then I get beaten up by Vogel's men, so she must have told him about the gold not being on the seabed.'

'But you know that there isn't any gold,' said Smiler.

'That's something that Vogel and Lucia don't know, and they

have assumed the Tiger's Head along with the car's gold body panels was melted into bullion. Remember, they don't know the panelling was covered in goldleaf, not solid gold.'

'Or maybe they've forgotten about the Tiger's Head, like we did for a while,' said Kirstie.

'Could be, but whatever way, they think I, or we, are searching for some gold bullion, and that's what they want.'

'So, what are you going to do?' asked Kirstie.

'Yuri and I have a plan, but what exactly we do depends on Vogel's reaction. I'll tell you when I see which way he jumps. Meanwhile, each of you take these burner phones. Any communications about anything to do with the Tiger's Ghost, only by burner, unless otherwise instructed.'

'Is there anything for us to do now, Guv?' asked Smiler.

'Not right now. Vogel's my first priority, then when he's dealt with, Kirstie and I can get back to Tegan's mystery lamb.'

Smiler went back to work, and Kirstie and I to the office.

'How you going to make contact?' asked Kirstie.

'That may be the tricky part, but it's possible he's still monitoring our phones and emails. He doesn't realise we know, so to keep that secret from him I'll have to send him an email and hope it's still active.'

Kirstie looked over my shoulder as I typed away.

Vogel, I'm sending this blind, in the hope that this address is still active. I know you were behind the attack on me a few days ago. I thought we had concluded our business satisfactorily, but it seems you feel differently. I admit I was wrong about the gold being on the U-3000 submarine, but I only found out that was the case after we last were in contact.

I am now in possession of all the gold bullion, about 1,638 kilos, which at today's trading price is worth around seventy-five million Pounds Sterling.

I am not a greedy person and so to get you and your principal to stop your vendetta against me, I am prepared to give you half of the gold.

My conditions are that you and your principal alone will personally come to collect your share. I shall be unaccompanied, will meet you both at a railway station and will drive you to where the bullion has been safely hidden since 1940, and where your half still remains. We will then go our separate ways. There will be a van waiting for you to load the gold and drive away. How you get it out of the country will be your problem.

Vogel, should you have in mind to harm or kill me, be advised that my half of the bullion is now safely out of your reach, and my newfound wealth has allowed me to engage security that will not only protect me, but will hunt both you and your principal down in the event of an attempt on my life.

Benedict Ross.

'Supposing they decide to come after you, kidnap you like they did Mitch, but torture the whereabouts of all the gold out of you?' said Kirstie.

'I asked the same question of Yuri. He told me not to worry and that I would be looked after. I suppose rather like Oisin said to us, we would see and hear nothing unless there was trouble. I think it's a chance I'm willing to take to catch the bastards.'

'Bearing in mind you are effectively in bed with the Russian FSB, do you think you should run all this past Howly?'

'Hmm! That, Kirstie, is a bloody good point. I'll do it. If all goes well, we shouldn't hear from Vogel until he's had time to contact his principal, the darling Lucia, so we'll have to wait a while and hope this address is still live.'

'I have to be in London for a few days. Let me know if there's any developments,' said Kirstie.

As soon as she was on her way, I dialled Howly on my burner phone and explained the plan. He listened without comment and then asked a few pertinent questions, saying he would call back later in the day.

At 6:00pm he did so. 'Benedict, dear boy, I have looked into your situation, and after the usual initial negative comments, the powers that be now see no reason to interfere. Herr Vogel being unknown to them he would expect a degree of protection as a visitor to our fair shores. But it seems his real name of Herr Richter is known, and his becoming a guest of the FSB is deemed to be a satisfactory ending to his career, without of course any British involvement. In whatever way he leaves the country with Mr. Propopenkov he is unlikely to be delayed.'

I thanked Howly and phoned Kirstie to tell her the good news. A minute later an email notification popped up. It was Vogel.

Mr. Ross, I have spoken to my principal, who like you is a pragmatist. We were most disappointed to have only received such a small percentage of the jewels from the Tiger's Ghost, but such is the way that the dice falls. I am instructed to tell you that your proposals are acceptable. It will be convenient to meet you in four days' time, as my principal and I will be flying to Heathrow from different countries. I shall await the details of the railway station to which we must travel, when you feel confident enough to inform me.

Vogel's response was really as good as it could be. I didn't trust him an inch, but I wasn't anticipating any skulduggery from him until he thought he had his share of the non-existent gold in sight.

After again calling Kirstie, I dialled Yuri, to agree the time and day for the meeting that we had planned for Vogel and Lucia. His simple reply was that all would be in place. I had no doubt at all that it would.

CHAPTER FORTY

Four days before, when Vogel had agreed to my plan, I had not told him of where the bullion was ostensibly concealed, nor which station he must travel to. That way I had minimised the likelihood he would do me harm, or more likely find out the whole thing was a scam. Forty-eight hours after that I sent him an email telling him when to take a train to Thetford in Norfolk.

I arrived there before 10:00am, in plenty of time to park the Defender where it allowed the best view of the station and its surroundings. Being a Sunday morning, the car park had few vehicles to impede my lines of sight. I would let Vogel and Lucia wait for a few minutes, so I could look for any covert accomplices.

The train pulled in on time and amongst the few Sunday passengers that emerged there was no sign of Vogel or Lucia. I waited for five minutes to be sure they had not been lingering on the platform, when a Mercedes van pulled up in the drop off and collection area. Vogel opened the driver's door and stood by the front wing. He was dressed much as he had been on the Eurostar and in his London taxi. Against the glare of the sun I could just see the outline of another person in the passenger seat. I hurried over as I was keen to confront Lucia.

The van was left-hand drive, had a Dutch registration and its signwriting advertised it as belonging to a tulip grower. Vogel offered me his gloved hand and his cold-eyed smile.

'Mr. Ross, forgive the little subterfuge of travelling by ferry to Felixstowe in our own transport. Now let me introduce you to my principal.'

The passenger door opened and out stepped not Lucia, but an immaculately dressed Indian, wearing a Nehru jacket and silk turban. Tall and slim, he had an air of refinement and culture about him.

'Sir, this is Mr. Benedict Ross, your one-time employee and now it seems, benefactor. Mr. Ross, this is Mr. Sharma, our principal in the matter of the Tiger's Ghost,' said Vogel.

Sharma did not offer his hand but gave a curt nod.

'Vogel, where is Lucia Bassoli?' I asked.

'Ah, the young lady who works for Mr. Mitchelletti. I have not met her and certainly have no reason to involve her with our negotiations.'

This was a shock: I had been convinced that Lucia was Vogel's employer, his principal. How badly had I misjudged her, and did I owe her something after all? Her vitriolic outburst in the restaurant certainly showed her true nature, but she wasn't responsible for Mitch's kidnap, my beating, or the chloroforming of Columbus. Now was not the time to worry about that. 'But I thought she was your principal,' I blurted out.

Sharma spoke up, his voice quiet, his English pronunciation near perfect, marred only by the slightest cadence, and smudge of the letters W and V. 'Mr. Ross, I assure you I am Herr Vogel's employer in this matter. I am a servant of the court of the Maharajah of Cooch Sebah and am acting on behalf of His Serene Highness. It is the gold stolen from his ancestor that I wish to reclaim.'

I nearly replied that the gold had been returned to Cooch Sebah by the British government in 1909 and ask him why the present ruler was unaware of the fact. I checked myself in time, realising that to do so would ruin the trap I was about to spring on Vogel.

'My mistake!' I said to both of them. 'You'd better follow me; the journey will take less than half an hour.'

'Why not drive us in our transport, and then you will be able to take the unneeded van you have arranged for us from the site of the bullion,' said Vogel.

'And I would very much like to know where we are going and how you discovered the gold was not in a sunken submarine,' added Sharma.

'You'll see when we get there,' I replied, not wanting to yet give away our destination. 'But in answer to your second question, Herr Vogel will tell you that he employed me to search for what remained of the Tiger's Ghost because he thought I had the required abilities as a hunter of rare old cars. It turns out he was right. That, coupled with clues I found at Clarecourt, the house in Ireland, some hunches and just plain good fortune brings us here today.'

Sharma gave another of his curt nods.

Elston Manor, halfway between Thetford and the American airbase at RAF Lakenheath was our destination, a suitable site selected by Yuri. The British government had allocated the use of the house and estate to Kuldeep Singh from the time of his arrival in England until his departure in 1912. It then had various government uses until the Second World War, during which it was used to house American air crews. After the war it became a base for residential government training courses, until 1993 when it was taken out of use. It had remained secured by the Ministry of Defence ever since. There's a perimeter fence and a private security firm checks the house twice a day, but Yuri had assured me that would not be a problem.

'Tell me, Mr. Sharma, what brought the Rolls to your attention in the first place?' I asked.

'The story of the Tiger's Ghost and of the criminal Kuldeep Singh is legendary in the state of Cooch Sebah, but it was always accepted that the car and the thief of the State treasures were lost on the Titanic. The importance of stories can fade with time, and the present Maharajah is more of a titular Head of State than all-powerful. In fact, the Royal Palace is now an hotel. The Tiger's Ghost was never foremost in his mind, that is until we learnt that his grandfather, the Maharajah Ajit Singh had commissioned an American news-filing agency to notify him of any references to the Tiger's Ghost. It seems that although long forgotten, the agreement with the agency was ongoing and paid annually by an unnoticed standing order.'

'And after all these years they spotted the article about Angelo Mitchelletti and the car in an English newspaper?'

'Yes, unbelievably, that is the case, Mr. Ross, and so the Maharajah of today asked me to investigate the situation and see what could be done to regain what he feels rightfully belongs to our State treasury.'

'As I see it, Mr. Sharma, the problem you have is that Kuldeep Singh may have broken the spirit of your tradition by using a car to carry his share of the State treasures, but he kept to the letter of the law, or tradition, by not being assisted by man nor beast. It seems unlikely that any international court would uphold your claim.'

'Indeed Mr. Ross, I concur with your assessment of the situation, which is why we have reluctantly accepted your offer of receiving only half of the gold that has survived to be available to us.'

I was almost beginning to feel sorry for him, but the beating he had arranged for me, knocking out Columbus and virtually destroying the Jaguar E-Type kept me well short of actual sympathy. 'Something I don't understand, if Lucia Bassoli is not involved with you, how did you discover the gold wasn't on the submarine and I was searching for it?'

Vogel replied, and I could hear the smile in his voice. 'Miss Bassoli had called you to arrange an evening meeting in London. I was aware of this conversation and decided it would be prudent to have one of my employees follow you both. Miss Bassoli's outburst in the restaurant made it obvious that you had told her there was gold still to be found.'

'You must have been tempted to let me keep up the search and then intervene at a later date, so why arrange for Vogel here to warn me off with a beating?' I asked Sharma.

For the first time I saw a smile flicker momentarily across his face. 'We felt with your acquisition of the house in Ireland, coupled with what you had achieved so far made it most possible that you would not only find the gold, but secure it away from us, all before Herr Vogel could remake your acquaintance. Now, here we are, so it seems we underestimated your tenacity and except for your surprising generosity in giving back half of the gold, you would have it all and we would have nothing. Why have you been so generous, Mr. Ross?'

'I have been successful in finding what happened to the Tiger's Ghost, I can't deny, but really I'm a car broker. I search for old cars of merit for clients who haven't the time to do so, or who wish to remain out of the public gaze. I enjoy it, I don't enjoy being threatened and hounded by the likes of Herr Vogel here. Ever since he introduced me to his umbrella on the Eurostar, I have been looking over my shoulder, waiting for a fatal attack. I just want to drive away today knowing that's an end to it all.'

'Umbrella! What has an umbrella to do with this?' asked a

puzzled Sharma.

'When we first met, Mr. Ross and I had a chat about concealed weapons of old, that is all.'

'Are we nearly at our destination, Mr. Ross?'

'Five minutes or so,' I assured them.

We drove along the lane, past the main entrance to Elston Manor with its Georgian gateway and brick wall tucked well inside the Ministry's wire perimeter fence. Various warning signs reading 'Ministry of Defence – Keep out' were regularly spaced along the perimeter, all with a private security company's name and logo. After half a mile, I turned by the fence down a single-track lane, finally pulling in to face chain-link gates. There was a small but empty guard hut just inside. I jumped out and fiddled with the chain and padlock that secured the gates. Yuri had done his job well. The padlock was open and just holding the chain together. Gates opened and closed again, I drove slowly along the cinder track, now showing signs of relaxed maintenance. It curved gently to the side of the house and the main drive. At the back, I turned onto the once pristine lawn, now looking like a horse paddock. We bumped along until a fully glazed Victorian orangery came into view, with a van parked by it on a gravel pathway.

'What is this?' shouted Vogel. 'The security people are here.'

The van had on its side the same name and logo as the perimeter fence's warning signs.

'Don't worry Vogel, that's the van I have arranged. No one is going to suspect a security vehicle on or near the grounds. Hidden in plain sight I think they say.' Sharma gave another of his curt nods and Vogel said nothing.

The heat of the day was building, without a breath of wind, and an aggressive robin tried to discourage us from invading his territory. I led the way to a boarded, once-glazed door into the main house, just a few feet from where the orangery was attached. I took a key from my pocket, pretended to turn it in the lock with some effort. I pushed down on the door handle and gave a hefty shove with my shoulder and upper arm. The door resisted in its damp-swollen frame. Another shove, as hard as I could manage and the door snapped open, the oil-starved hinges resisting all the way. We had a short but dark passage to walk along, until another door which this time easily opened, allowing us into the corridor that gave access to the orangery. Two ornate full-height cast-iron and glazed doors gave access to the exotic room of the same construction. It was a long time since any plant had been nurtured here. The room was bare except for a small heap of broken tubular-framed chairs. Along the length of the windowed walls ran a tiled trough, and below that a trio of heating pipes. On the floor by the chairs were the feathery skeletons of two pigeons.

'We are in the country house that Maharajah Kuldeep Singh lived in during his time in England,' I explained.

Sharma walked to the centre of the room and looked down at the tiled floor. He pointed to the patterned black and white tiles. 'The Sri Chakra, I think Maharajah Kuldeep Singh has left a tribute to his heritage,' he said with reverence.

'I am not familiar with this design,' said Vogel.

Sharma answered him with a radiant smile. 'The Sri Chakra is a form of mystical diagram used in Hinduism. It consists of interlocking triangles that surround a central point known as a Bindu. These triangles represent the cosmos and the human body.'

It was similar to the pattern at Clarecourt, also with its outer rings and lotus pattern, except for the lack of Sanskrit numbers.

I walked over to the stylised lotus petal, the tip of which was central to the points of two of the four matched equilateral triangles that touched the inner circle of the design. I tapped the petal with my shoe. 'Gentlemen, beneath these tiles are the gold bullion bars I have promised you.'

Vogel looked doubtful. 'And where were the bars that you have taken for yourself?'

I hoped to God that Yuri had done his job as agreed. I walked across to the other side of the Sri Chakra, bent over, and picked up one of the recently loosened tiles that mirrored the other side. 'My bullion was here.' I dropped the tile back in place.

'I think, Mr. Ross, it would be a helpful gesture if you were to assist us in the recovery of our gold, rather than leave us to it,' said Sharma.

'Fair enough!' I agreed. 'There are tools in the security van, I'll fetch them.'

My heart was thumping like a steam engine, for my going to the van was the signal for Yuri and whoever he had bought with him to capture Vogel and now Sharma. I waited a minute, closed the van doors, and walked back to the orangery. I was worried, as I could hear neither a scuffle nor any shouting.

CHAPTER FORTY-ONE

Yuri stood holding a single-use syringe. Vogel was unconscious and being fireman-lifted out of the orangery by a man with the build of an Olympic weightlifter. Another of Yuri's helpers stood by Sharma who looked truly shaken. He was seated on one of the least damaged tubular chairs. It looked as though the capture of Vogel and Sharma had been so fast that neither had time to react.

'Is everything okay?' I asked Yuri.

'All as planned, my friend. Herr Vogel will wake up in Moscow. Our transport will be here in a few minutes, along with our doctor who will keep our patient safe on his journey.'

'I'm sorry about Lucia, Yuri. It turns out this is Vogel's boss, Mr. Sharma he calls himself. He says he represents the present Maharajah and State of Cooch Sebah.'

Yuri walked over to Sharma, squatted in front of him and patted his knee. 'What shall we do with him, Benedict? I have an expert in interrogation with me, or when Viktor returns from taking Herr Vogel to the truck, he would be most happy to teach Mr. Sharma how to behave.'

All the while Yuri held Sharma's petrified stare. I too walked over to the Indian, as Yuri rose to stand over him.

'Mr. Sharma, how am I to be sure you will not hire another man like Vogel to pursue me and my share of the gold?' I asked.

'There is only one way for sure,' said Yuri.

Sharma let out a little yelp of fear, then his whole body seemed to relax, as did his fear-stricken face. After two deep breaths he looked up at us both. 'If it is the will of Brahman that

I suffer for my misdeeds, then so be it. But first, let me make peace with Mr. Ross. Yes, I did allow Herr Vogel's men to beat you, but I would never condone the killing or injury of your dog. All animals are sacred to Hindus and are considered to have souls. I am deeply upset that I have instigated actions that resulted in the ill-treatment of your dog. I beg forgiveness from you and from the spirit of the dog.'

My need for revenge towards Sharma melted away, as I believed he was sincere about Columbus. 'Mr. Sharma, there is no point in you pursuing the matter further. There is no gold here, and I have found none for myself. All the gold bullion from the Tiger's Ghost was, as I originally told Herr Vogel, sunk on the German U-boat,' I lied. 'This whole story of the gold being here is just the bait to catch Vogel. I wanted him off my back and Yuri, here, would like to take him to Moscow.'

I had to perpetuate the lie about the gold to keep my word to Howly not to break the Official Secrets Act. I was still puzzled why Sharma, and the current Maharajah, didn't seem to know that the gold had been returned to Cooch Sebah in 1908. Maybe there had been some double-dealing in the royal court and the young Maharajah had kept the gold secretly for himself, or some high official had never revealed its return. I doubted I would ever know the truth.

'Your Maharajah will have to settle for the few jewels that were saved from the submarine.'

'You mean the diamond from the submarine?' Sharma said.

'And the thirty-nine other stones.' I replied.

'Mr. Ross, Herr Vogel has only given me one stone, a large and very valuable red diamond, but no others.'

I pulled Yuri aside. 'Yuri, it looks like Vogel double-crossed his principal. Do you think you could persuade Vogel to give up all the gems to Sharma? That way he will save face in Cooch Sebah, and the Maharajah will have something of value to feel good about and stop his search.'

'I regret, Ben, that once in Moscow any gems revealed will fall into the hands of the government, well, one high-ranking official, for safe keeping, you understand. Your idea is good. I will have Vogel awakened and personally discuss the matter with him before he leaves England. When retrieved, I will hand them to the Maharajah's representative here.' Yuri turned to him, 'Mr. Sharma, it seems that your friend Herr Vogel has not been truthful to you concerning the gems from the submarine. Mr. Ross gave him forty gems, all large and of the highest quality. Herr Vogel will tell me where they are, so that you may collect them to present to your Maharajah. But that must be an end to the matter. As important as Cooch Sebah is in the world, any future interference in the life of Mr. Ross will incur the displeasure of the Russian government. Do we understand each other?'

I listened in awe to Yuri and hoped Sharma would believe my mythical importance to Russia.

Sharma looked truly relieved. 'Mr. Ross, you have my word and my gratitude for giving me a chance to redeem myself in the eyes of His Serene Highness, and to lead a better life. You need have no further concerns about your safety, I swear before Brahman.'

'Can you drive?' I asked him.

He nodded yes.

'Then you can take me back to Thetford Station in your van and be on your way. Sit here until I call you.'

I beckoned Yuri out of the orangery. What will you do now?'

'Follow me,' he said.

We walked around to the front of the house and there on the drive was a large truck. 'Sunrise Bakery' was emblazoned on the side, with a stylised sunrise shining down on a loaf of bread which had a smiling face. Yuri walked to the rear and looked up above the double doors for a few seconds.

'Camera!' he explained.

The click of an electronic lock sounded, and Yuri opened the truck's doors. Loaves and sliced bread sat in plastic boxes on racked shelving. The smell of fresh warm bread wafted out. Yuri leant inside the truck by the nearside door and punched in a code. He stood back and waited as the entire shelving unit, the plastic boxes and the loaves opened out and up, rather like the opposite of a covered car-transporter's fold-down ramp. At the same time steps appeared from under the truck-bed.

Come!' said Yuri.

He led the way up the steps and through what turned out to be an airlock. The rest of the truck's cargo body was a positive air-pressure medical facility. It looked for all the world like a private ICU room. On one of the two beds, lay a comatose Vogel, a drip was running into the back of his left hand, and a monitor bleeped away regularly. A doctor, judging by her white coat with a stethoscope stuffed into the pocket, made notes on a clipboard and a nurse was raising the safety bars on the bed. I noticed the two chairs by each of the beds were fixed to the floor and had seat lap-belts.

'Herr Vogel will travel like this to one of the east coast's smaller commercial airports. There, the Sunrise Bakery will supply a privately hired Aeroflot business-jet with its requirements. Before take-off I shall speak to Herr Vogel about the gems. The plane can be delayed for as long as it takes me to persuade our friend to talk. I do not envisage it will be long, for I will have the help of my colleagues, Viktor, and the doctor here.'

Yuri checked his watch. 'Come, now we must go. The clocks are running, as you would say.'

As soon as we were clear of the truck, the false bread-racks descended, the steps retracted and Yuri closed and locked the rear doors, giving the worldwide signal to a driver that it was safe to go: two loud slaps on the truck's body.

CHAPTER FORTY-TWO

I set off for home, my mind racing with the events of the day. I could hardly believe that Vogel was finally out of our lives.

The satphone rang, it was Yuri. 'Benedict, I thought you would like to know that one of my men apprehended an armed man in the grounds of Elston Manor. Vogel had fitted a tracking device to his own van so that his associate could follow him. His task was to shoot you once he had received a command from Herr Vogel that he was in possession of the gold.'

'It seems I owe you my life, Yuri,' I said.

'Not really, Benedict. No gold, no signal from Herr Vogel to shoot you. You were safe.'

'Well, it sounds bloody unsafe to me. Do you know who the gunman was?'

'He had no identification on him, but by your description to me of Conrad, it was him.'

'And what has happened to Conrad?'

'I explained to him that Vogel would not be needing his services in the future, and a healthy life would best be served by forgetting Vogel ever existed. Having been unable to rescue him, and being nothing more than hired muscle, he has been sensible enough to agree to look for other employment.'

'Thanks, Yuri, I still feel I owe you one.'

'Ah, one day, perhaps, who can say. Goodbye, my friend.'

It was dark by the time I reached home. Smiler, Kirstie, and Tegan were waiting for me, anxious to hear what had transpired. I thought it best not to go into details, so all I said was Yuri's plans had been faultless, and we would not be hearing anything more from Vogel or his principal. My three helpers were all as surprised as I had been that Lucia was not Vogel's employer.

'So, she's just a scheming little bitch, out of her depth,' said Kirstie.

'That's about it, although I can see why she feels hard done by, being a descendant of Kuldeep Singh.'

'If Kuldeep didn't have a will leaving anything to his descendants, then surely she has no legal claim,' said Tegan.

'No, I guess not. So, it's back to the search for the Tiger's Head tomorrow, but now I'd better phone my grandfather and give him the good news.'

The three went to their various homes, all pleased with the outcome and excited to see what the morning would bring. I tapped out Howly's number on the burner phone, now, more to use up the time on it than for security. Howly answered immediately, so I guessed he was at his study desk waiting for me to call and give him a detailed account of the day.

'The bread lorry is an interesting new means of covert transport. I haven't heard of that one before,' he said.

Retired he may be, but every now and then his comments make me quite sure that my grandfather still has access to many MI5 and MI6 secrets.

'Tomorrow, I plan to return to Ireland and see what progress I can make with finding the Tiger's Head.'

'I've been thinking about that dear boy. I spoke to a chum of mine, retired now of course but spent some time at GCHQ. Given the clues you have, he thinks what you are looking for is either at Clarecourt itself, or if the artefact is elsewhere, there will almost certainly be more definitive clues at the house. This he bases on years of experience in the psychology of codedinformation.'

I thanked him, wished him goodnight, and took myself off to bed, still reeling from the thought that I could easily have been shot, never mind what Yuri said.

The next morning when everyone was back in the office, I explained the simple plan. 'Smiler, back to normal duties for you, at least until something develops, but hang on while I tell Tegan and Kirstie what I have in mind for them. Kirstie, we will go back to Ireland and do a follow-up search for the sheep connection. Maybe Oisin will have some news on that for us.'

'He hasn't found anything yet,' piped up Tegan. 'Got a WhatsApp from him just now.'

'Okay, Tegan, if you stay here could you come into the office a couple of times a day to keep the normal business running? There's a list of what needs to be done this week on the computer. If we need you, or Smiler, you can fly over ASAP.'

'Yes, I can do that,' said Tegan, 'but I just thought of something, should have mentioned it earlier, sorry. In Miss Whelan's small sitting room, the one beside the dining room, I noticed there's a book about the house, on one of the side tables, The History of Clarecourt. I only glanced through it briefly as it has nothing to do with the library books that I had to catalogue for Dublin. It has drawings and watercolours of the house and important contents from its heydays, along with a written history from Georgian times. Anyway, it also contains photos taken in 1895 when the book was published. It may be worth a look for something to do with a sheep.'

'Sounds like a good place for us to start,' agreed Kirstie.

'All right, let's all get to it,' I said.

CHAPTER FORTY-THREE

We took the Land Rover over to Clarecourt, to be met on the steps of the house, just as before, by Oisin.

'Welcome back, Lieutenants,' he said. 'I'm sure Tegan told you I have no fine news about the search for the sheep.'

'Yes, she did. But we have a new lead, and if that doesn't work out we'll just have to keep ferreting. Anyway, Oisin, I'm pleased to say that you can stand your team down. There's no longer a risk of an attack on the house.'

Oisin pulled an impressed and approving face. I left him to speculate on what might have happened to our enemy. 'Will you and Jacko carry on as normal security guards, please?' I gave Oisin a wad of cash. 'Give all the lads a bonus for a job well done, and here's something for yourself.'

'Thank you, Lieutenant, it's always good to be appreciated. I'll continue as I started then, just myself and Jacko, in the house and grounds at all times.'

Kirstie and I took our bags upstairs and met again in Miss Whelan's sitting room. Kirstie had changed into an old pair of jeans and a checked shirt, her hair now kept in place with a bandana. I couldn't help noticing that however dressed down, she still looked pretty good.

Sure enough, just as Tegan had said, on a side table away from the windows was the book about Clarecourt. It was large, leather bound and close to A2 in modern paper size. I carried it through to the dining room and placed it on the table. Seated on two fine examples of Irish Georgian chairs we started to scan the book. External views were first, showing the house and then the gardens. We turned to the interior shots and marvelled at the exquisitely designed Irish furniture, some Victorian but mostly Georgian by their looks. Paintings were hung everywhere. Who knows how good they were or how valuable they would be in today's market?

Few of these decorative items and furnishings had survived at the house, and even fewer were reminders of Kuldeep Singh's tastes. Page sixty-three showed a photo of the hall, taken from the entrance doors, looking towards the main staircase. No sign of the later Sri Chakra lotus-leaf floor tiles, but the marble sills either side of the staircase supported bas-reliefs, which the photo caption said were hewn from Connemara marble. Annoyingly, the photo was not clear enough to positively identify what each portrayed.

We scooted through the remainder of the photos of the main rooms, until reaching the pages showing important artistic details of the house. Included were lithographs of the bas-reliefs. Each of the six seemed to represent an item of Irish farming heritage. They included a milkmaid complete with yoke and buckets, against a backdrop of cows and calves; a farm girl with a basket brimming with potatoes in a potato field; a farm worker scything a field of wheat; some cattle being driven down to a market scene; a woman spinning flax to make linen; and a shepherd with his crook, a lamb in his arms.

Kirstie let out a yelp and clapped her hands. 'Yess,' she said excitedly.

We both had the same idea: Could we now identify which sill had supported the bas-relief of the shepherd and lamb? Kirstie flicked back to the photo of the hall. We peered at the image, but despite our new knowledge it was still not clear.

'Hang on,' I said, 'look, there's a magnifying glass on the side table by Miss Whelan's chair.' Grabbing it we both used it to look at the image, our heads touching. I could smell Kirstie's lingering perfume, or maybe it was just her. I took a slow, deep breath.

Now we knew what we were looking for, the first bas-relief on the immediate right of the stairs looked to be the shepherd and his lamb, or maybe it was wishful thinking.

'Do you think this is what Kuldeep Singh's clues referred to?' asked Kirstie.

'Wait for me in the hall, I've got to fetch something from the Defender.'

'A metal detector,' exclaimed Kirstie. 'I didn't know we'd brought that with us.'

Turning it on and selecting the gold and bronze setting I scanned the walls beneath the sills to the right of our target. As expected, no response at all. I walked back to the sill identified as having supported the shepherd's marble, just to the right of the staircase. Again, no response.

'Well, back to the drawing board,' I said.

Kirstie tugged my arm. 'Hang on, Ben, suppose something gold or bronze was inside an iron box of some sort. Would you get a response then?'

'Perhaps not. This is the first time I've used the thing, only bought it a couple of weeks ago.'

I changed the setting to 'iron' and pointed it once again below where the shepherd's bass-relief had been. The noise was deafening, so much so that I jerked the detector's scanning-head away from the wall by reflex. Gently returning it, the strengthening signal pinpointed a large iron item at floor level directly below the sill. There was no signal at all beneath the other sills.

'This looks promising,' I said.

'What now, Ben?'

'Time to undertake some architectural vandalism,' I replied with a smile. 'We're going to knock a hole in the lath and plaster wall. It can easily be mended.'

Another trip to the Defender and I came back with a lump hammer, crowbar, pad saw and cold chisel. Kirstie chiselled around the edge to form an oblong panel centred on the detector's strongest signal, and I followed, sawing through the wooden laths.

Pulling out the newly created plaster panel, revealed that the wall either side was structural and nearly two feet thick, appearing solid either side of where we had forged the opening. The square cavity beyond contained an iron chest, reinforced with iron bands. There were two keyholes on the front. I brushed the debris, dust and cobwebs off with my hand, and tried to lift it out. It didn't seem to be fixed in any way but resisted my efforts completely.

My heart was thumping, as I scooted back, so Kirstie could see what we had uncovered. She couldn't resist leaning into the hole, trying to heave out the chest herself.

'Have we done it, have we found it?' she asked with a grin and eyes as wide as could be. 'Don't suppose you brought anything to remove a solid gold Tiger's Head from a wall?'

'As a matter of fact, yes, but you'll have to give me a hand to bring it in.'

We manhandled a foldable engine-hoist from the Defender. Once set up on its A-frame base, by pumping the hydraulic ram, it raises the crane-like arm with its lifting hook attached.

Kirstie and I pushed and pulled it up onto the top step of the entrance, then wheeled it to our hole in the wall. Two of the reinforcing iron bands on the chest had iron loops riveted on. I threaded a strop through them and attached it to the hoist's lifting hook.

'Kirstie, if you pump the ram slowly, I'll reach in and check the chest is lifting squarely and clearing the sides.'

Despite her excitement, she pumped with care.

'Stop now,' I said. 'The chest's about a foot off the stone base, and about six inches clear of the bottom of the hole in the wall.' I backed out of the way and stood up. It was going to be a real effort to drag the hoist backwards on its tiny roller-wheels if the head was in the chest. It could weigh half a ton and that would cause a lot of friction.

Just then Oisin walked through the hall on his way to distributing the bonus payments to his men. 'Here, Oisin, would you give us a hand with moving this? It's bloody heavy.'

With the two of us pulling as gently as we could, and Kirstie stopping the load from swaying and crashing into the wall, we managed to free the chest from its unknown decades of concealment. I could see Oisin was dying to ask about it.

'We don't know what's in it, Oisin,' I volunteered. 'I'm hoping it's something that Mr. Singh hid when he lived here.'

'It's none of my business, Lieutenant, I'll get on just now,' he replied disappointedly, and left us to it.

Kirstie and I pushed the chest to a corner made by the wall and the staircase, where we lowered it to the marble floor. I measured it, then placed a chair from the library in front of it, folded the engine lift and dragged it to Miss Whelan's sitting room and stashed it in a cupboard.

When I returned, Kirstie was on her knees examining every square inch of the chest, almost caressing it. 'Look, there's no hinges on the back, just another two key holes.'

'I suppose hinges would be easier to saw through than four concealed deadbolts. Anyway, it should be safe here with you, Oisin, and Jacko about the place. Let's face it, no one's going to tuck it under their arm and run off with it.'

Kirstie frowned as she put her hands on her hips. 'And where will you be?'

'I've been thinking. With luck we've got a solid gold artefact here. If we tell the Irish authorities, they're bound to seize it as treasure trove or something. I'd rather take it quietly back to England, see what it is and ask Howly what our best course of action should be.'

'You mean smuggle it out of Ireland.'

'I wouldn't put it like that, but I suppose so. I'm going to take the first ferry I can tomorrow, then drive back here to collect you and the chest. I should be back by Friday afternoon.'

'Why don't we both take it now?' asked Kirstie.

'I don't want to risk the chance of a customs official finding it and demanding to see inside. I've a plan to minimise that risk, but I must phone Smiler.'

Back in the Defender I did so and gave him my instructions. If all went to plan everything should be ready for me by the time I reached the Clock House.

CHAPTER FORTY-FOUR

The motoring gods were with me. Light traffic to the ferry, a space available on the next sailing and a calm crossing followed by a traffic-free drive home. There, Smiler met me looking seriously pleased with himself.

'All done, Guv, worked out like a dream.'

'Great,' I replied. 'I've got a booking on the first ferry back to Ireland tomorrow, so I'll drive back to Pembroke this evening, stay with a friend who only lives twenty minutes from the port, then off the ferry and drive straight through to Clarecourt.'

Smiler took me over to one of the cars from my private collection, a 1929 Speed Six Bentley, to show me what he had done. Below the back-seat cushion was a neatly installed metal box, just big enough to hold the chest that we hoped contained the Tiger's Head. Smiler had screwed down a metal sheet over it across the width of the seat and replaced the seat cushion. From underneath the car, all that could be seen was the box, with a thick insulated wire protruding from it and bolted to the chassis. For all the world it looked like a typical battery box with an earth cable.

'If the bleeders find that, they deserve to,' said Smiler.

'Brilliant job,' I confirmed.

The rest of the day was spent in the office with Tegan until it was time to leave for Pembroke.

I chucked enough luggage for a couple of weeks' holiday in the back, just for the look of it, and climbed over the side of the car, sliding into the seat – no driver's door on this sporting car, just an outside handbrake. I went through the starting procedure and the six-and-a-half-litre engine burst into life. If Thor or Mars had a car, this would be their choice. As she warmed up, I looked down the length of the bonnet, held tightly closed by two leather straps, to the winged 'B' mascot on the radiator. A thrilling sight I never tired of. This car is a road-going version of the thundering racing cars that won Le Mans in 1929 and 1930. The car's creator Walter Owen Bentley preferred the Speed Six to all the other models he had designed, and I wouldn't disagree with him.

The drive to Pembroke was a pure joy. Fast and furious though a Speed Six can be, its turbine-like engine, good brakes and beautifully balanced chassis make driving at any speed feel safe. I drove in the same manner from the ferry to Clarecourt, the car's burbling, throaty exhaust announcing my arrival.

Kirstie had been in the garden and came running over to the car.

'You never showed me this beauty. Take me for a drive, right now.' She demanded, jumping into the passenger seat.

Half an hour later we were back at the house, Kirstie windswept and joyous. 'It beats my Morgan hands down,' she said, patting the dashboard.

I explained about the hiding place and with Oisin's help, using the hoist, we lowered the chest into it, screwed the plate back down and replaced the seat cushion. Oisin lent us his pickup truck to drive to the Bay View Bar for supper.

'Why the old Bentley, and not a modern car or van?' Kirstie asked.

I took a good long swig of my Guinness. 'A modern car's suspension wouldn't cope with the weight, and it would be much more difficult to hide the box. Yes, a van could handle the weight, but again difficult to hide something this cumbersome.

The main reason is the ferry company's number plate recognition camera will show the vehicle is returning after only a day. That, and an empty-looking van could seem suspicious to the customs.'

'Won't they think the same about the Bentley?' asked Kirstie.

'Not likely. A ninety-year-old Bentley with a young couple like us in it, all flying helmets, and goggles, might raise a smile but not their suspicions. In case it does draw their attention, I booked a return ferry for a fortnight's time. The reason we are cutting short our touring holiday is because our dog has been injured, and you're beside yourself with worry.'

'We're a young couple, are we?' she asked with just a hint of seriousness beneath the teasing retort.

We held each other's gaze for a couple of silent seconds, but I decided to sidestep that issue for now. A decision that I immediately hoped I wouldn't regret. 'When we're at the customs do you think you could work up a tear or two if need be?'

'Easily! I'll imagine Columbus dying from his chloroforming.'

CHAPTER FORTY-FIVE

In the event, we sailed through both Irish and English customs, the only special attention paid to us being a thumbs up for the car from the duty inspectors in Pembroke.

Now, Kirstie and I stood looking at the locked chest that Smiler had winched onto one of his work benches. Tegan rushed over from her flat being as excited as the rest of us to see what was inside.

Smiler puffed fruitlessly on his dormant roll-up. 'Clever bastard, whoever made this. See, no hinges: too easy to cut through. Two locks either side with bloody great deadbolts on each one I'll bet, and a recessed lip all the way around.'

'Is it going to be difficult to open?' asked Tegan.

'Nah, back in them days they didn't have angle grinders. I'll have to be careful though, I don't want to damage whatever's inside.'

Smiler got to work, while we stood back away from the noise and spraying sparks.

'It's wrought iron, not steel, I can tell from the colour of the sparks,' shouted Smiler over his shoulder.

After ten minutes, he switched off the angle grinder, took off his safety goggles and stood back. A wisp or two of smoke rose from the newly cut metal.

'Give it a couple of minutes to cool off, and you should be able to open it, Guv,' he said, handing me a pair of work-gloves.

After the suggested couple of minutes that had all of us fidgeting with anticipation, I tried to lift the lid; it only wobbled slightly. I tried again, this time with more effort, but the result was the same.

'Hang on,' said Smiler as he gently moved the lid from side to side a few times, then picked up a lump hammer and smashed it into one of the corners. 'Try it now, Guv.'

Tegan and Kirstie crowded either side of me, each with a hand on my shoulders. Their excitement was palpable, their faces radiant with hopeful expectation. I could feel their heartbeats were as fast as mine, and Smiler's roll-up now had a continually glowing red tip.

Not only was my pulse racing, but the feeling of excitement in the pit of my stomach was as strong as a bungee-jumper must feel as they lean into the big drop. Was it gold fever?

I grabbed the lid. It turned out to be as heavy as it looked, but now came off the box with ease. Everyone crowded even closer to see inside. The contents were wrapped in a red velvet bag pulled closed with a silk drawstring. All around was tightly packed straw, here and there singed by Smiler's work. I pulled out as much of the packing as possible and unknotted the drawstring. As the bag dropped away, we all stood silently in awe of the Tiger's Head looking straight back at us. Being made of gold, it had lost none of its brightness or colour. Even the black tiger stripes looked as if they had just been painted. The eyes were made from numerous green and amber-yellow gems, all faceted and each the size of small peas, about three or four millimetres across. They sparkled and flashed in the workshop lights, giving the Tiger's Head an illusion of fiery temper.

In the mouth, clenched between the front teeth was an oval blood-red gemstone, the size of a duck's egg. Given the provenance of the Head, my guess was a genuine ruby.

'It's magnificent, look at the eyes,' said Kirstie.

'Bloody hell, Guv. You got it,' exclaimed Smiler.

'I feel like Howard Carter at Tutankhamun's tomb,' added Tegan.

Kirstie was last to speak. 'Ben, if this is real, you're going to be famous in the art world.'

'It's real, you can't fake that weight,' said Smiler.

After what seemed an age, Kirstie broke the silence. 'How are we going to lift it out? it's so heavy.'

'We're not,' said Smiler. 'The Guv and me will lay the chest down on its side, put some plastic over the rough edge, and we'll be able to slide it out.'

The space around the Head was too small to get a good grip on such a heavy item, and it wouldn't move. Smiler found some nylon rope, which I fed around the back of the head and the base. While Kirstie and Tegan held the box steady, Smiler and I tugged at the rope. Bit by bit, gently pulling first to the left and then to the right, the head inched its way out. The more the weight on the slippery, protective plastic sheet, the easier it came. Once fully clear of its home of decades, and with all of us helping, and using the rope, we managed to stand the Tiger's Head upright on its base. Its size was perhaps slightly larger than a football.

Both Tegan and Kirstie ran their hands over every inch of it, with admiration in their eyes, and giggles of joy in their throats.

'I've never seen anything so beautiful, even at the V&A,' said Tegan.

'I've never really understood the lust that some people have for jewels and gold, but I do now. It's almost addictive to be near,' added Kirstie.

'God! How rich were those Maharajahs back then?' wondered Tegan.

'What we going to do with it now, Guv?' said the ever-practical Smiler.

'I think we need the gemstone specialist, Mo Katz, who I met in London. I'll call himright away. I've got a burner phone up in the office, just in case.'

Mo answered on the third ring, and he remembered me.

'Mr. Katz, I have had some luck with my car search, and I have something that I would like your opinion on, and which I think you will want to see.'

'Bring it to my workshop and we'll see what we shall see.'

'Afraid I can't do that Mr. Katz, it's rather heavy.'

'How heavy can heavy be?' said Mo a little impatiently.

'Give or take half a ton maybe.'

Mo was quiet for a while. I could almost hear his brain assimilating what I was saying, trying to imagine what I had found.

'Can't you extract what you want me to see, or do I need to view the whole half ton?'

'Mr. Katz, you really will want to see the whole article.'

'I think you mentioned that you lived near Newbury. I shall take a train tomorrow morning, as early as I can. What station should I come to?'

'Newbury is easiest. Call me when the train leaves Reading, and I'll meet you.'

The thought crossed my mind that we should find a safe hiding place for the head. It was going to be difficult for anyone to steal it, but better safe than sorry. I walked back down to Smiler's workshop, and my heart missed a beat: the head was no longer on the bench. Just oily rags, some tools and an ancient, battered Castrol oil drum, one of the five-gallon cylindrical ones, with a conical top.

'How did you move it without me, and where the hell is it?'

I asked.

All three of them smiled like idiots, as Kirstie grabbed the oil drum and lifted it off the bench. There was the Tiger's Head, safe and sound. Smiler had cut the bottom out of the old can and placed the rest of it over the Head.

'Anyone looking for treasure isn't going to think it's inside a dirty old oil drum right in front of their eyes, are they, Guv?'

'Brilliant, Smiler, bloody brilliant.' I said, as they laughed at the joke on me.

'I'd offer to take you all to the pub for dinner, but I daren't leave it alone, even hidden where it is.'

'How does Mr. Katz fit in?' asked Kirstie.

'I want his opinion on what we have in terms of value, financially and as an historic artefact. Then I shall consult my grandfather about the chances of establishing ownership, treasure trove, national claims, those sorts of problems.'

'Good luck with that, Guv,' said Smiler.

That was something I didn't need to be told.

CHAPTER FORTY-SIX

Before leaving for Newbury station, I had cleared everything off the bench, except the Tiger's Head, now sitting beneath its red velvet bag, under Smiler's watchful eye. Just the theatrical side of my nature governing the reveal to Mo Katz.

Bringing him into the workshop, I introduced him to Kirstie, Tegan, and Smiler.

'Am I giving a master class?' he asked.

Kirstie flashed one of her smiles at him. 'No, Mr. Katz, we're just super-excited to hear the opinion of a real expert.'

'Don't schmooze a schmoozer, Miss Laing,' he replied, but a brief twitch at the corners of his mouth betrayed his pleasure at the compliment.

Mo had with him a large aluminium suitcase, of the kind professional photographers use for their equipment. I had carried it from the car, and he now gestured for me to place it on the bench.

'So, what have you brought me all the way from London to see?'

I whisked the velvet bag away from the Tiger's Head. The lights immediately caught the gems that made up the eyes, and the red stone in its mouth seemed to glow from within.

We all looked at Mo, in time to see the colour drain from his face, as he swayed slightly on his feet. Kirstie quickly fetched a work-stool, as Tegan and I moved towards him.

'No, no, I'm alright, I'm alright,' he said. 'Let me sit.'

He did so, without saying anything for at least half a minute, all the while scrutinising the golden, bejewelled sculpture.

'This is magnificent, I've never seen such workmanship. Do you know who made it?' he asked.

'I suppose Willard's set the stones, but who formed the gold head and how, I've no idea.'

Mo scooted his stool closer and lightly ran his fingers over the head. 'In my view, the head was cast in India by a craftsman of the highest order. Probably by the cire perdue method.'

'The what?' asked Kirstie.

'Cire perdue or lost wax process. First you make a wax sculpture, then you surround it with a mixture of casting-plaster. Once set, you gently heat it to the point when the wax melts and runs out, leaving a perfect negative image of the wax sculpture. Next, fill the plaster cast with whatever molten metal you choose, usually bronze, silver or gold. When it's cooled down you smash off the plaster and with a final fettling you have a perfect replica of your wax sculpture, but in the precious metal of your choice. They've been doing it in India for six thousand years.'

I smiled inwardly to myself, as I knew that six millennia later Rolls-Royce still use that same method to cast their Spirit of Ecstasy mascots.

'Thanks, Mr. Katz,' she said.

'Call me Mo, everyone calls me Mo,' he exclaimed, without taking his eyes off the Head.

'So, Ben, to work, let us see what we have here.'

Mo stood his case on edge, handle uppermost, and unclipped both sides which folded down leaving a centre section with several pieces of testing equipment secured in place. The two sides contained bottles of liquids and laboratory paraphernalia.

'First we shall see how pure is the gold.'

He took a flat, black pebble from the case and rubbed it

gently by the base of the head. Flecked gold streaks rubbed off on the stone, which he placed in a petri dish. He took a rack of small plastic eye-dropper type bottles from the case.

'Each of these bottles contains acid. This one aqua fortis, that's a smart name for nitric acid. It will dissolve anything that is not gold.'

Mo squeezed a drop onto the gold smear on the black stone. 'No reaction! It's gold. Now we have to ascertain how pure.'

'You mean what carat it is?' asked Kirstie.

'Yes, my dear. And to do that we use various strengths of aqua regia. That's a mixture of nitric and hydrochloric acid. The greater the strength needed to dissolve the gold, the purer it is.'

'Why wouldn't it be completely pure gold?' asked Kirstie.

'Pure gold is soft, it will dent or scratch too easily to maintain its shape. Pure gold is twenty-four carat. My guess would be that this is eighteen carat, made up with silver,' explained Mo.

He started with the aqua regia for ten carats, then that for fourteen: both showed a need for a stronger solution. Mo's final test showed the head to be made of twenty-two carat gold. It quickly dissolved the smear from the black stone.

'So, the gold on the surface of this head is 91. 67 percent pure. Now let us see if it is just a covering of an iron casting.'

'Surely, it's too heavy not to be solid gold?' I asked.'

'You have an exact weight and an accurate volume of the head?' asked Mo.

'Well, no,' I answered.

'Another test then. For a small item I could use a powerful magnet, but for something as large as this I will need my electro-magnet.'

Mo took out an instrument that looked a bit like a hairdryer. He plugged it into a bench socket and fiddled with a dial on the back. He placed it against the surface of the Tiger's Head in half a dozen places, each time checking a display screen, also on the back of the electro-magnet.

'There is no ferrous metal inside,' announced Mo.

'So, it's solid twenty-two carat gold?' asked Kirstie.

'The metal here is, yes. But we must know how much it weighs and what is its volume. Then we will know if it's solid, has a non-ferrous core or is hollow.'

'We don't have scales that will take that weight,' said Smiler.

'I know someone who does,' I replied. 'But how do we allow for the weight of the gems?'

'I will be able to give you a weight for all the stones. I will extract two from the eyes, a yellow one and one of the olive-coloured that give an illusion of the pupil in the eye. The red stone will have a fixing that keeps it safe against the Tiger's teeth. It will be no problem to free it.'

Mo felt behind the red gem and nodded that he was right. Using tools to free the stones, similar to those a dentist could need in their work, he looked at each stone through a powerful jeweller's loupe, under the light of several differing lamps from his kit. He said nothing, but many soft sounds of surprise and approval rose from his throat. When he had finished with all three extracted stones, he moved his attention to those still in the Tiger's Head, again moving his lamps around the multitude of gems. Lastly, he weighed the three he had removed for examination, then replaced them.

Mo finally sat back, rubbed his eyes, and moved his glasses back down from his forehead. We all moved closer to him, like expectant disciples of a guru.

He cleared his throat. 'The eyes are a mixture of two types of diamonds. You should understand that when grading diamonds, we examine the four Cs: Colour, Clarity, Cut and Carat. For clear, so-called Colourless diamonds their colour is rated D, H, L, P, U, Z, running from Colourless to Light Yellow. Colourless is best. There are also grades of true Coloured diamonds, which few people realise can be shades of any colour, or mixtures of some. A Pure Red diamond is the rarest and most valuable of all.

'The head's eyes are a combination of Canary Yellows, the rarest of the Fancy Yellows, and the darker stones are Fancy Chameleons. They change their colour from the olive green you can see now to orange, depending on the temperature and the type and intensity of light.

'The Clarity is the degree of flawlessness. There are six grades for Clarity. These stones are of the finest: no internal inclusions or external blemishes.

'The Cut refers, as you may suppose to the way the rough diamond has had its facets proportioned, angled, and polished. There are many ways the finished diamond can be presented. These here are a traditional form known as Round Brilliant Cut. It shows off well the Brilliance, that is the light reflected, the Fire, the dispersion of light into the colours of the spectrum, and Scintillation, the flash and sparkle of the light, all of which should reflect out from the Table, that's the top of the diamond, in a rainbow blaze of colours.

'The Carat is not as is often thought to be the size of the stone but it's simply the weight. Is all this clear?' asked Mo.

We all nodded, but I for one wouldn't remember much more than the four Cs.

'All the diamonds are of the highest quality for their types, and the ruby, for it is a ruby, is an equally fine example. The size, about that of a duck's egg, is substantial. The colour, a Pure

Red, with just the slightest hint of silk-thread-like inclusions that prove it to be natural, probably Burmese. No external blemishes and not synthetic or heat treated. It's what is called an Oval Cut. I could re-cut and make much more of it, if it was just a stone by itself,' added Mo.

'All what you say sounds great. Are there any buts?' I asked him.

Mo looked each of us in turn before he spoke. 'There are no buts. What you have here is many million pounds' worth of gold, several million pounds worth of jewels, and an artefact that is probably worth substantially more than the sum of its parts.'

CHAPTER FORTY-SEVEN

Sleep had not come easily that night. My mind had been racing with Mo's summation of what we had found. I had known all along that if we ever did find the Tiger's Head, and it was as real as legend recorded, it would be a magnificent historic artefact and worth millions. But to be told so by a leading expert, and to have the Tiger's Head here at the Clock House was just overwhelming. Even so, now that all the travelling, all the meetings, and frankly all the good luck that had seen us make progress was over, my excitement was tinged by feelings of disappointment. The thought of whatever financial gain I would receive, was nowhere near as uppermost in my mind as the simple fact that the chase was over, and the certainty of once again being just a classic car broker was a bit deflating.

Fortunately for me the black dog of despond never sits for long on my shoulder, and there was still plenty to do before the finding of the Tiger's Head could be announced to the world.

Silas Brown was the man who had scales in his scrap yard that were strong enough to weigh the Tiger's Head, and the first problem was how to transport it to his yard.

We would need to move the Head around easily, and Smiler had come up with an answer. I'd heard hammering and the crack of flying welding sparks late into the evening, and now, on the workshop floor sat a cubic metal frame with a pyramid shaped top. It looked for all the world like a large old lantern missing its glass. The pyramid was topped off by an eyelet, and on the base of the cube rested the Tiger's Head chest.

'Here's the clever part, Guv,' said Smiler.

I watched as he lifted the Castrol oil can to reveal the Tiger's Head, now in a web of nylon lifting strops. He picked it up with the workshop engine hoist and wheeled it to the side of the lantern-like frame. He lifted off the pyramid top, and manoeuvred the Tiger's Head above the cube, and gently lowered it into its chest.

'Now all we have to do is place the lid on the chest and bolt the pyramid back on the cube, then the whole thing can be lifted by the eyelet onto a trolley that we can easily push.'

'Smiler, you're in danger of getting a pay rise, this is perfect.'

I backed the Defender into the workshop, and again using the engine lift, we guided the frame into it. Once secured, I set off for Silas Brown's yard.

Just as before, I was met with a smile, a bone-crushing handshake and momentary attention from the two dogs. This time I was even favoured by a desultory wag of two tails.

'So, what have you got for me now, boy?' asked Silas, as I opened the Defender's rear door.

'Here's the thing, Silas, no offence meant, but can we just weigh this, with no questions asked?'

'In my business, no questions asked is normal,' he said, tapping the side of his nose. 'I'll help you lift it on the scales'.

'We'd better use a hoist,' I said.

Silas gave me an old-fashioned look, as he tried to lift the lantern. It didn't move. He waddled over to a decrepit old fork-lift truck and drove it to position the forks over the lantern. We fixed a chain and hook to the eyelet, with the other end securely wrapped around the truck's pushed-together blades. Once weighed, Silas gave me the printout, then he skilfully replaced the load back in the Defender.

'I don't suppose this has anything to do with the U-3000

submarine, has it, boy?'

I couldn't help but smile. This was the man whose stock in trade was 'no questions asked'.

'Not really, Silas, but I will tell you all when everything is settled.'

As I started to move off, Silas signalled to lower my window. 'Can't think of much that size, that's so heavy. You owe me a drink next time, boy, mine's a pint of Strongbow Gold,' he said, with another tap on the side of his nose.

I used the journey home to phone Howly, bring him up to speed and ask if I could bring the Tiger's Head down for safe keeping. I also wanted his advice on what to do with it.

Smiler helped me remove the head, then we weighed the empty chest, lantern, and the lifting strops. I subtracted the weight from the total shown on Silas's print out. We now knew the precise weight of the Tiger's Head. Mo had explained how to assess the volume of an article by water displacement. Simply put, you lower the item into a brim-full container, collect the water displaced over the rim and measure the volume.

Once the head was safely back on Smiler's bench, I emailed the calculations for the Tiger's Head to Mo. Ten minutes later he phoned me back.

'Ben, are you sure your figures are correct?'

'Yes,' I answered, I'm sure.'

'In that case, bearing in mind I have allowed for the weight and volume of the diamonds that make up the eyes, and the ruby, your Tiger's Head has a cavity of some sort inside.'

'How big a cavity?'

'That I can't say, because it was almost certainly cast for a purpose, and may contain something, which of course would have weight of its own, or maybe important documents which weigh almost nothing. I suggest you see if you can find a way into the cavity. Maybe through the back of the mouth, or through the base. I have to catch a plane; I'm giving a lecture in Amsterdam. Text me if you find anything of interest.'

Smiler has an industrial endoscope camera for examining the inside of car components, which we used to probe the interior of the Tiger's mouth. There was no indication of a concealed cavity.

'Let's think about it, Guv. I'll put a brew on,' said Smiler.

We supped our tea and mulled over the problem.

'How would you easily make an access to a cavity in this thing?' I asked Smiler.

'The obvious way would be like Mo said, through the base. Once on the car, it would be concealed, and if you wanted to open it up, you wouldn't damage the look of the head at all.'

Tea finished; we laid the head on its side with the base just over the edge of the bench.

There were two drilled and threaded holes about four inches apart, that would have held the head on the car's scuttle by threaded studs, ahead of the windscreen.

Smiler had occasions to use a desk-top magnifying glass with a light source around its rim. I switched it on and peered around the base. There was no hint of a join that I could see.

'Tell you what, Guv. Let's screw a couple of studs in the holes and apply pressure on them with a pry-bar.'

We wedged the head between some wood blocks so that it wouldn't slide around on the bench. I held the blocks firmly, as Smiler placed the pry-bar under one stud and over the other. He gently applied anti-clockwise pressure and, sure enough, the studs began to rotate. A faint circular crack appeared on the surface of the base. Smiler was unscrewing a plug about five inches across. The thread was fine and ran about an inch up the plug, which then tapered to about three inches in diameter: a solid gold top hat shape. I pulled it free from the head but could see nothing inside.

'Here Guv, take a butcher's with the endoscope.'

We both watched the tiny VDU, as I fed the camera into the void.

'It looks empty, that's disappointing.'

'Yes, but the roof of the void, it's not gold. Hang on a minute,' said Smiler.

He grabbed a long screwdriver and fed it up next to the camera. Gently scratching at the different material.

'It looks like plaster of some kind,' I said.

Smiler grunted his agreement and shoved the screwdriver handle hard with the heel of his hand. A ragged hole appeared, and with several similar shoves while scraping away the loose plaster, we could see beyond there was a ball-shape wound from a strip of leather.

Smiler fetched a sprung grabbing tool, rather like an elongated, ultra-slim pair of scissors, with ends that curled inward. Just right for collecting dropped nuts and bolts from inaccessible places under a car's bonnet. He inserted the tool and closed it around a pinch of the soft leather. Pulling gently, he extracted the ball which was a snug fit in the cylindrical cavity.

'There must be something inside,' I said.

Carefully unwinding the strips that made up the leather ball, I uncovered the contents, just as Kirstie arrived.

'What have you boys been up to?' she asked, giving my arm a squeeze.

I gave a rough account of all we had done that had led to

Mo's thoughts there was a hollow void in the Head, how he was right, and what we had found.

It was an irregular shaped sculptured figurine of three entwined tigers. In fighting poses, their bodies and limbs formed a roughly oval shape, the whole containing a dull opaque stone of some type.

'The tigers are beautiful, look at the detail, you can sense their musculature. They look like gold,' said Kirstie.

'I should think so, but it's very delicate, if it wasn't for the glass lump inside, you could crush it with your bare hands.'

'But why was it hidden in the Tiger's Head?'

'Religious artefact or maybe something with royal importance,' suggested Smiler.

Kirstie held it up to the light and squinted at the supporting translucent centre. 'They wouldn't have used plain old glass, would they?'

'Probably not, it could be quartz or maybe topaz, they can be colourless like this,' I said.

'Not a diamond, then,' smiled Kirstie.

Taking it back I waved it around under the light. 'Not much sparkle for a diamond. I think Smiler's right, it could be historically valuable, religious maybe or have royal significance. I'll take it up to the office and text Mo. He's away for a few days, but he might be able to say what sort of thing it is.'

Meanwhile, the beautiful tigers around the ugly glass, quartz or whatever it was found a temporary home concealed in the back of a filing cabinet drawer.

I now needed to organise taking the Tiger's Head to Penhydrock. Neither Howly nor Farrell were strong enough to help manoeuvre the chest into the house, so I would need to take someone young and fit with me.

Back in the yard, I shouted across to the workshop, 'Kirstie, fancy a trip to Cornwall tomorrow?'

CHAPTER FORTY-EIGHT

First thing the next day, Smiler and I had placed the Tiger's Head in its chest on the carrying frame, then onto the workshop trolley. Once secured, we hoisted the whole thing into the back of the Defender, with just a quarter of an inch to spare either side of the doorframe. The engine hoist, when folded, rested across the top of the load, leaving plenty of room for overnight bags.

Kirstie appeared dressed in a smart designer outfit of jeans and a brown leather biker-jacket over a white tee-shirt with I'm a Limited Edition printed on the front. Her hair was in a ponytail and her sunglasses were perched on top of her head. The whole look was set off by zip-up ankle boots with block heels. She was dressed sensibly for helping with moving our treasure, but still managed to look gorgeous.

I must have stared noticeably, for Kirstie gave a twirl and struck a fashion-model pose.

'You like, Mr. Ross?' she asked with a giggle.

There was only one answer to that, but Kirstie went on before I could speak.

'I thought I'd better dress smartly if I'm going to meet your grandfather. So, sensible and fashionable seemed the order of the day.'

We stopped on Dartmoor, just outside Two Bridges, for a late picnic lunch. The views in all directions were stupendous over lake and heath. To the southwest we could see the rooftops of the famous Dartmoor prison at Princetown. Kirstie had bought cheese and tomato sandwiches and some fresh fruit for us both plus a pork pie for me, a delicacy that I remembered from our army days that she could not abide. All was washed down with a half-pint of beer each.

Up until now, as we set off again, talk had been of the old days, and more of what we had each been up to since leaving the army; subjects that sparked off our own views on life, which we found coincided in nearly all matters. Not a word about the adventures with our search for the Tiger's Ghost car. It was Kirstie who finally broached that subject.

'Ben, you haven't told me why we're bringing the head down here for safe keeping. Wouldn't it be better with Mo, or at your bank maybe?'

'Mo probably hasn't a safe big enough or accessible enough for it, and banks ask too many questions these days. Besides, the fewer people that know what we've found the better. By the way, I'll introduce grandfather as Sir Howel when you meet, but he's bound to ask you to call him Howly, as we all do, I mean did.' It was still hard to remember that my father and his second wife had both died in the helicopter crash.

Kirstie didn't answer, but she squeezed my hand on the steering wheel, and we drove on with the radio replacing our friendly chatter.

Our easy talk was back to normal by the time we turned into the drive at Penhydrock House. The rhododendrons along the drive reminded us of Clarecourt, except these were well kept, and soon gave way to views over the lawns to the gardens that run down to the river's edge and its tiny beach. The house is imposing enough on its own, but when all is in bloom and at its best, the eye is rarely on the house itself.

The Farrells were first to greet us, having heard the crunch of tyres on gravel. He as butler, and she, as always, to see if this time I had brought the future Mrs. Ross.

Introductions done, I asked where Howly was.

'He's taking a walk amongst the gunneras, Master Benedict,' said Farrell.

'What on earth is a gunnera, Ben?' asked Kirstie.

'Look, down there, between the large pond and the river, those huge rhubarb-like plants, they're gunnera manicata. They were introduced in 1867 to the UK and thrive in the Cornish micro-climate. You need to stick to the paths though, as they grow close together, and the stems have tough prickles all over.'

'How big do they get?' she asked.

'Anything up to fifteen feet high with three-foot diameter leaves. Howly's are about eight to ten feet tall.'

'I'll take your bags up, Master Benedict,' said Farrell. 'You are in the King's room and Miss Laing is in the Chinese room. I'm sure you would both like to freshen up after the journey, so please come down when you are ready. Sir Howel will see you in the music room, at six for a drink before dinner.'

'Mr. Farrell, there's something we must do first. We have a rather heavy and valuable artefact that I would like to put in the gun-room safe. Does my grandfather still have the wheelchair ramp from when he broke his ankle? We'll push our trolley up the steps to the kitchen entrance and go along the corridor from there.'

'Yes, Master Benedict, it's in the old stables. I fear it's a little too heavy for me these days.'

'Don't worry, I'll fetch it, and please leave the bags for us.'

By the time I had dragged the ramp to the kitchen steps and walked back to the Defender, Kirstie had unloaded the hoist, set it up and connected it to the lantern and its trolley. We lowered the cargo to the ground, and between us easily pushed it to the ramp, just managing to heave it up. Wheeling it along the flagstone floor from the kitchen door to the gun room was a much easier manoeuvre.

'This is real English Country House stuff,' said Kirstie, as we entered the gun room.

Nowadays most of the glass-fronted gun cases were empty as they no longer satisfied the insurance and police requirements. Two cases still held guns, but these were old muzzle-loading flintlocks, that wouldn't be much good to villains. At the far end of the room was a heavily armoured door, the entrance to the walk-in safe. Chatwood-Milner 1888 was stamped onto a round plaque above the massive handle and keyholes. Nowadays the sporting guns that are still in use are kept with their ammunition here under lock and key.

I know where Howly keeps the massive pair of keys that the old safe-door needs, and once turned in their locks, it took only a few seconds to heave the weighty door open. We pushed the trolley inside and manoeuvred it to the end of the room-safe. Kirstie took a while to admire Howly's guns, some less than twenty years old, some made over one hundred years ago. Once back in the gun room, I re-locked the safe's door and replaced the keys in their hiding place.

Having told Farrell that we would take our own bags up, I threw mine on the bed, and showed Kirstie next door to the Chinese room.

'Wow! What a room, Ben. I see how it got its name. Just look at the silk wallpaper, and the furnishings, and the rugs. Look, even the tapestry bedhead has a Chinese scene.'

'The wallpaper is quite special, the pattern's called trailing cherry blossom on a yellow background. My great-grandfather loved to travel in the orient, he amassed a seriously good collection of jade figurines, I'll show you tomorrow. First things first though, I'll escort you to your bathroom, no en-suites here, I'm afraid.'

At five to six, I knocked on Kirstie's door to take her down to meet Howly. She had changed from her travelling outfit, into a chic black evening trouser suit, styled like a man's shawl-lapelled dinner jacket, but perfectly cut to fit a woman's curves. No wonder she liked the yellow Chinese wallpaper; her silk blouse was just a shade lighter than the bedroom walls.

'You never wore that in Afghanistan,' I joked, which earned me a grin and a whack on my shoulder with her clutch bag.

Howly greeted us with his usual enthusiasm, and there was no doubt that he immediately approved of Kirstie, both as a stunningly attractive young woman and as a retired soldier. For her part, like many a girl before her, she fell for Howly's charm and the still active twinkle in his eye. I glanced at the oil painting above the piano, of Howly as a young army staff-officer. Undeniably dashing, I was glad I was not introducing him to Kirstie back in those days.

Farrell passed around the champagne, and it was soon time to go into dinner. The three courses, prepared by Mrs. Farrell, were as fine as a Michelin-star restaurant could serve. Howly was far too good a host not to try and balance the conversation between the three of us, but both Kirstie and I egged him on to tell of his army escapades, which all seemed to involve humorous incidents, whether bravery was called for or not.

Howly has a firm rule, at the stroke of ten he said goodnight and headed for his bed. The evening had sped along, and we were both surprised to see the time.

'If you and Miss Laing would like a nightcap, may I suggest you retire to the library. The fire is still alight, and you will be more comfortable, Master Benedict,' said Farrell.

I glanced at Kirstie, she met my eye and gave a nod of agreement.

'That's a good idea, Mr. Farrell. I'll have my usual Calvados.'

'Me too, please, Mr. Farrell,' said Kirstie.

'Certainly, Miss.'

Sitting on a sofa by the fire, Kirstie with her shoes kicked off and feet curled beneath her, we sipped our drinks, as they warmed in our hands.

'I love your grandfather, he's got so much life in him, and what stories he has to tell.'

'He's remarkable, I was brought up in this house, and as long as I can remember he has had an uncanny ability to get people to do what he wants and have them think it was their idea in the first place.'

'I shall watch out for that, then, in case it's a family trait,' smiled Kirstie, taking another sip of the fragrant brandy. 'Ben, apart from Howly asking if all was in the safe, when we met for drinks not a word has been said about the Tiger's Head.'

'Grandfather is still very much of the old school, and he wouldn't broach a business subject on a social occasion. At breakfast he'll invite us to come to his study around coffee time. That's when we'll discuss it.'

'I imagine he'll have some good advice.'

'Let's just say that Howly may be getting on for ninety and long retired from government service, but he is probably the best-connected civilian in the country. Tomorrow, we shall know exactly what the British Civil Service has decided about the Tiger's Head.'

We finished our drinks and walked up to our rooms. At Kirstie's door, she turned to me.

'Ben, that was a wonderful evening. I haven't laughed so

much in years. Your grandfather is a wonderful raconteur, and those stories of you as a little boy, what can I say?'

'Nothing, just a goodnight kiss will do,' I said, laughing.

She kissed me lightly on the lips. 'See you in the morning, Ben.'

It took a long while for me to get to sleep, not with thoughts of what lay in the safe, but thoughts of Kirstie sleeping with just a wall to separate us.

CHAPTER FORTY-NINE

Breakfast was always served at 8:00am in the small dining room. On the sideboard, to serve ourselves, Farrell had laid out hot dishes in silver trays over spirit burners, alongside brown and white loaves baked by Mrs. Farrell. Her husband would supply fresh tea and coffee as desired. How he knew when to appear at just the right time for this task I have never known but appear he did.

Howly and I heaped our plates with a full English breakfast. Kirstie was more restrained, taking only fresh grapefruit juice and some kedgeree. All three of us wanted some of Mrs. Farrell's homemade bread and marmalade, which I offered to slice and toast.

Pushing back my chair, I heard the distant ring of the front-door bell.

'Someone's at the front door, Howly. Are you expecting anyone this early?' I asked.

'Couldn't hear it, dear boy. The old ears aren't as good as they used to be, but no, not expecting anyone. Kept the day clear for you two. Farrell will see to it and let us know. Now, how about that toast.'

As I filled the ancient toaster, the door to the breakfast room was flung open with a crash, and Farrell was pushed through followed by a man in an army camouflage jacket, black gloves, and a ski mask. More alarmingly he was carrying an automatic pistol which he immediately pointed at me.

'All of you stand behind the table. No questions.'

There was the sound of more struggling and footsteps coming along the hall; Mrs. Farrell was half dragged into the room. Her attacker wore the mask I had last seen in the garage at Fir Tree cottage: Munch's Scream. The wearer seemed to recognise me, stopping in his tracks for a moment, looking quickly at his companion and then back at me.

Farrell started towards his wife, calling her name, 'Joan!'

The gunman waved the pistol momentarily at Farrell, hovered for a second at Howly whose eyes flashed with vengeance at the treatment of Mrs. Farrell, then back onto me. 'Nobody move until I command it,' he said, pushing Mrs. Farrell towards her husband, who put his arms around her trembling shoulders. 'Phones on the table,' shouted the ski-masked man.

Only Kirstie and I could comply, as the others never carried a phone with them in the house. Scream searched their pockets and silently shook his head.

Enough of the man's face in the ski-mask was exposed to recognise him, and a German accent confirmed his identity. I spoke without thinking. 'Conrad, you didn't take the Russian's advice to stay away.'

'No, Herr Ross, I am not as stupid as you all think. Even Herr Vogel underestimated me. He saw only muscle to do his bidding, but I watch, I remember, and I wait. Now it is my turn to be rich.'

I moved as directed to the far side of the table, with Howly, Farrell and his wife between Kirstie and myself. We were now as distant from each other as possible, so that if the opportunity arose, we could rush Conrad from two different angles, and both ends of the table. Our one chance of surprise could be if Conrad didn't know of Kirstie's military background and assumed her to be just a frightened young woman.

'You have brought the Tiger's Head with you. Give it to me and none of you will be harmed,' said Conrad.

I didn't know if he had it in him to be a killer, but if he did then I, having been stupid enough to identify him, was in trouble for sure. All the others could also tell the police that a German named Conrad was the thief. They too could be in mortal danger.

'It's in a safe with a time lock on the door. It can't be opened until six this evening,' I lied.

'I think not, Herr Ross. No more delays, or it will be the worse for the cook woman.' With that, Conrad pushed Kirstie out of the way and grabbed Mrs. Farrell's hair, pulling her away from the rest of us, holding the pistol barrel against her cheek. Bravely, her only reaction was a tight-lipped grimace of disobedience.

Howly had been standing as straight and as resolute as ever, but with Mrs. Farrell in danger he sagged at the shoulders and let out a feeble cry. 'Alright. I'll show you where it is, just let her go. It's in the gun-room safe. Just don't lock us in, I can't bear small spaces, I'll do anything you say, but don't lock me in the room-safe.'

I had never seen my grandfather collapse and kow-tow to anyone before, and the looks on Kirstie and Mrs. Farrell's faces showed them to be just as shocked. I never knew that Howly had serious claustrophobia.

Farrell turned to support him, and with his back three-quarters on to Conrad and The Scream, he caught my eye and gave the slightest shake of his head, and half a wink. It was a setup; Howly was luring them to take us to the room-safe, and I realised why.

'So, you and your old servant, lead the way. You, girl, help the old woman and you, Herr Ross, you stay at the back,' sneered Conrad, as Scream took a pistol from his pocket.

Our two captors shoved us along to the gun room, with Howly all the while playing the frightened, cowardly old man on the verge of collapse. Howly reluctantly fetched the key from its hiding place, and I unlocked the safe door.

'All of you go in and push the Tiger's Head outside the door,' ordered Conrad.

As I prepared to step forward with the others Conrad grabbed my arm. 'Not you, Herr Ross, you will push the trolley to your Land Rover, and you will load it using the hoist that you have so kindly left beside it.'

He then panned his pistol slowly across the others. 'Do not worry, we shall make Herr Ross immobile, but I expect he will manage to free himself before you all die of oxygen starvation.'

He gave an almost dog-like yelp of a laugh as he swung the door shut and locked it, throwing the keys onto a window ledge. 'You two push the trolley to the car. Schnell, quickly,' he yelled to me and Scream.

Conrad knew his stuff, he stayed far enough back, so that I couldn't just turn, attack, and seize the gun. He hadn't identified his accomplice, who also stayed out of reach and to one side. My next instruction was to unlock the Defender, give Conrad the keys, then hoist the Tiger's Head on its trolley into the back. I did so, but fiddled with the securing strops, taking care that the trolley was not secure at all.

'There you are, Conrad. But just one question. How did you know where we were?'

'So simple. I have been watching your Clock House home and workshop. Yesterday, I quietly visited your employee Tegan Jones and her husband in their apartment. With just a little encouragement she told where you were going and what you carried. Fortunately, her husband has an exceptionally low threshold of pain, so no long-lasting damage to him. Someone will find them. They are safely out of the way, somewhere quiet.'

Tegan wasn't to blame, as I knew Gwyn had a weak heart as well as his asthma. Conrad had probably been a lot nearer killing him than he realised.

'Now we go down into the gardens where you will be secured. By the time you are found and have freed the others we will be away. No need for killings that will attract the full force of the British police. It will be just another robbery for their files,' Conrad explained.

He had thought it out the best he could, but I was determined that was not going to be good enough. Scream was acting nervously, but he pushed me towards the steps leading down to the gardens. The German stayed well back as ever. I decided the best time to try and overcome them would be just as they started to tie me up, so I complied with the instructions.

They steered me onto the path that wound through the ten-foot-high gunnera plants; not trees, but tall enough to look like a forest on an alien world. In most places the gunnera were too close together with their thorny stems to force our way off the path, but as we reached a slightly sparser patch Conrad called out, 'Stop here', and threw some cable ties to Scream. 'Secure him in there, use these and this duct tape. Also gag him.'

Despite my desire to thwart Conrad, I had no real opportunity to fight back, as he maintained his safe distance with the pistol unwaveringly pointed at my heart. It now seemed I was to be left immobilised, as Conrad had put it, and not shot, so I decided trying to free myself when they had gone was my new best-bet.

Scream was expert at the task, and it only took him a couple of minutes to have me trussed and gagged with the cable ties and duct tape. At least I was going to live, as promised. Conrad squatted down beside me and gently tapped my forehead with his pistol. 'I'm afraid I have not been entirely truthful, Herr Ross. Your knowledge of my connection with Herr Vogel, and how easily you could identify me makes it most appropriate to kill you.'

He stood up and turned to Scream. 'Give me time to get back to Herr Ross's Land Rover. When I sound the horn shoot him, then drive our auto back to London, and dispose of it as you have said you know how best to do.'

Scream didn't answer for a second. 'Right, Boss,' he exclaimed with the chalky growl of a London East End accent.

CHAPTER FIFTY

It would be a lie to say I wasn't scared out of my wits. My heart was pumping adrenalin like it was supercharged and my breathing rate was out of control. But for the gag I would have shouted to Scream to get on with it.

As soon as Conrad was out of sight, Scream leant over me, pulling off his mask. He looked tough, but older than I had expected, like a retired boxer who still kept fit in a gym. He put the gun away and took out a lethal-looking knife. Even in such dire circumstances my mind still registered that Scream was about to do the sensible thing with a silent knife and no shot to arouse suspicion anywhere.

He ripped the tape from my mouth, saying 'Not a word,' turned me onto my front and sliced through the tape on my elbows and the cable ties on my wrists, then the same around my knees and ankles. Finally, he hauled me into a sitting position.

I had no idea what to say, army training or not, I just looked at him like a questioning idiot.

Scream spoke. 'I didn't know who you was until we got here. It was just another job. In, out and away. But after we gave you a smack in that garage, and the Kraut knocked the dog out, Smiler Harris's family put the word about how you was to be left alone in the future, and we owe the Harris family a favour or two.'

'Honour amongst thieves,' I said.

'Do what?' asked Scream.

'Whatever your name is, thanks. I thought I'd had it.'

'You'd better thank Smiler Harris. I'm off out of it now.'

'You could stay and help me catch Conrad,' I suggested

hopefully.

'Nah, mate! The word was not to cause you no bother. Nothing about helping you out.' Scream turned on his heels and jogged away towards the woods that bordered the gardens, keeping out of Conrad's line of sight.

I pulled off the remaining bits of duct tape and stood up. My wrists were fine, but one of the cable ties had cut into my ankle. Regaining my composure found me in a mood to catch Conrad, whatever it took, and that would need some speedy planning.

Any second I expected to hear the Defender's horn, the redundant harbinger of my immediate death. What Conrad did not know is that Howly's great-grandfather, who had installed the safe, had suffered from terrible claustrophobia and he had ordered Chatwood-Milner to supply a door that could be unlocked from both sides. If Conrad went back up to the house, the Farrells, Howly and Kirstie would no longer be in the room-safe, having used the set of keys always kept inside. They would be free to lay a trap for Conrad, and I'd bet that was already planned.

Just then I heard the crack of a snapping dead branch. My stomach turned, and a prickly shiver went down my spine. Had Scream changed his mind about Conrad's bidding?

'Ben! it's me,' whispered Kirstie.

'What the hell are you doing here?' I asked as relief swept over me.

'Trying to rescue you. What else?'

'Are the others okay?'

'They're all fine.'

She was carrying a rifle from the room-safe gun cabinets. 'Do you and Howly have a plan?' I asked, hopefully.

'I was all for taking an incapacitating shot at Conrad, but

Howly said there could be serious legal implications if he wasn't actually threatening us with death or injury. He said conning him into a face-to-face shootout would be too dangerous. Anyway, I was really worried he planned more than just tying you up.'

'You weren't wrong there, but you won't believe what the Scream did.'

'I was within earshot, I heard it all. I was sure he was going to kill you. I was just about to apply pressure to the trigger when he took the mask off and put his gun down. Lucky for him he explained what he was doing, otherwise he'd be dead now.'

I had a strong desire to give Kirstie a big hug, but this wasn't the time or the place. 'How about this for a plan. We'll make our way back towards the house. We can follow Scream's route and take the flank through the woods and come around from the side. If Conrad's still there I want to scare him into driving off at speed.'

'But we'll be between the Defender and the end of the drive. That'll put him off.'

'Good point, Kirstie. Could you take an accurate shot from say a couple of hundred yards away, in the trees? That way the drive will be clear for him to race along.'

Kirstie held up her gun. 'Howly gave me his favourite deer stalking rifle, a . 275 calibre Rigby. The sight's calibrated and he gave me some Hornady ammo. Don't forget I have an army marksman rating, so where do you want me to aim?'

'Wait for him to start the engine, then put the shot through both front side-windows. A bullet between the windscreen and his nose should have the desired effect.'

We scurried into the woods, and Kirstie stopped me around the two hundred yards I had guessed at.

She peered through the telescopic sight. 'This is close

enough, and the angle's not bad, but there's no sign of Conrad.'

'Look! Here he comes now.'

'Greedy boy!' Kirstie said, looking through the gunsight. 'He's nicked some of the family silver from the dining room. If he'd been happy with a few million quid's worth of gold he could be away by now, but he just had to have that little bit extra.'

I moved away from Kirstie as she wriggled into a more supportive position to take aim. I could see her relax as she exhaled and breathed in slowly. Her voice was low, calm, and quiet. 'I have the shot,' she said dispassionately.

I jumped a fraction as Conrad started the engine and sounded the horn, the signal for Scream to kill me. He lowered the passenger side-window, the better to hear my demise. Kirstie didn't flinch an iota.

'I still have the shot,' was all she said.

'He wants to hear a shot, so let him.'

Kirstie breathed in, and as she breathed slowly out, she gently squeezed the trigger.

The driver's side-window shattered, before the sound of the shot could reach Conrad's ears. It only took him a split second to realise what had happened. He glanced at the trees as he selected drive and mashed the throttle to the floor. All four wheels spun on the gravel momentarily, then the Defender shot forwards at a pace.

Physics being what it is, the half-ton of unsecured cargo hurtled into the Defender's back door, smashed it open and flew out, crashing down onto the gravel drive. Conrad stepped hard on the brakes causing the door to jam firmly shut against its bent and broken latch. He looked at the empty rear of the Land Rover, trying to make up his mind what to do.

I quietly said to Kirstie, 'Okay, another shot, please. Through the back window and out the rear side window.' It was a tight angle for the shot.

The words were hardly out of my mouth before the two sheets of glass crazed to smithereens. Conrad decided he was better off somewhere else, and again set off at speed. He was out of our field of vision in a couple of seconds.

'That's what I wanted. Conrad and the Tiger's Head separated. Now let's go get him.'

CHAPTER FIFTY-ONE

'How are we going to catch him?' asked Kirstie.

'Come on! I'll show you,' I said, leading the way to the old stable yard and carriage house. No horses now, but in an open-fronted tractor shed Howly kept a Morris 1000 Traveller for local trips and for the Farrells' use. I ran towards it and grabbed a key from the hook just inside the shed's entrance.

'We'll never catch him in that,' said Kirstie, pointing at the Morris.

'No, we won't, but we will in this,' I said, as the key was not for the Traveller, but for the old carriage house doors where Howly kept his 1954 Bentley Continental Fastback. It was far from my first choice for speeding along narrow, twisting Cornish lanes, but when Conrad reached a major road or a motorway, the Bentley's top speed of one hundred and twenty miles an hour would give us the edge. Especially with the Defender's smashed windows and damaged door.

Carriage house doors opened, we pulled off the Bentley's dust cover, and jumped in the car, with Kirstie carefully sliding the Rigby rifle onto the floor, between her seat and the door. Howly kept the ignition key under the lambswool carpet, just by the driver's seat. I found it immediately, turned on the ignition, and after a few seconds, when the fuel pumps stopped ticking and with the gauge showing full, I pressed the starter button. The 4.9-litre engine sprang into life, and the oil pressure gauge quickly rose to the operating pressure. Into first gear and we stormed out of the yard and along the drive.

The brakes are powerful, even by today's standards, only

the car's size was going to make our journey difficult through the narrow, twisting Cornish lanes with their high-sided stone walls and hedges.

'Clear left!' said Kirstie as I swung out onto the public lane.

'My guess is that he'll head for the A39 to pick up the A30 towards London. He may get baulked by a tractor or farm wagon in these lanes, but I don't want to confront him here.'

I reached under the dashboard and lifted an old-fashioned press-button handset from its cradle. 'It's an old radio-telephone, cutting edge in its day, but updated as a satphone now,' I said, handing it to Kirstie. 'Dial 01, Howly should answer.'

'Howly, it's me, Kirstie. Are you all okay there? Thank goodness. We're in your Bentley chasing after Conrad in Ben's Defender. The idea is to catch up and just keep him in sight, that is if we've guessed right which road he took.'

'Let me speak to him,' I said.

The old phone didn't have a speaker, so Kirstie held the handset by my ear as I needed both hands to control the car in the winding lanes. 'Howly, I need you to activate the anti-theft tracker. If we can catch up with Conrad, the police can home in on us and then grab Conrad.'

'What did he say?' asked Kirstie, as she disconnected the line.

'He's going to activate the tracker right away, and he's already notified the police of the situation at the house as soon as they all left the room-safe. The police are on their way there right now. Howly's going to try and divert them to us. Better call him back and tell him Scream's left as well and so there's no danger to them, otherwise the police might not leave the place to come after us.'

The Bentley's tracker was Civil Service issue, one of the government perks that Howly still enjoyed. As soon as he informed the duty officer of the situation, the nearest armed response team would join the search for us, by then hopefully close to the target vehicle. All this was dependent on us finding the Defender and keeping it in sight.

We were nearing the junction with the A390 when I spotted Conrad. I eased off the speed and maintained a distance that would not spook him. I kept the gap steady until the turn onto the A39, where we had to wait for an old Volvo estate to pass by before following Conrad on to the faster road.

A helicopter zoomed low behind us. 'I hope that's a police helicopter.' I said to Kirstie, both of us straining to see, but unsuccessfully.

We caught the Volvo in about half a mile. Nothing was coming the other way, so I changed down to third and surged passed it. Conrad was three hundred yards or so ahead, with no traffic between us, as we came up to the tight right-hand bend just before Calerick.

'Once he's out of sight round the bend I'm going to close the gap a bit. I don't want some tractor pulling out between us.' The speedo needle climbed to eighty, as the apex of the corner came up. Just at the point where I could see around it, I slammed on the brakes with as much force as I could muster, shouting 'Hang on Kirstie, brace!' The stationary Defender loomed closer and closer. No ABS brakes on our old car, so the final few yards were accompanied by an ear-splitting screech of rubber on road.

'A good job Howly fitted seat belts,' I said.

We sat silently looking at the back of the Defender and could see through the broken rear window that Conrad was staring at the road ahead of him. In the way was a military helicopter, hovering about twenty feet above the road. Fast-roping descent lines were hanging from it and five soldiers, Royal Marines, in combat dress stood blocking the road, their automatic weapons at the ready.

Kirstie and I recognised the helicopter as a Wildcat, both of us having been deployed in them during our tours of duty in Afghanistan. These aircraft take two crew and up to six passengers. In this case, the sixth man was running back along the road to stop all oncoming traffic. Once we had halted, one of the five remaining soldiers ran past us to stop any traffic about to come around the bend from our direction.

'How the shit did Howly manage that?' asked an incredulous Kirstie.

Before I could answer, the reversing lights on the Defender lit up and the car shot backwards to within a few feet of the Bentley's Flying B mascot. We had stopped just short of a field entrance between the stone-bank hedges. Conrad smashed his way through the gate, and started across the field, wheels spinning furiously, but the Defender was fishtailing across the slippery grass at only the pace of a running man.

The Marines most probably would have been taking part in an exercise on Dartmoor. They wouldn't have had live ammunition, but they had taken off the bright yellow blank-firing adaptors from the muzzles of their weapons. I guessed it would be up to us to stop Conrad. Kirstie had the same idea. As soon as the Land Rover crashed its way into the field, she leapt from the Bentley and ran the few steps to the gateway, at the same time activating the bolt action of the Rigby. Resting an elbow on the gatepost, she simultaneously fired at the Defender, hitting the offside rear tyre. It exploded, sending shards of rubber into the wheel arch, and the air. Conrad's progress slowed even more and the rims of the tyreless wheel dug furrows into the land. The four-wheel-drive systems fought hard to keep the slowing Land Rover moving, but Conrad panicked, leapt out and started to run away, pistol in hand.

The Marines were already in the field, and set off after him, the Sergeant in charge firing a shot over Conrad's head. 'Stop now! Drop your weapon and lay face down on the ground.'

Conrad ran on for another few yards or so, then he tripped, falling flat on his face as the gun span away out of his reach. We all heard the yell of pain, as he rolled over clutching his ankle.

Kirstie and I knew that if we went after him, the Marines would consider us a nuisance and a liability, so we stayed at the gate. By the time they reached Conrad he was over the first shock of pain and realised he was neither going to run any further nor reach his gun to shoot his way out of an arrest. He didn't lie face down, and the soldiers didn't force him. An obvious broken ankle was deemed to be sufficient for their personal safety during the arrest. A soldier with Corporal's stripes expertly frisked him for other weapons. Finding none and sure that Conrad had seriously given himself up, two soldiers lifted him upright. They placed their crossed and linked wrists under his seat and with his arms around their shoulders they carried him to the helicopter, which by now had landed on the road.

The sergeant jogged across to us. 'Sergeant Rapson, sir, ma'am. We received instructions to detour to your aid. Judging by your shot, ma'am, you probably didn't need us.'

'We both served in Afghanistan, Sergeant, Intelligence Corps. We guessed you might not have live ammo on your exercise,' said Kirstie.

Sergeant Rapson nodded his appreciation of our guess. 'As luck would have it, we do have live ammo. Helps the new recruits to keep their heads down when they see branches splinter above them.'

'What happens now?' I asked.

'We take laddo here back to the exercise area, we have a fully equipped field hospital there. Then the local police will take him away.'

'Will Kirstie be in trouble for discharging a firearm on a public highway?' I asked.

Sergeant Rapson looked at Kirstie, then at me. 'Sorry, don't know what you mean, sir, didn't see any shooting here, just an exploding tyre in a stony field.'

Kirstie and I shook the Sergeant's hand. 'Thanks, Sergeant, much appreciated. We'll get the Bentley clear of the road and change the Land Rover's wheel.'

Sergeant Rapson saluted us, and spoke into his radio, telling the two traffic guards to ask the front drivers of the queueing cars to wait until they saw the now-landed helicopter depart. The Wildcat spooled up as he ran back, and it was soon in the air. Before the road was open, I dragged the smashed field gate aside and backed the Bentley in. I wasn't going to leave a derelict-looking Defender with a fortune in accessories unguarded. I lifted a flat stone from the dry-stone wall and used it to support the Defender's jack so that I could change the wheel.

'Kirstie, I'll drive the Bentley, and you follow me. Time we got back to Penhydrock to see how everyone is doing with the local police, and to tell them the army's got Conrad.'

Once we were ready to set off, Kirstie pulled up beside the Bentley. 'I hope no one's pinched the Tiger's Head off the drive,' she shouted, half in humour, half in concern.

CHAPTER FIFTY-TWO

At Penhydrock, we weaved our way around two police cars, a police van, and an ambulance. A constable stopped us from going closer to where the Defender had been parked when Kirstie had shot at it.

'I'm Sir Howel's grandson, is everyone all right?' I asked.

'Wait here please, sir,' was the only answer, but a plainclothes officer was fetched in a few seconds.

He looked at the Bentley, then across to Kirstie in the Defender, then me. 'Inspector Lamphier. Mr. Ross and Miss Laing, is it?'

'That's us. Is everyone all right?' I asked, pointing at the ambulance.

'Yes sir, just a precaution. The cook, Mrs. Farrell was a bit shaken up, but she's all right now, and your grandfather and Mr. Farrell are just fine. They don't make'em like that any more,' he added with a wry smile.

'Too right, Inspector. Can we go and see them?'

'Yes sir, we'll use the main entrance, forensics are around the back, there seems to have been some shots fired at your Land Rover. Broken glass and two bullets have been found. Would you know anything about that?'

Kirstie had locked Howly's Rigby rifle in the boot of the Bentley while I was changing the Defender's wheel, so I hoped the police would not want to search the car.

Kirstie had joined us. 'It's only a guess, Inspector, but Conrad had an accomplice. Both of them had guns, maybe there was a falling out over something.'

'That's more or less what Sir Howel suggested, Miss Laing,' said the Inspector.

'I imagine you know that Conrad was after the Tiger's Head?' I asked Lamphier.

'Sir Howel has explained all about it. He's even shown it to me. Quite an impressive item, I have to say. Some of the lads have pushed it on its trolley back into the room safe.'

More police were in the house, doing God knows what, but all looking busy as hell. Howly and the Farrells were in the library, with a medic and a uniformed policewoman.

You two are all right, I trust,' asked Howly.

'We're fine, but what about you, and Mrs. Farrell, Mr. Farrell?' I said, glancing at the elderly couple.

'No harm done at all, dear boy. Farrell's made of iron and Mrs. Farrell is as imperturbable as a D-Day beachmaster.'

'Are you really all right, Mrs. Farrell?' asked Kirstie.

'Yes, dear. Just a bit shaken when that man in the mask dragged me into the breakfast room, but a nice drop of Sir Howel's brandy has seen me right.'

'Look, Inspector, Conrad told me that he found out where we were by questioning one of my employees and her husband back in Berkshire. He said they were tied up somewhere quiet. What can you do?'

'We'll contact the local police right away. Have you any idea where he might have taken them?

'From what he said, and the time between Kirstie and me driving down here and his arrival, I think they are probably somewhere close to their home. That's where he said he interrogated them.'

'Then I expect they'll use a dog to follow a scent,' said Lamphier.

He left to give instructions to his station at Truro but was back in the library no more than five minutes later. 'No need to worry about Mr. and Mrs. Jones. They're safe and sound back at home. Seems that Herr Lehmann, the man you know as Conrad, is spilling the beans, hoping to reduce his sentence. He'll soon be safely locked up in Plymouth,' said the Inspector.

'Did he say anything about being shot at?' asked Kirstie.

'He didn't see who it was but could only imagine it was his accomplice trying to get the Tiger's Head all for himself. Wouldn't give us a name though. Like many of his kind, they draw the line at being a grass.'

And what will happen to the Tiger's Head, will you require it as evidence?' I asked.

'No, I have received instructions from the Chief Constable that it should be released into Sir Howel's safekeeping.'

It was 8:00pm before the police had finished interviewing us all, packed up and left. Mrs. Farrell had insisted on supplying a substantial meal, a collation of cold meats, a memorable veal and ham pie and a green salad with a dressing that a restaurant in rural France would have been proud to serve. By 10:00pm Kirstie and I had hit a wall of tiredness, and when Howly wished us a good night's sleep, we were both happy to retire as well. No awkward moment by Kirstie's door tonight. A brief hug and a chaste kiss were just right for both of us. I was asleep as soon as my head hit the pillow.

By the time I was shaved and showered, Kirstie had beaten me to breakfast by only a few minutes, and Howly was long gone to his study. Today there were no interruptions from armed thugs, and Mrs. Farrell's offerings could be enjoyed to the full.

'Master Benedict, Sir Howel has asked if you and Miss Laing would be good enough to join him in his study, for morning coffee.'

'Of course, Mr. Farrell,' I glanced at my watch. 'Sorry we're late. Please apologise to Mrs. Farrell for us.'

'No need, Master Benedict. Quite understandable after yesterday's troubles,' replied the unflappable Farrell.

Howly's morning coffee was always at 10:30am, and Kirstie and I joined him just as his George Graham long-case clock struck the half-hour. He waved us to the chairs by his desk. Farrell had left the coffee tray by Howly, who poured out three cups, pushing the milk and sugar towards us.

'We can forget yesterday's unpleasantness,' said Howly. 'There's news about the Tiger's Head. I have spoken to the appropriate authorities, and it seems that you have two choices. You can apply for ownership under the rules of Treasure Trove, as it used to be called, or you can accept a full and final offer for it from the government.'

'What are the implications?' I asked.

'If you apply to keep it, you will have to counter claims by the British, Irish, and Indian governments as to ownership. This will almost certainly take many months, if not years and be expensive. If you agree to what the British government will offer you, then payment will be immediate, and the government will take on the onus of battling with the inevitable Irish and Indian appeals.'

'What do I have to do if I accept the government proposal?' I asked.

'You must swear an affidavit listing all factors concerning your search and discovery of the artefact. All will be checked rigorously, and an offer will be made to you based on the perceived strength of your case.'

'If I fought to keep it and won, I would offer it only to British museums on a sealed bid basis.'

'That's exceptionally good of you, my boy. But it would appear there's more to it than just as a valuable artefact. It seems there is a political angle to its future ownership. A chum of mine at the Foreign and Commonwealth Office has indicated for that reason the British government will be most generous if you cooperate with them.'

Kirstie was looking fascinated by Howly's comments, and I was once again reminded just how close to the seat of power he remained.

'Is there anything you don't know about government matters?' I asked.

'A few old pals give me titbits now and again, that's all, just for old time's sake.'

'And you never have any advice for them?'

He waved a hand dismissively. 'Perish the thought, dear boy, perish the thought.'

'Howly, will you be safe with the Tiger's Head locked up here?' asked Kirstie.

'Oh yes! Some soldiers are coming down from Hereford to keep an eye on things, along with experts from the V&A to examine it. I wouldn't let them take it away, as they wished. I expect we shall have an offer from Whitehall within a week after receipt of your affidavit.'

'I'll get on with it right away. I can't thank you enough for all your help, Howly. We'll sit tight until you hear from Whitehall. The police are holding the Land Rover as evidence, so Mr. Farrell has ordered us a taxi to Truro station, for the train to Newbury.'

Kirstie gave my grandfather a hug. 'Thanks for everything, Howly, I've really enjoyed meeting you, I hope I do so again soon. One thing I nearly forgot, your rifle is locked in the boot of your Bentley, I'm sorry I didn't fetch it in.'

'Probably better that you left it there with all the police comings and goings,' he replied.

We collected our bags, thanked the Farrells and wished them well.

Kirstie and I sat opposite one another in First Class, a treat that was warranted after all we had been through. She had been quiet, reading a book since leaving Truro, and I had business matters to catch up with on my tablet, with phone calls to make. We had just left Exeter St. Davids when the refreshment trolley came around, so we chose a couple of sandwiches and two glass-size bottles of wine. Filling the two plastic glasses, I couldn't help noticing Kirstie was looking down-at-heart.

'You look a bit glum,' I said. 'Just think how successful we've been. We started with a legendary car supposedly sunk on the Titanic, discovered that to be untrue. Found the complete chassis, solved the mystery of the golden coachwork and the whereabouts of the gems, actually found some of them and then the pièce de résistance, the Tiger's Head.'

Kirstie didn't answer immediately. I could see she was collecting her thoughts. 'That's the problem, Ben. What do we do now it's finished; I mean what do I do now?'

Kirstie's eyes were glistening, and her face was flushed with worry. What I thought was, you could let me kiss you, but what I said was, 'If we hadn't met up again, what would you be doing?'

'After the police force, I thought the only thing I could really do would be to start up as a private investigator, but that would probably only be about cheating spouses, shoplifters, and thieving employees. Really, really boring stuff. It's nothing like

Cormoran Strike or V. I. Warshawski in real life.'

'I've been thinking. If the treasure trove pay-out on the Tiger's Head is enough, I'm going to stop chasing cars for other people. It's interesting but I'm at the beck and call of the clients. When they snap their fingers, I have to come running, put up with the moods and whims of some of them, and in the end only earn a commission. If I have enough funds to buy and sell cars myself, I can make much more than a commission percentage,' I looked at Kirstie carefully to judge her reaction before continuing. 'We've done pretty well together on the Tiger's Ghost, and I could do with an assistant, a partner really, if this new venture is possible. What do you say?'

'A car detective! I say yes, please,' replied a happy-looking Kirstie, to a happy me.

CHAPTER FIFTY-THREE

My first job, back at the Clock House, was to go across and see Tegan and her husband Gwyn, assure them that I didn't blame them for telling Conrad where I was, and to check that they had suffered no lasting damage.

'Well, you know Gwyn, he's been reliving the kidnapping a bit, full of vengeful thoughts, but he knows he can't do anything about the German since he's already been caught. As for me, neither of us was hurt, so I don't even think about that side of things. I do feel I let you down though, but thank you for being so understanding.'

I assured her with a hug that she had not had a choice.

Normal business now called as I had to fly out to Oman, where my newest client wanted valuations and a purchase negotiated on two cars, a 1924 Doble steam car and a 1949 Talbot Lago SS, both belonging to a collector in Abu Dhabi. First class return on Oman Air, and the client's private jet from Muscat to Abu Dhabi and back; all paid for by the Omani sheik.

Two days later Kirstie dropped me off at Heathrow on her way home to her parents' Norfolk farm. Pulling up at the drop-off zone, she jumped out and hauled my one bag from the back of the Morgan, as I extricated myself from the small door-space.

'Call me when you know you're leaving Muscat and I'll see you back here as you come through customs.' She made her usual hurried airport farewell with a peck of a kiss and a wave.

On the return flight, I looked out from my window seat to admire the city beneath, as the plane briefly flew along the course of the Thames, buffeting in its slow descent towards

Heathrow. I was feeling as excited as when I had found and purchased my first car for my first client. But now the excitement was manifold. I had negotiated the purchase of the two cars at particularly good prices for the sheik. The commission was already in my bank, and as a gift of gratitude, he had given me a wristwatch made by the late George Daniels.

Then, Howly had phoned me with news of the British government's offer to secure the Tiger's Head for the nation. They wouldn't say what value they had put on the artefact but were prepared to make me an offer in full and final payment, providing I would relinquish all and any future rights to its ownership. The sum offered was seven million pounds. Howly advised me to accept it, and I quickly agreed. A funny thing, coincidence. In the same week that I was given a George Daniels watch, I could finally afford to buy one.

Most exciting of all was the thought of seeing Kirstie again and telling her of what a week it had been. Now that the adventure of finding the Tiger's Ghost and all its parts was completed, I had made up my mind to let Kirstie know for sure my feelings for her.

Passport Control cleared and baggage claimed, I headed out through the green customs channel. The meeting and greeting area was packed with family and friends and of course the ever-present drivers with their passengers' name cards held out in front of them. Scanning the faces as I walked to the end of the crowd barrier, I couldn't see Kirstie. The pleasurable butterflies in my stomach turned to those of apprehension; had something happened to her, an accident, trouble at home, or even a kidnapping like Mitch's? I negotiated past the throng, looking for a quiet spot to call her, but there was no need, for there she was standing by a pillar away from the crowd. Relief and pleasure washed over me with equal power. She saw me at the same time, and only a few feet apart our meeting was blocked momentarily by an Indian woman pushing a trolley loaded with cleaning implements; not an assassin from Cooch Sebah, just a kindly airport worker.

'Fate's keeping us apart,' I laughed.

'Oh no, it's not!' she said, as we fell into each other's arms. Did I kiss her, or did she kiss me? No matter, the kiss was long and passionate. I felt her body meld with the whole length of mine, her arms around my neck, and mine pulling her as close as possible.

We parted and held each other at arm's length. 'Wow!' she said. 'I wasn't expecting that.'

'On my part it was wish fulfilment,' I said laughing.

'It seems your wish is my command?'

'That'll be the day,' I said.

'All right. Your wish is my pleasure, then. What do we do now, Ben?' she said with a throaty giggle.

'You drive me back to the Clock House; we see the others and I send them home early.'

'Why's that, then?' she asked with a coy look, and a blush of colour on her cheeks.

I answered with a lascivious smile, and a squeeze of her hand.

We walked to the Morgan and kissed again once we were in the car. I was left in no doubt that having the Clock House to ourselves was going to be a very good idea. Just over an hour later, Kirstie pulled up by the workshop, where Smiler acknowledged our arrival with a wave of a hand holding a grubby fuel pump. Columbus rushed over from his workshop bed, still having the decency to welcome me first, briefly, before making a greater fuss of Kirstie.

'I'm going to freshen up, while you dismiss the troops. I bought a new dress in Diss, let's see if you like it.'

'Don't change just yet,' I said. 'I want to speak to you all together. See if Tegan's in the office, while I get Smiler to come on up.'

'Sounds ominous. Are we all going to get fired?'

'No! You're all going to get something, but not the sack.'

Tegan welcomed me back, and we waited a few minutes while Smiler cleaned the worst of the day's grease and grime from his hands and made a new roll-up for the meeting.

Tegan stayed at her desk, Kirstie sat in the old, battered armchair that was Columbus's favourite. I remained standing as Smiler walked in and settled down on the sofa.

'I wanted to see you all together now that the search for the Tiger's Ghost is successfully over. You've all played a part, and one way and another I've done pretty well out of it, so I have a bonus for each of you.' I leant over to my desk and picked up three small plastic boxes, the sort that cheap rings are sold in. 'This is for you, Tegan, this one's for you, Smiler, and this is yours, Kirstie. Open them up. Tegan, yours is a ruby, Kirstie, yours is a sapphire, and Smiler you've got a diamond.'

None of them spoke. They all looked at each other, then me, all momentarily rendered speechless. Then they all spoke at once. Tegan and Kirstie both raced over and gave me a kiss and a hug, and Smiler sat where he was and made his usual comment when surprised pleasantly: 'Fuck me, Guv!'

'You may remember that there were forty-five gemstones in the compressed-air cylinder that Harold Tyler gave me. Well, I kept four back when I gave the rest to Vogel, three for you and one for me. As you can see, they are each large enough to split into whatever you want, earrings, necklace, rings, or of course set as single stones. I've been in touch with Mo Katz and he's keen to re-cut, polish, and set them however you wish. Phone him tomorrow and tell him what you want. He'll do some sketches, and you can confirm the designs with him. My treat.'

'Oh, sorry Benedict, I almost forgot,' said Tegan, 'a foreign man, Indian by the sound of his voice telephoned on Monday. Name ofSheema, Sharma, something like that. It was a bad line. Anyway, he said to tell you that Mr. Propopenkov had organised for him to collect the thirty-seven gems that had been in Herr Vogel's possession, and to thank you for arranging it all.'

Two stones for Yuri, then, and I bet they weren't the smallest ones in the cylinder.

'Tegan, I want you and Smiler to take the rest of the day off and have a think about what you want Mo to do for you, but before you go, there's one more thing. Here!'

I gave all three of them an envelope. Inside each was a cheque for two-hundred and fifty thousand pounds. 'I'm about to be paid quite a lot by the British government in exchange for the Tiger's Head. It's enough to start buying and selling cars for myself and keep you all busy. I'll let you know when the funds are transferred to me, and you can cash your cheques. You'll have to sort out your own tax liabilities. By the way, Kirstie is now on the permanent staff.'

'I'm not retiring, Guv,' said Smiler, waving his cheque. 'You can't get rid of me with this.'

'Oh well, it was worth a try. Push off now, and I'll see you both in the morning.'

Tegan wiped away some tears. 'A grand holiday for Gwyn

and me, and then something special for my collection of Asian art. The rest is going into a pension fund for our old age. You've no idea how good the security of this feels. I'll go now and tell Gwyn. See you tomorrow then.'

I flopped down on the sofa and Kirstie came across and slid down next to me. 'You didn't have to give me a cheque, Ben, but thank you so much, and as for the sapphire, wow!'

'What will you do with it?'

'I already know,' she said, tucking her legs up under her. 'I've always wanted a really stunning necklace, and I don't want to break up the sapphire, with all its history. It's a fantastic souvenir of our adventure. I shall have it all my life as a reminder of what we did. So, I'll ask Mo to set it in a necklace, leaving it as a single stone, cut to perfection.'

There was one more thing to tell Kirstie, and I wasn't sure how she would feel about it. 'The fourth stone, the one I chose for myself,' I started.

'Yes, what did you select?'

'I didn't know what to choose, not being a gem expert. I thought of asking Mo which one was the most valuable, but that isn't appropriate. So, I laid them all out on a white towel, under Tegan's desk lamp. I looked at them for a good five minutes, and my eye kept going back to a Fancy Chameleon. You know, a large version of the ones that make up the Tiger's Head eyes; the ones that Mo says can change colour dependent on temperature and light. So, I did just that. Changed the light and warmed it up. It's actually quite noticeable. It goes from green to a golden yellow. That's the one I selected.'

Retrieving it from its hiding place in the office, I handed it to Kirstie. She held it up to the window, turning it between thumb and index finger, much the same as Vogel had done with the diamond I had given him in his taxi. 'What are you going to do with it, Ben?'

'I'm going to send it to Lucia Bassoli.'

Kirstie came back to me. 'Why would you do that, Ben?' She asked, with an edge to her voice.

'Lucia may or may not have intended to fess up to Mitch about her claim on the Tiger's Ghost, and I'm pretty sure she was stringing me along until she lost her temper and blew it. But, without her realising what the old photo-plates in Mrs. Saparowitz's loft really were, the whereabouts of the car, the gold and the gems would still be unknown. Plus, she's a direct descendant of Kuldeep Singh. It was she who got the ball rolling on the whole thing.'

'So, you think she deserves something?'

'Honest truth, Kirstie, I feel guilty about her getting nothing. I'm just tying up a loose end, by doing what I consider to be the honourable thing.'

'Then I think you should, and maybe there's no need to mention her again?'

'Only once more, and that's to Howly. I'm going to ask him to arrange to have the diamond sent to her in the diplomatic bag bound for our Consulate in San Francisco. That will save questions of provenance by the US customs, and God knows how much import duty.

Then that will be it,' I said pulling her towards me and kissing her again. Now, alone, there was no need to control our passion.

'Time for me to take a post-flight shower, I think.'

'Ben, I've always admired the look of your state-of-the-art shower. I bet there's room for two.'

CHAPTER FIFTY-FOUR

Sleep came late on our first night together, and I awoke at half past nine to find Kirstie next to me with an arm across my chest, head nestling against my shoulder. Trying to slide from the bed without waking her, my manly effort came to nothing, for she stirred, stretched and was immediately as bright as could be. Grabbing me for a morning kiss, she said. 'I'm ravenous. What's for breakfast?'

'I'm glad to know that romance and lust are not dead.' I quipped.

'Just wait'till we've eaten,' she laughed.

It was 11:00am before we were fed and watered, Kirstie's promise kept, and the shower capacity once again tested. With Tegan at home and Smiler busy in the workshop, there was no one to make sarcastic comments about our late arrival together in the office.

Regretfully, I dragged my mind from Kirstie to work, starting with the letters that had come in during my week away, and gave Kirstie some auction catalogues to introduce her to the type of cars that she would be dealing with in her new role.

In the excitement with the Tiger's Head, I had forgotten all about the paperweight-sized interlinked tigers, wrapped around the crystal, but searching for a folder in the filing cabinet in which I had hidden it jogged my memory and I fished it out.

'Smiler might be right about this being some sort of religious relic. Let's kill two birds with two stones. I'll ask Tegan to contact one of her pals at the Victoria and Albert Museum. We'll see what they think of it. While we're in town we can show Mo your sapphire, and you can tell him you would like it to be set as a pendant.'

'He may know what the tigers around the crystal represent,' she replied.

By late afternoon Tegan had arranged a meeting with an Indian-artefact specialist at the V&A, for 3:00pm the following day, and Mo had agreed to see us at 10:00am.

No lovemaking tonight, as Kirstie needed to go back to her place for changes of clothes and a supply of essentials. Our first goodbye as lovers was a long and sweet kiss, all the more exciting with the promise of the next day's shared adventure. Neither of us had mentioned her moving into the Clock House just yet, but if all continued to go well, I was certainly happy with the thought of her being here for more than two or three nights a week,– and Columbus would be happy too, the little sycophant.

Kirstie was waiting on the platform at Newbury, and the journey to Paddington passed quickly as we chatted away. Mo's premises were in Hatton Garden, London's traditional diamond and jewellery centre. I pressed the video-entry-phone button and announced who we were. A young lad dressed in the same traditional clothes that Mo wore let us in and showed us down to the workrooms in the cellars below his shop, typical of underground Hatton Garden.

'So, what have you got to show me?' asked Mo, straight to the point as usual.

Kirstie gave him her sapphire, wrapped in the yellow duster that I had used for Vogel's diamond. Mo examined the stone and called over his young apprentice. He pointed out some details to him, commenting in Yiddish, then shooed him back to his work.

'This is a magnificent sapphire,' he said, looking at Kirstie. 'Do you know yet how you want me to cut and mount it?'

'I'd really like it to be left a single stone and mounted as a pendant,' said Kirstie.

'A good choice, my dear. The colour, it's the best for a sapphire, a cornflower blue. Yes, I suggest you let me re-cut the stone to what is called a Mixed Cut. It's a combination of an Octagon and a Brilliant Cut. That will minimise waste and give you the best balance of colour and sparkle. Ideal for a pendant on such a figure as yours.'

Kirstie involuntarily placed a hand below her throat and blushed a little. 'Why, thank you, Mo.'

He lifted his gaze to Kirstie's face and hair, narrowing his eyes slightly. 'With your fair skin and light hair, I suggest platinum will be best. A little more expensive, Ben, but what a result.'

'We'll leave it in your hands to come up with the best setting, then,' said Kirstie, as I nodded my agreement. She couldn't resist squeezing my arm and giving a little jump and squeal of excitement.

'While we're here Mo, this is the artefact we found concealed in the Tiger's Head; we assume it's a religious object or has royal significance in India. My guess is the centre is more likely quartz than glass. What do you think?'

Mo examined it under a powerful magnifier. Using one of his dental-like tools he unclipped the legs and tails of the tigers from one another. 'Twenty-four carat I should say,' he mumbled to himself.

Putting down the gold, he hefted the crystal in his hand, and held it to a light, examining every facet. His eyes became hooded, and his voice wounded. 'What is this, a test? You want to tease an old Jew like me with this stupid trick?' He chucked the crystal on an electronic scale. The numbers settled at one eight six.

'I'm sorry, Mo, we meant no offence, it's just as we found it concealed in the Tiger's Head, honestly.'

Mo still looked disbelieving and peeved. 'Ha! You even got the weight right, but I'll show you.' He picked up an electronic probe and touched it against the stone. 'Conductivity,' is all he said by way of explanation. Then with a frown and a grunt of disapproval, he reset the instrument and tried again. Hurriedly he picked up another probe. This time he said worriedly, 'This measures heat dissipation.'

Mo sat down hard on his work stool. His face was as pale as a sheet, and his hand was shaking. 'You say this was what you found in the Tiger's Head cavity?' His eyes darted from mine to Kirstie's, back and forth.

'Yes!' I answered. 'What's wrong, Mo?'

'Go! I must do more tests, some research. Come back at three, now go, go.'

Kirstie and I both had a sixth sense not to mention that we planned to take the artefact to the V&A. The lad was called to show us out, and Mo said not another word to us.

'Well, that was odd,' said Kirstie.

'It certainly was, but whatever we did to upset him, we'll find out at three. Seems to me he suspects the thing is a worthless fake, some kind of ancient scam. I'll just phone and cancel our meeting at the V&A, then how about lunch at the Royal Automobile Club in Pall Mall?'

'Perfect!' said Kirstie, 'I've always wanted to go there.'

After a quick tour of the club facilities, including the finest swimming pool in London, we each had a glass of champagne in the cocktail bar, a fine lunch in the Brooklands Room, and were back at Mo's premises ten minutes early. The same lad let us in, and instead of taking us down to the workshop, he showed us upstairs to Mo's office. The room was cluttered with old trade magazines, folders, and reference books. Judging by the gaps, nothing seemed to have been put away once taken off a shelf, but Mo's desk was orderly, with just four books, a laptop, and our putative paperweight on the worn leather surface.

Mo greeted us and gestured at two folding chairs by his desk and introduced us to a huge bear of a man seated in a more robust Edwardian swivel chair. He was older than Mo, with a white bushy beard and payots.

'I have asked my friend Noam Rosenberg to be here and speak to you. He's an elder of my synagogue, but more importantly for you, he's London's leading expert on Indian diamonds.'

Kirstie and I shot a glance at each other, and simultaneously exclaimed, 'Diamonds!'

Noam raised a hand and smiled. His voice was quiet and soft for such a big man. 'I shall explain. Do you know of any famous diamonds?' he asked us.

Kirstie spoke first. 'I've heard of the Koh-i-Noor in one of The Queen's crowns.'

'And I know about the Cullinan, from South Africa, because Rolls-Royce have named one of their models after it.'

Noam nodded. 'The Koh-i-Noor, The Mountain of Light. Let me tell you a little of its history. It's rumoured to have been found some six thousand years ago, but the earliest reliable mention of it comes at the time that Babur, a descendant of Genghis Khan, founded the Mughal Empire in 1526. Babur acquired a diamond that was likely the Koh-i-Noor, as part of a tribute when he won the Battle of Panipast and conquered Delhi and Agra. The diamond passed down through Babur's successors to the sixth Mughal ruler, Aurangzeb. It was during his reign that the alleged seven hundred and ninety-three carats gem was cut into a more attractive shape, but sadly reduced in weight to a mere one hundred and eighty-six carats. That was the weight and shape that it remained until 1852.'

'What happened in 1852?' I asked.

'Let me take you back, just a few years. In 1843 Maharajah Duleep Singh, a close relative of your Kuldeep Singh, became the last Indian ruler of the Punjab, before the British took control in 1849. They seized all of Duleep Singh's wealth and possessions. In return, by the Treaty of Lahore, he was to be given a stipend of fifty thousand pounds a year. One of the seized treasures was the Koh-i-Noor, which Queen Victoria requested be sent to her in England. It was given to an officer of the Punjab government, John Lawrence, for safe keeping, but unbelievably he left it forgotten in a coat pocket. Six weeks later when plans for its journey to England were ready, he was reminded that he had been given the stone. In a panic he asked his personal servant if he had seen the small box it was kept in. The servant remembered having put it away, and handed the box to Lawrence, saying not to worry, it only contained an old piece of glass.'

I thought I was ahead of Noam. 'Are you going to tell us my paperweight is an exact copy of the Koh-i-Noor?'

'No, Mr. Ross I am not going to tell you that. Let me continue. Once in The Queen's possession, the diamond was put on display at the Great Exhibition in the Crystal Palace in Hyde Park. Not only were the public disappointed in its lacklustre appearance, but so was The Queen's husband, Prince Albert. So much so that he arranged with Garrard, the Crown Jewellers, to propose a suitable company to re-cut it. Their choice was Messrs Coster of Amsterdam, who would do the work at Garrard's shop in Panton Street, here in London.'

Noam leant forward in his seat and pointed to Kirstie and me in turn. 'And now, my friends, comes the most interesting point. Mr. Voorzanger and Mr. Fedder of Coster's, although confident, were concerned about the cutting they were about to undertake. The diamond showed yellow inclusions, also some blemishes, probably made to secure it in a previous mount. They were right to be concerned. After thirty-eight days the finished stone, now cut as an Oval Brilliant, weighed one hundred and five point six carats. Prince Albert was furious about the serious reduction in weight and size, and both Coster's and Garrard came in for severe criticism. Today, we know that they had done the best they could under the restrictions of the inclusions and blemishes, the end result being as fitting for a Royal crown as it could be.'

'Forgive me for being dense, but what has this intriguing tale got to do with us?' I asked.

Mo cut in. 'Ben, Kirstie, both Noam and I have completed definitive tests, and what you have shown me is a diamond the exact cut, weight and size of the Koh-i-Noor as it existed in its one hundred and eighty-six carat form, before its 1852 re-cut.'

Noam added. 'Except there are no blemishes nor any inclusions, and it's a grade D Colourless. In short, it's as perfect a diamond as can be.'

'But why would someone copy the old shape of the Koh-i-Noor if the stone itself is so good?' I asked.

'Mo and I have come up with the same answer, my friends. Up until Garrard arranged for the stone to be assessed by Costers, no substantiated mention was ever made of the flaws, just that it was an outstanding diamond, in size and colour. There is no concern at all about the integrity of Garrard or

Coster, so there can be no doubt that the diamond that arrived in England did have inclusions and blemishes, but did the one owned by Duleep Singh in Lahore have any? Maybe you have here his original stone, and the flawed near twin was cut to be a substitute to fool the British. The swap could have been at any time, but most likely after the British took the Punjab and before it arrived in England on HMS Medea.'

Both Kirstie and I were having a hard time taking in what Noam and Mo had told us. 'Are you saying that the diamond in The Queen's crown is a fake?' I asked.

'No, not a fake. It's the same diamond that Prince Albert had re-cut, but neither Mo nor I now think it to be the original diamond that Babur seized around 1526, known as the Koh-i-Noor.'

Mo made it crystal clear. 'We think the diamond now in the Crown Jewels is made from a good but flawed stone cut to look like the Koh-i-Noor, before its arrival in England and its 1852 recut.

Kirstie pointed at our diamond. 'Then what's this stone here?' she asked with a frown.

Mo looked at Noam. 'I'm sure,' he said.

Mo spoke for them both. 'Your stone, here on my desk, is the superior, original and true Koh-i-Noor diamond.'

No one spoke for what seemed an age. Mo was the one to break the silence. 'Here, take it, you are the first person in six thousand years to possess, without stealing, the Koh-i-Noor; but not for long, I think. The government will take it as part of the Tiger's Head treasure, and maybe rightly so.'

'Take my advice, my friends,' said Noam, 'find somewhere safe to keep it until the powers that be collect it. The discovery of special gems has a way of becoming known to those who would steal them. Who knows how?'

'We could take it down to Cornwall to be reunited with the Tiger's Head that's underpolice and army guard,' said Kirstie.

'Cornwall's a long way, anything could happen,' said Mo.

'You're making me nervous,' I said.

'With good cause. A taxi to Paddington, a few hours on the train, another taxi maybe, anything could happen. With a gem such as this, I wouldn't risk it.'

'I have a solution,' said Noam. 'I advise the V&A museum on matters of Asian sourced diamonds. I could call and arrange for the Koh-i-Noor to be held in one of their safes, while you inform the government of the situation.'

'It's your call, Ben,' said Kirstie, 'but I would do as Noam suggests.'

'The V&A does sound a good place to keep it safe. I suppose you want an armed guard to take us there.'

Noam smiled, 'I think low-key is best for that short trip. I shall only tell the chief conservator of Indian jewellery that two people will be bringing an artefact that she may agree should be kept safe at the museum, for a few days at most. Mo and I will remain shtum, silent, until we hear from the British Government. They are bound to question us as having identified the real Koh-i-Noor. If they decide to go public on the find, then we shall talk to claim our just place in the history of the Mountain of Light. Until then, shtum.'

CHAPTER FIFTY-FIVE

Mo sent his apprentice to hail us a black cab, while we waited in the ground floor shop, with its ultra-secure door and window. The taxi pulled up, and Mo bundled us towards it, telling the cabbie, 'V&A, quick as you can.'

We shook hands with Mo and Noam. 'I'll call you when we're home,' I said.

Neither of us spoke for a while, our own thoughts all-embracing. A light drizzle was falling, enough to obscure the view from the windows with zigzagging water droplets. I had the diamond zipped into an inside pocket. Every few seconds I pressed against it with my forearm; just to make sure it was still there. Kirstie had its three gold tigers in her shoulder bag.

'Ben, let me see it.'

I quickly glanced outside the cab, imagining every pedestrian to be a potential diamond thief. Silly of course, so I took the stone from my pocket, and holding it low, out of sight of the driver's rear-view mirror, passed it to Kirstie. 'Probably best not to hold it up to the window, just in case.'

'I know, it makes me nervous too,' she said. Clasping it in cupped hands as if it were a rescued butterfly, she caressed the stone on every facet, gently hefting its weight. 'You can almost sense its history by holding it.'

I nodded. 'Just think, for six thousand years it's been passed from conqueror to conqueror. Until I bought it with Clarecourt House, never sold, always taken. Battles fought over it and murder done, all to possess a piece of compressed carbon.'

Kirstie gave a huff of a laugh. 'This huge diamond has

glorified monarchs and Princes, been worn by Queens and Maharanis and graced statues and thrones, and now here it is with us in a London taxi.'

'You know, Kirstie, it's the history, not the value that makes my heart race. I just want to keep it safe for the brief time we have it. Daft I suppose to think that way.'

Kirstie slid the Koh-i-Noor back into my hand, with a squeeze. 'No Ben, not daft at all.'

The phone vibrated in my pocket. It was Yuri of all people. 'Yuri, how are you?'

'I'm well, Benedict, but I need to see you as soon as possible. I have important news about the Maharajah of Cooch Sebah and your golden Tiger's Head. Are you at home?'

'No, I'm with Kirstie and we're on our way to the Victoria and Albert Museum; where are you?'

'I am at the Russian Embassy in Kensington Palace Gardens, so I can meet you at the museum in ten minutes. If what you are doing there has anything that concerns the Tiger's Head wait until we have spoken, it is most important for you, I think.'

'Okay, we'll see you in ten minutes, traffic permitting.'

As soon as I saw it was Yuri calling, I had put the phone on speaker so that Kirstie could hear.

'That sounds a bit disturbing,' she said.

'I don't think so, it's too late for the Maharajah to interfere, Vogel and Conrad are out of the picture, Yuri can't know we've got the diamond, and the Tiger's Head is locked in Howly's safe, guarded by the police.'

We pulled up at the museum just seven minutes after Yuri had called. He was waiting on the entrance steps, pacing back and forth. The rain had all but stopped.

I introduced Kirstie, and before pleasantries could be

exchanged Yuri hurried us inside the Museum's Dome entrance hall. The place was busy with tourists, their guides tirelessly trying to keep them from straying, a task made more difficult by groups of school children being shepherded around them and all the other visitors.

'Come. Let us find a quiet place to talk.' Yuri seemed nervous, something I had never seen before. His eyes darted around the vast vestibule, and perspiration was beading on his forehead. He looked up at the second-floor gallery balustrades, just beneath the domed ceiling that gave the entrance hall its name. 'I think there are fewer people up there, we go,' he said, guiding us both gently by an arm.

Part of the second-floor space is called the Belinda Gentle Gallery and houses a collection of decorative metalwork from the Bronze Age to modern times. It was deserted, but for us. I walked over to look down on the ground floor, from where a gentle hubbub of conversations could be heard, even this high up.

'Ben,' Kirstie called.

Her voice had an urgent tone to it, enough for me to quickly return my gaze from the scene below. Yuri was standing close to Kirstie, with his left arm around her shoulders, his hand on her neck, beneath her hair. In his right hand was a small pistol and it was pointed at me. I wasn't worried, Kirstie was well able to disarm him, and I was sure I could instantly rush him and put him down, despite his KGB training.

'Kirstie would be wise not to try and disarm me, for I have a knife at her jugular vein.' Yuri's hand flicked her hair aside momentarily, long enough for me to see he held a finger-ring knife: its small razor-sharp blade, no longer than an inch, could be lethal with just a twitch of his hand.

'What the hell is all this about Yuri, it's a bloody poor joke,' I said.

'No joke, my friend. I am forced to be serious. Give me the Koh-i-Noor and you will both survive unharmed.'

My mind was racing, and I couldn't see a way out of this without doing what Yuri wanted. I needed to play for time. 'How the hell do you know about the diamond?'

A smile crossed Yuri's face. 'My gift to you Benedict, your beautiful phone case. It is also a, how do you say, a state of art radio transmitter. When your phone is with you, I hear everything. I listen with interest when Mo Katz is perturbed by what you have brought him, and then when he tells of what you now own, I think fate has turned for me at last.'

I felt a mixture of fear for Kirstie, rage at Yuri for what he was doing and sadness for the end of our long-time friendship. 'Yuri, why are you doing this? Is it the lure of owning the Koh-i-Noor? You're one of the richest men in Russia, so it can't be for money.'

Yuri gave a bray of a laugh. 'It is for the money, Benedict. Putin has taken against me. Now I am a renegade oligarch. He has seized all my assets, houses, businesses, and bank accounts. He has put a price on my head, my life is in danger and so is that of my wife and my son. The Koh-i-Noor will enable me to get my family out of Russia and for all of us to disappear into a new life.'

'If that's all true then how come you phoned me from the Russian Embassy?' I thought I could add 'lying bastard' to Yuri's crimes.

'A small lie to explain the coincidence of me being so close to the V&A. Had I been at the Embassy, then I would already be drugged to be taken back to Russia for interrogation and death.

Now, please Benedict, the diamond and we can all be on our ways unharmed.'

I couldn't see a solution; Yuri looked desperate enough to kill us if need be to save his family and have a future. 'Okay, Yuri, how are we going to do this?'

'You will place the diamond and your phone on that display case. You will stay here and lean over the balcony so that I can see you until I leave the building. Kirstie will walk with me. We will look a happy couple. When we reach the street, I shall release her and be gone. Is that clear for you?'

'Yes, it's clear. Don't worry, Kirstie, I'll do what he says, soon as he's gone come back in so I can see you're okay. I'd rather have you safe and sound than the diamond.'

'I know that, Ben, but just now it's good to hear,' she said.

Yuri picked up my phone and the diamond and led Kirstie back to the staircase. He stopped and turned at the arched entrance to the gallery. 'Benedict, I am very sorry our friendship has to end like this, but I have no choice if my family and I are to survive.'

Peering over the balcony, I could see them descending past the first floor and down to the Dome hallway. They made their way, weaving through the increasing number of visitors. Just by the ticket counters, they passed two security guards, neither of whom would be capable of rescuing Kirstie from Yuri, the ex-KGB and FSB man. She, too, made that assessment, making no move to gain their help.

They were two thirds of the way to the main entrance and the revolving doors, when twenty or so excited primary-school children, all with blue and yellow backpacks, swarmed around Kirstie and Yuri, the teacher in front trying frantically to keep them all together. She had two younger assistants at the group's sides, encouraging the kids to stay together. At the rear an older woman shooed stragglers with her collapsible umbrella. Her attention on her charges, she bumped into Yuri and Kirstie, dipping her head, and raising her free hand in an apology. In a second she scooted back to her task.

As Kirstie and Yuri reached the doors, she looked back up at me, worry etched on her face. Yuri stood stock still, seemingly studying something on the ground. He took his arm from around Kirstie's shoulder and stepped away from her, reaching out to the door frame for support. A second later he slowly collapsed onto the floor. I raced down the stairs, nearly sending an elderly couple flying, the man's complaint echoing after me. Reaching the entrance, a small crowd had gathered to see what had happened. I elbowed my way through and joined Kirstie kneeling by Yuri's side. He was deathly pale, his lips tinged blue. His breath was shallow and fast. He looked to be on the verge of unconsciousness.

'What happened?' I asked Kirstie.

'I don't know, Yuri just let me go, staggered to the doorway and collapsed.'

'Has he said anything?'

'Yes, "Putin wins", that's all he's said.'

'Yuri, can you hear me?' I asked.

His eyes slowly focused on me. 'Ah! Benedict, the woman with umbrella, I think she is FSB, not schoolteacher. I am sorry for everything.'

Yuri took a few shuddering breaths before he could continue. 'Kirstie, I would not have harmed you, it was bluff for me to beat Putin. Now I die and my family will be poor but left alone, so maybe is best.'

'Can I do anything for you, Yuri?' I asked.

'Yes, take back the diamond before police arrive, your phone and my phone. Tell my wife all, and I love her.' Yuri swallowed with difficulty, and foam bubbled at his mouth. 'Also, sell my beautiful car and send her money, all details in phone.'

I'll do that, Yuri,' I said, as Kirstie shielded me from the onlookers so that I could discreetly slip the diamond and phones from Yuri's pockets.

'Ambulance is on its way, sir,' said one of the security guards.

A woman pushed through the rubber-neckers. 'I'm a doctor,' she barked.

Standing, I squeezed her arm to get her attention, and whispered close to her ear. 'He's a Russian diplomat and has been poisoned with a nerve agent, I don't know if it's safe to touch him.'

For a few seconds she looked at me hard to judge if I was a raving lunatic or someone to believe.

'Everyone stand well back,' she shouted. 'This man may be contagious, so please stay back for your own safety.'

She knelt by Yuri, pulling me down with her. 'You'd better be telling the truth,' She said.

Benedict, are you there, I can no longer see?'

'I'm here Yuri,' I said, but it was the last thing he heard in this world.

CHAPTER FIFTY-SIX

Despite a call to Howly and from him to one of his 'chums' it was after midnight before the police and Special Branch had finally done with us, our story of coincidently bumping into Yuri, an old client, eventually believed. Too late for the last train home, we had to take a taxi.

Kirstie elbowed open our bedroom door, her turn to fetch the morning tea and newspaper. Columbus was through the door and on the bed in a second. I took a sip, and put the cup on the bedside table, pushing the two phones, now divested of their Fabergé look-alike covers, and the Koh-i-Noor aside to make room.

Back in the bed, Kirstie snuggled down against me, brushing her hair from her face. 'Does the paper say anything about yesterday?' she asked.

I flicked through, and on page six, a short piece related that a foreign tourist had collapsed and died at the V&A. No mention of Russians, assassins, or oligarchs.

'Will you do what Yuri asked you, contact his wife and sell the car?' she asked.

'Yes, despite what he did to us.'

'Hmm!' was Kirstie's only answer.

'I'll have to find a translator as his phone is all in Russian. But I've been thinking, we'll take the Koh-i-Noor down to Cornwall today, to be reunited with the Tiger's Head in Howly's safe, then while the authorities start working out what compensation I should get for it, how about a short holiday? There's something I want to do.'

'Where to?' asked Kirstie excitedly.

We'll fly to San Miguel in the Azores, spend a few days visiting the islands, and then hire a yacht to take us for a couple of days cruising to a spot in the Atlantic Ocean about five thousand feet above the wreck of the Stokesay Castle.'

'Harold Tyler's wartime ship,' exclaimed Kirstie. 'But I thought he said its exact position was unknown.'

'He was right at the time. The Royal Navy didn't know where it went down, but the U-boat that sank it did record its exact location. The details of the engagement were in the German Kriegsmarine files, all of which the Allies took charge of after the war. Silas Brown only recently found out and tipped me off. He found the Stokesay Castle's last position recorded in the National Archives at Kew.'

'What are we going to do when we get there?' asked Kirstie.

'Harold told me that the ship's crew were the finest friends he had his entire life, and all but two went down with the ship. If we hire a boat with side-scan sonar, we can pinpoint the site exactly, because I think the Stokesay Castle is the best place for Harold Tyler's ashes to be laid to rest.'

Kirstie's eyes glistened. 'Ross, you just get better and better the more I know you. Now, put that dog of yours outside the bedroom and come back here.'

Printed in Great Britain
by Amazon